Contents

Jane Austen (1775–1817)

Revd George Austen,
Jane's father

Revd James Austen,
Jane's brother

Comtesse Eliza de Feuillide,
Jane's cousin

Revd Henry Austen,
Jane's brother

Front view of Steventon Rectory, Jane's birthplace
(drawing by her niece Anna Lefroy, 1814)

The Vyne (Hampshire), home of the Chutes,
friends and neighbours of the Austen family

The Austens' residence in Chawton (above) and
Jane's lodgings in Winchester, where she died in 1817 (below)

Lady Susan

Letter 1

Langford, December

My dear brother,

I can no longer refuse myself the pleasure of profiting by your kind invitation, when we last parted, of spending some weeks with you at Churchill, and therefore, if quite convenient to you and Mrs Vernon to receive me at present, I shall hope within a few days to be introduced to a sister whom I have so long desired to be acquainted with. My kind friends here are most affectionately urgent with me to prolong my stay, but their hospitable and cheerful dispositions lead them too much into society for my present situation and state of mind; and I impatiently look forward to the hour when I shall be admitted into your delightful retirement. I long to be made known to your dear little children, in whose hearts I shall be very eager to secure an interest. I shall soon have occasion for all my fortitude, as I am on the point of separation from my own daughter. The long illness of her dear father prevented my paying her that attention which duty and affection equally dictated, and I have but too much reason to fear that the governess to whose care I consigned her was unequal to the charge. I have therefore resolved on placing her at one of the best private schools in town, where I shall have an opportunity of leaving her myself, in my way to you. I am determined you see, not to be denied admittance at Churchill. It would indeed give me most painful sensations to know that it were not in your power to receive me.

Your most obliged and affectionate sister

Susan Vernon

Letter 2

LADY SUSAN TO MRS JOHNSON

Langford

You were mistaken, my dear Alicia, in supposing me fixed at this place for the rest of the winter. It grieves me to say how greatly you were mistaken, for I have seldom spent three months more agreeably than those which have just flown away. At present nothing goes smoothly. The females of the family are united against me. You foretold how it would be, when I first came to Langford; and Manwaring is so uncommonly pleasing that I was not without apprehensions myself. I remember saying to myself as I drove to the house: "I like this man; pray Heaven no harm come of it!" But I was determined to be discreet, to bear in mind my being only four months a widow and to be as quiet as possible – and I have been so: my dear creature, I have admitted no one's attentions but Manwaring's; I have avoided all general flirtation whatever; I have distinguished no creature besides of all the numbers resorting hither, except Sir James Martin, on whom I bestowed a little notice in order to detach him from Miss Manwaring. But if the world could know my motive *there*, they would honour me. I have been called an unkind mother, but it was the sacred impulse of maternal affection, it was the advantage of my daughter that led me on; and if that daughter were not the greatest simpleton on earth, I might have been rewarded for my exertions as I ought. Sir James did make proposals to me for Frederica – but Frederica, who was born to be the torment of my life, chose to set herself so violently against the match that I thought it better to lay aside the scheme for the present. I have more than once repented that I did not marry him myself, and were he but one degree less contemptibly weak I certainly should, but I must own myself rather romantic in that respect, and that riches only will not satisfy me. The event of all this is very provoking. Sir James is gone, Maria highly incensed, and

4

Mrs Manwaring insupportably jealous; so jealous in short, and so enraged against me, that in the fury of her temper I should not be surprised at her appealing to her guardian if she had the liberty of addressing him – but there your husband stands my friend, and the kindest, most amiable action of his life was his throwing her off for ever on her marriage. Keep up his resentment therefore I charge you. We are now in a sad state; no house was ever more altered; the whole family are at war, and Manwaring scarcely dares speak to me. It is time for me to be gone; I have therefore determined on leaving them, and shall spend I hope a comfortable day with you in town within this week. If I am as little in favour with Mr Johnson as ever, you must come to me at No. 10, Wigmore St – but I hope this may not be the case, for as Mr Johnson with all his faults is a man to whom that great word "Respectable" is always given, and I am known to be so intimate with his wife, his slighting me has an awkward look. I take town in my way to that insupportable spot, a country village, for I am really going to Churchill. Forgive me, my dear friend: it is my last resource. Were there another place in England open to me, I would prefer it. Charles Vernon is my aversion, and I am afraid of his wife. At Churchill however I must remain till I have something better in view. My young lady accompanies me to town, where I shall deposit her under the care of Miss Summers in Wigmore Street till she becomes a little more reasonable. She will make good connections there, as the girls are all of the best families. The price is immense, and much beyond what I can ever attempt to pay.

Adieu. I will send you a line, as soon as I arrive in town.

Yours ever,
Susan Vernon

Letter 3

MRS VERNON TO LADY DE COURCY

Churchill

My dear mother,

I am very sorry to tell you that it will not be in our power to keep our promise of spending the Christmas with you; and we are prevented that happiness by a circumstance which is not likely to make us any amends. Lady Susan, in a letter to her brother, has declared her intention of visiting us almost immediately – and as such a visit is in all probability merely an affair of convenience, it is impossible to conjecture its length. I was by no means prepared for such an event, nor can I now account for Her Ladyship's conduct. Langford appeared so exactly the place for her in every respect, as well from the elegant and expensive style of living there as from her particular attachment to Mrs Manwaring, that I was very far from expecting so speedy a distinction, though I always imagined from her increasing friendship for us since her husband's death that we should at some future period be obliged to receive her. Mr Vernon I think was a great deal too kind to her when he was in Staffordshire. Her behaviour to him, independent of her general character, has been so inexcusably artful and ungenerous since our marriage was first in agitation that no one less amiable and mild than himself could have overlooked it at all; and though as his brother's widow and in narrow circumstances it was proper to render her pecuniary assistance, I cannot help thinking his pressing invitation to her to visit us at Churchill perfectly unnecessary. Disposed however as he always is to think the best of everyone, her display of grief, and professions of regret, and general resolutions of prudence were sufficient to soften his heart and make him really confide in her sincerity. But as for myself, I am still unconvinced; and, plausibly as Her Ladyship has now written, I cannot make up my mind till I better understand her real meaning in coming to us; you may guess therefore, my dear madam, with what feelings

6

I look forward to her arrival. She will have occasion for all those attractive powers for which she is celebrated to gain any share of my regard; and I shall certainly endeavour to guard myself against their influence, if not accompanied by something more substantial. She expresses a most eager desire of being acquainted with me, and makes very generous mention of my children, but I am not quite weak enough to suppose a woman who has behaved with inattention if not unkindness to her own child should be attached to any of mine. Miss Vernon is to be placed at a school in town before her mother comes to us, which I am glad of, for her sake and my own. It must be to her advantage to be separated from her mother; and a girl of sixteen who has received so wretched an education would not be a very desirable companion here. Reginald has long wished, I know, to see this captivating Lady Susan, and we shall depend on his joining our party soon. I am glad to hear that my father continues so well, and am, with best love etc.,

Catherine Vernon

Letter 4

MR DE COURCY TO MRS VERNON

Parklands

My dear sister,

I congratulate you and Mr Vernon on being about to receive into your family the most accomplished coquette in England. As a very distinguished flirt, I have always been taught to consider her; but it has lately fallen in my way to hear some particulars of her conduct at Langford which prove that she does not confine herself to that sort of honest flirtation which satisfies most people, but aspires to the more delicious gratification of making a whole family miserable. By her behaviour to Mr Manwaring, she gave jealousy and wretchedness to his wife, and by her attentions to a young man previously attached to Mr Manwaring's sister deprived an amiable girl of her lover. I learnt all this from a Mr Smith now in this neighbourhood – (I have dined with him at Hurst and Wilford) – who is just come from Langford, where he was a fortnight in the house with Her Ladyship, and who is therefore well qualified to make the communication.

What a woman she must be! I long to see her, and shall certainly accept your kind invitation, that I may form some idea of those bewitching powers which can do so much – engaging at the same time and in the same house the affections of two men who were neither of them at liberty to bestow them – and all this without the charm of youth. I am glad to find that Miss Vernon does not come with her mother to Churchill, as she has not even manners to recommend her and, according to Mr Smith's account, is equally dull and proud. Where pride and stupidity unite, there can be no dissimulation worthy notice, and Miss Vernon shall be consigned to unrelenting contempt; but by all that I can gather, Lady Susan possesses a degree of captivating deceit which must be pleasing to witness and detect. I shall be with you very soon, and am

your affectionate brother Reginald De Courcy

Letter 5

LADY SUSAN TO MRS JOHNSON

Churchill

I received your note, my dear Alicia, just before I left town, and rejoice to be assured that Mr Johnson suspected nothing of your engagement the evening before; it is undoubtedly better to deceive him entirely: since he will be stubborn, he must be tricked. I arrived here in safety, and have no reason to complain of my reception from Mr Vernon; but I confess myself not equally satisfied with the conduct of his lady. She is perfectly well bred indeed, and has the air of a woman of fashion, but her manners are not such as can persuade me of her being prepossessed in my favour. I wanted her to be delighted at seeing me – I was as amiable as possible on the occasion – but all in vain – she does not like me. To be sure, when we consider that I *did* take some pains to prevent my brother-in-law's marrying her, this want of cordiality is not very surprising – and yet it shows an illiberal and vindictive spirit to resent a project which influenced me six years ago, and which never succeeded at last. I am sometimes half disposed to repent that I did not let Charles buy Vernon Castle when we were obliged to sell it, but it was a trying circumstance, especially as the sale took place exactly at the time of his marriage – and everybody ought to respect the delicacy of those feelings, which could not endure that my husband's dignity should be lessened by his younger brother's having possession of the family estate. Could matters have been so arranged as to prevent the necessity of our leaving the Castle, could we have lived with Charles and kept him single, I should have been very far from persuading my husband to dispose of it elsewhere; but Charles was then on the point of marrying Miss De Courcy, and the event has justified me. Here are children in abundance, and what benefit could have accrued to me from his purchasing Vernon? My having prevented it may perhaps have given his wife an unfavourable impression – but where there is a disposition to dislike a motive will never be wanting; and as to money matters, it has not withheld him from being very useful to me. I really have a regard for him; he is so easily imposed on!

The house is a good one, the furniture fashionable and everything announces plenty and elegance. Charles is very rich I am sure; when a man has once got his name in a banking house he rolls in money. But they do not know what to do with their fortune, keep very little company and never go to town but on business. We shall be as stupid as possible. I mean to win my sister-in-law's heart through her children; I know all their names already, and am going to attach myself with the greatest sensibility to one in particular, a young Frederic, whom I take on my lap and sigh over for his dear uncle's sake.

Poor Manwaring! – I need not tell you how much I miss him – how perpetually he is in my thoughts. I found a dismal letter from him on my arrival here, full of complaints of his wife and sister, and lamentations on the cruelty of his fate. I passed off the letter as his wife's to the Vernons, and when I write to him, it must be under cover to you.

Yours ever, S. V.

Letter 6

MRS VERNON TO MR DE COURCY

Churchill

Well, my dear Reginald, I have seen this dangerous creature, and must give you some description of her, though I hope you will soon be able to form your own judgement. She is really excessively pretty. However you may choose to question the allurements of a lady no longer young, I must for my own part declare that I have seldom seen so lovely a woman as Lady Susan. She is delicately fair, with fine grey eyes and dark eyelashes; and from her appearance one would not suppose her more than five and twenty, though she must in fact be ten years older. I was certainly not disposed to admire her, though always hearing she was beautiful; but I cannot help feeling that she possesses an uncommon union of symmetry, brilliancy and grace. Her address to me was so gentle, frank and even affectionate that, if I had not known how much she has always disliked me for marrying Mr Vernon, and that we had never met before, I should have imagined her an attached friend. One is apt, I believe, to connect assurance of manner with coquetry, and to expect that an impudent address will necessarily attend an impudent mind; at least I was myself prepared for an improper degree of confidence in Lady Susan; but her countenance is absolutely sweet, and her voice and manner winningly mild. I am sorry it is so, for what is this but deceit? Unfortunately one knows her too well. She is clever and agreeable, has all that knowledge of the world which makes conversation easy and talks very well, with a happy command of language, which is too often used I believe to make black appear white. She has already almost persuaded me of her being warmly attached to her daughter, though I have so long been convinced of the contrary. She speaks of her with so much tenderness and anxiety, lamenting so bitterly the neglect of her education, which she represents however as wholly unavoidable, that I am forced to recollect how many successive springs Her Ladyship spent in town, while her daughter was left in Staffordshire to the care of servants or a governess very little better, to prevent my believing whatever she says.

If her manners have so great an influence on my resentful heart, you may guess how much more strongly they operate on Mr Vernon's generous temper. I wish I could be as well satisfied as he is that it was really her choice to leave Langford for Churchill; and if she had not stayed three months there before she discovered that her friends' manner of living did not suit her situation or feelings, I might have believed that concern for the loss of such a husband as Mr Vernon, to whom her own behaviour was far from unexceptionable, might for a time make her wish for retirement. But I cannot forget the length of her visit to the Manwarings, and when I reflect on the different mode of life which she led with them, from that of which she must now submit, I can only suppose that the wish of establishing her reputation by following, though late, the path of propriety occasioned her removal from a family where she must in reality have been particularly happy. Your friend Mr Smith's story, however, cannot be quite true, as she corresponds regularly with Mrs Manwaring; at any rate it must be exaggerated: it is scarcely possible that two men should be so grossly deceived by her at once.

Yours etc., Catherine Vernon

Letter 7

LADY SUSAN TO MRS JOHNSON

Churchill

My dear Alicia,

You are very good in taking notice of Frederica, and I am grateful for it as a mark of your friendship; but as I cannot have a doubt of the warmth of that friendship, I am far from exacting so heavy a sacrifice. She is a stupid girl, and has nothing to recommend her. I would not therefore on any account have you encumber one moment of your precious time by sending her to Edward St, especially as every visit is so many hours deducted from the grand affair of education, which I really wish to be attended to while she remains with Miss Summers. I want her to play and sing with some portion of taste, and a good deal of assurance, as she has *my* hand and arm, and a tolerable voice. *I* was so much indulged in my infant years that I was never obliged to attend to anything, and consequently am without those accomplishments which are necessary to finish a pretty woman. Not that I am an advocate for the prevailing fashion of acquiring a perfect knowledge in all the languages, arts and sciences: it is throwing time away; to be mistress of French, Italian, German, music, singing, drawing, etc., will gain a woman some applause, but will not add one lover to her list. Grace and manner after all are of the greatest importance. I do not mean therefore that Frederica's acquirements should be more than superficial, and I flatter myself that she will not remain long enough at school to understand anything thoroughly. I hope to see her the wife of Sir James within a twelvemonth. You know on what I ground my hope, and it is certainly a good foundation, for school must be very humiliating to a girl of Frederica's age; and by the by, you had better not invite her any more on that account, as I wish her to find her situation as unpleasant as possible. I am sure of Sir James at any time, and could make him renew his application by a line. I shall trouble you meanwhile to prevent his forming any other attachment when he comes to town; ask him to your house occasionally, and talk to him about Frederica, that he may not forget her.

Upon the whole I commend my own conduct in this affair extremely, and regard it as a very happy mixture of circumspection and tenderness. Some mothers would have insisted on their daughter's accepting so great an offer on the first overture, but I could not answer it to myself to force Frederica into a marriage from which her heart revolted; and, instead of adopting so harsh a measure, merely propose to make it her own choice by rendering her life thoroughly uncomfortable till she does accept him. But enough of this tiresome girl.

You may well wonder how I contrive to pass my time here – and for the first week it was most insufferably dull. Now, however, we begin to mend; our party is enlarged by Mrs Vernon's brother, a handsome young man, who promises me some amusement. There is something about him that rather interests me, a sort of sauciness, of familiarity which I shall teach him to correct. He is lively and seems clever, and when I have inspired him with greater respect for me than his sister's kind offices have implanted, he may be an agreeable flirt. There is exquisite pleasure in subduing an insolent spirit, in making a person predetermined to dislike acknowledge one's superiority. I have disconcerted him already by my calm reserve, and it shall be my endeavour to humble the pride of these self-important De Courcys still lower, to convince Mrs Vernon that her sisterly cautions have been bestowed in vain, and to persuade Reginald that she has scandalously belied me. This project will serve at least to amuse me, and prevent my feeling so acutely this dreadful separation from you and all whom I love. Adieu.

Yours ever,

S. Vernon

Letter 8

MRS VERNON TO LADY DE COURCY

Churchill

My dear mother,

You must not expect Reginald back again for some time. He desires me to tell you that the present open weather induces him to accept Mr Vernon's invitation to prolong his stay in Sussex that they may have some hunting together. He means to send for his horses immediately, and it is impossible to say when you may see him in Kent. I will not disguise my sentiments on this change from you, my dear madam, though I think you had better not communicate them to my father, whose excessive anxiety about Reginald would subject him to an alarm which might seriously affect his health and spirits. Lady Susan has certainly contrived in the space of a fortnight to make my brother like her. In short, I am persuaded that his continuing here beyond the time originally fixed for his return is occasioned as much by a degree of fascination towards her as by the wish of hunting with Mr Vernon, and of course I cannot receive that pleasure from the length of his visit which my brother's company would otherwise give me. I am indeed provoked at the artifice of this unprincipled woman. What stronger proof of her dangerous abilities can be given than this perversion of Reginald's judgement, which when he entered the house was so decidedly against her? In his last letter he actually gave me some particulars of her behaviour at Langford, such as he received from a gentleman who knew her perfectly well, which if true must raise abhorrence against her, and which Reginald himself was entirely disposed to credit. His opinion of her, I am sure, was as low as of any woman in England, and when he first came it was evident that he considered her as one entitled neither to delicacy nor respect, and that he felt she would be delighted with the attentions of any man inclined to flirt with her.

Her behaviour I confess has been calculated to do away with such an idea: I have not detected the smallest impropriety in it – nothing of vanity, of pretension, of levity – and she is altogether so attractive that I should not wonder at his being delighted with her, had he known nothing of her previous to this personal acquaintance; but against reason, against conviction, to be so well pleased with her as I am sure he is does really astonish me. His admiration was at first very strong, but no more than was natural; and I did not wonder at his being struck by the gentleness and delicacy of her manners; but when he has mentioned her of late it has been in terms of more extraordinary praise, and yesterday he actually said that he could not be surprised at any effect produced on the heart of man by such loveliness and such abilities; and when I lamented in reply the bad-ness of her disposition, he observed that whatever might have been her errors, they were to be imputed to her neglected education and early marriage, and that she was altogether a wonderful woman.

This tendency to excuse her conduct, or to forget it in the warmth of admiration vexes me; and if I did not know that Reginald is too much at home at Churchill to need an invitation for lengthening his visit, I should regret Mr Vernon's giving him any.

Lady Susan's intentions are of course those of absolute coquetry, or a desire of universal admiration. I cannot for a moment imagine that she has anything more serious in view, but it mortifies me to see a young man of Reginald's sense duped by her at all. I am, etc.

Catherine Vernon

Letter 9

MRS JOHNSON TO LADY SUSAN

Edward St

My dearest friend,

I congratulate you on Mr De Courcy's arrival, and advise you by all means to marry him; his father's estate is, we know, considerable, and, I believe, certainly entailed. Sir Reginald is very infirm, and not likely to stand in your way long. I hear the young man well spoken of, and though no one can really deserve you, my dearest Susan, Mr De Courcy may be worth having. Manwaring will storm, of course, but you may easily pacify him. Besides, the most scrupulous point of honour could not require you to wait for his emancipation. I have seen Sir James – he came to town for a few days last week and called several times in Edward Street. I talked to him about you and your daughter, and he is so far from having forgotten you that I am sure he would marry either of you with pleasure. I gave him hopes of Frederica's relenting, and told him a great deal of her improvements. I scolded him for making love to Maria Manwaring; he protested that he had been only in joke, and we both laughed heartily at her disappointment and in short were very agreeable. He is as silly as ever.

Yours faithfully,
Alicia

Letter 10

LADY SUSAN TO MRS JOHNSON

Churchill

I am much obliged to you, my dear friend, for your advice respecting Mr De Courcy, which I know was given with the fullest conviction of its expediency, though I am not quite determined on following it. I cannot easily resolve on anything so serious as marriage, especially as I am not at present in want of money, and might perhaps till the old gentleman's death be very little benefited by the match. It is true that I am vain enough to believe it within my reach. I have made him sensible of my power, and can now enjoy the pleasure of triumphing over a mind prepared to dislike me, and prejudiced against all my past actions. His sister too is, I hope, convinced how little the ungenerous representations of anyone to the disadvantage of another will avail, when opposed to the immediate influence of intellect and manner. I see plainly that she is uneasy at my progress in the good opinion of her brother, and conclude that nothing will be wanting on her part to counteract me; but having once made him doubt the justice of her opinion of me, I think I may defy her.

It has been delightful to me to watch his advances towards intimacy, especially to observe his altered manner in consequence of my repressing by the calm dignity of my deportment his insolent approach to direct familiarity. My conduct has been equally guarded from the first, and I never behaved less like a coquette in the whole course of my life, though perhaps my desire of dominion was never more decided. I have subdued him entirely by sentiment and serious conversation, and made him, I may venture to say, *half* in love with me, without the semblance of the most commonplace flirtation. Mrs Vernon's consciousness of deserving every sort of revenge that it can be in my power to inflict, for her ill offices, could alone enable her to perceive that I am actuated by any design in behaviour so gentle and unpretending. Let her think and act as she chooses, however; I have never yet found that the advice of a sister could prevent a young man's being in love if he chose it. We are advancing now towards some kind of confidence, and in short are likely to be engaged in a kind of platonic friendship. On *my* side, you may be sure of its never being more, for if I were not already as much attached to another person as I can be to anyone, I should make a point of not bestowing my affection on a man who had dared to think so meanly of me.

Reginald has a good figure, and is not unworthy the praise you have heard given him, but is still greatly inferior to our friend at Langford. He is less polished, less insinuating than Manwaring, and is comparatively deficient in the power of saying those delightful things which put one in good humour with oneself and all the world. He is quite agreeable enough, however, to afford me amusement, and to make many of those hours pass very pleasantly which would be otherwise spent in endeavouring to overcome my sister-in-law's reserve, and listen to her husband's insipid talk.

Your account of Sir James is most satisfactory, and I mean to give Miss Frederica a hint of my intentions very soon. – Yours, etc.

S. Vernon

Letter 11

MRS VERNON TO LADY DE COURCY

I really grow quite uneasy, my dearest mother, about Reginald, from witnessing the very rapid increase of Lady Susan's influence. They are now on terms of the most particular friendship, frequently engaged in long conversations together, and she has contrived by the most artful coquetry to subdue his judgement to her own purposes. It is impossible to see the intimacy between them, so very soon established, without some alarm, though I can hardly suppose that Lady Susan's views extend to marriage. I wish you could get Reginald home again, under any plausible pretence. He is not at all disposed to leave us, and I have given him as many hints of my father's precarious state of health as common decency will allow me to do in my own house. Her power over him must now be boundless, as she has entirely effaced all his former ill opinion, and persuaded him not merely to forget, but to justify her conduct. Mr Smith's account of her proceedings at Langford, where he accused her of having made Mr Manwaring and a young man engaged to Miss Manwaring distractedly in love with her, which Reginald firmly believed when he came to Churchill, is now, he is persuaded, only a scandalous invention. He has told me so in a warmth of manner which spoke his regret at having ever believed the contrary himself.

How sincerely do I grieve that she ever entered this house! I always looked forward to her coming with uneasiness – but very far was it from originating in anxiety for Reginald. I expected a most disagreeable companion to myself, but could not imagine that my brother would be in the smallest danger of being captivated by a woman with whose principles he was so well acquainted, and whose character he so heartily despised. If you can get him away, it will be a good thing.

Yours affectionately,

Catherine Vernon

Letter 12

SIR REGINALD DE COURCY TO HIS SON

Parklands

I know that young men in general do not admit of any enquiry, even from their nearest relations, into affairs of the heart; but I hope, my dear Reginald, that you will be superior to such as allow nothing for a father's anxiety, and think themselves privileged to refuse him their confidence and slight his advice. You must be sensible that, as an only son and the representative of an ancient family, your conduct in life is most interesting to your connections. In the very important concern of marriage, especially, there is everything at stake: your own happiness, that of your parents and the credit of your name. I do not suppose that you would deliberately form an absolute engagement of that nature without acquainting your mother and myself, or at least without being convinced that we should approve your choice; but I cannot help fearing that you may be drawn in by the lady who has lately attached you to a marriage which the whole of your family, far and near, must highly reprobate.

Lady Susan's age is itself a material objection, but her want of character is one so much more serious that the difference of even twelve years becomes in comparison of small account. Were you not blinded by a sort of fascination, it would be ridiculous in me to repeat the instances of great misconduct on her side, so very generally known. Her neglect of her husband, her encouragement of other men, her extravagance and dissipation were so gross and notorious that no one could be ignorant of them at the time, nor can now have forgotten them. To our family, she has always been represented in softened colours by the benevolence of Mr Charles Vernon; and yet, in spite of his generous endeavours to excuse her, we know that she did, from the most selfish motives, take all possible pains to prevent his marrying Catherine.

My years and increasing infirmities make me very desirous, my dear Reginald, of seeing you settled in the world. To the fortune of your wife, the goodness of my own will make me indifferent; but her family and character must be equally unexceptionable. When your choice is so fixed as that no objection can be made to either, I can promise you a ready and cheerful consent; but it is my duty to oppose a match which deep art only could render probable, and must in the end make wretched.

It is possible that her behaviour may arise only from vanity, or a wish of gaining the admiration of a man whom she must imagine to be particularly prejudiced against her; but it is more likely that she should aim at something further. She is poor, and may naturally seek an alliance which may be advantageous to herself. You know your own rights, and that it is out of my power to prevent your inheriting the family estate. My ability of distressing you during my life would be a species of revenge to which I should hardly stoop under any circumstances. I honestly tell you my sentiments and intentions. I do not wish to work on your fears, but on your sense and affection. It would destroy every comfort of my life to know that you were married to Lady Susan Vernon. It would be the death of that honest pride with which I have hitherto considered my son; I should blush to see him, to hear of him, to think of him.

I may perhaps do no good, but that of relieving my own mind, by this letter; but I felt it my duty to tell you that your partiality for Lady Susan is no secret to your friends, and to warn you against her. I should be glad to hear your reasons for disbelieving Mr Smith's intelligence; you had no doubt of its authenticity a month ago.

If you can give me your assurance of having no design beyond enjoying the conversation of a clever woman for a short period, and of yielding admiration only to her beauty and abilities without being blinded by them to her faults, you will restore me to happiness; but if you cannot do this, explain to me at least what has occasioned so great an alteration in your opinion of her.

I am, etc.,

Reginald De Courcy

Letter 13

LADY DE COURCY TO MRS VERNON

Parklands

My dear Catherine,

Unluckily I was confined to my room, when your last letter came, by a cold which affected my eyes so much as to prevent my reading it myself, so I could not refuse your father when he offered to read it to me, by which means he became acquainted to my great vexation with all your fears about your brother. I had intended to write to Reginald myself, as soon as my eyes would let me, to point out as well as I could the danger of an intimate acquaintance with so artful a woman as Lady Susan to a young man of his age and high expectations. I meant moreover to have reminded him of our being quite alone now, and very much in need of him to keep up our spirits these long winter evenings. Whether it would have done any good can never be settled now; but I am excessively vexed that Sir Reginald should know anything of a matter which we foresaw would make him so uneasy. He caught all your fears the moment he had read your letter, and I am sure has not had the business out of his head since; he wrote by the same post to

Reginald, a long letter full of it all, and particularly asking for an explanation of what he may have heard from Lady Susan to contradict the late shocking reports. His answer came this morning, which I shall enclose to you, as I think you will like to see it; I wish it was more satisfactory, but it seems written with such a determination to think well of Lady Susan that his assurances as to marriage, etc., do not set my heart at ease. I say all I can, however, to satisfy your father, and he is certainly less uneasy since Reginald's letter. How provoking it is, my dear Catherine, that this unwelcome guest of yours should not only prevent our meeting this Christmas, but be the occasion of so much vexation and trouble. Kiss the dear children for me.

Your affectionate mother,
C. De Courcy

Letter 14

MR DE COURCY TO SIR REGINALD

Churchill

My dear sir,

I have this moment received your letter, which has given me more astonishment than I ever felt before. I am to thank my sister, I suppose, for having represented me in such a light as to injure me in your opinion, and give you all this alarm. I know not why she should choose to make herself and her family uneasy by apprehending an event which no one but herself, I can affirm, would ever have thought possible. To impute such a design to Lady Susan would be taking from her every claim to that excellent understanding which her bitterest enemies have never denied her; and equally low must sink my pretensions to common sense if I am suspected of matrimonial views in my behaviour to her. Our difference of age must be an insuperable objection, and I entreat you, my dear sir, to quiet your mind and no longer harbour a suspicion which cannot be more injurious to your own peace than to our understandings.

I can have no view in remaining with Lady Susan than to enjoy for a short time (as you have yourself expressed it) the conversation of a woman of high mental powers. If Mrs Vernon would allow something to my affection for herself and her husband in the length of my visit, she would do more justice to us all; but my sister is unhappily prejudiced beyond the hope of conviction against Lady Susan. From an attachment to her husband, which in itself does honour to both, she cannot forgive those endeavours at preventing their union, which have been attributed to selfishness in Lady Susan. But in this case, as well as in many others, the world has most grossly injured that lady by supposing the worst where the motives of her conduct have been doubtful.

Lady Susan had heard something so materially to the disadvantage of my sister as to persuade her that the happiness of Mr Vernon, to whom she was always much attached, would be absolutely destroyed by the marriage. And this circumstance, while it explains the true motive of Lady Susan's conduct, and removes all the blame which has been so lavished on her, may also convince us how little the general report of anyone ought to be credited, since no character, however upright, can escape the malevolence of slander. If my sister, in the security of retirement, with as little opportunity as inclination to do evil, could not avoid censure, we must not rashly condemn those who, living in the world and surrounded with temptation, should be accused of errors which they are known to have the power of committing.

I blame myself severely for having so easily believed the scandalous tales invented by Charles Smith to the prejudice of Lady Susan, as I am now convinced how greatly they have traduced her. As to Mrs Manwaring's jealousy, it was totally his own invention; and his account of her attaching Miss Manwaring's lover was scarcely better founded. Sir James Martin had been drawn in by that young lady to pay her some attention, and as he is a man of fortune it was easy to see that *her* views extended to marriage. It is well known that Miss Manwaring is absolutely on the catch for a husband, and no one therefore can pity her for losing by the superior attractions of another woman the chance of being able to make a worthy man completely miserable. Lady Susan was far from intending such a conquest and, in finding how warmly Miss Manwaring resented her lover's defection, determined, in spite of Mr and Mrs Manwaring's most earnest entreaties, to leave the family. I have reason to imagine that she did receive serious proposals from Sir James, but her removing from Langford immediately on the discovery of his attachment must acquit her on that article with every mind of common candour. You will, I am sure, my dear sir, feel the truth of this reasoning, and will hereby learn to do justice to the character of a very injured woman.

I know that Lady Susan in coming to Churchill was governed only by the most honourable and amiable intentions. Her prudence and economy are exemplary, her regard for Mr Vernon equal even to his deserts and her wish of obtaining my sister's good opinion merits a better return than it had received. As a mother she is unexceptionable. Her solid affection for her child is shown by placing her in hands where her education will be properly attended to; but because she has not the blind and weak partiality of most mothers, she is accused of wanting maternal tenderness. Every person of sense, however, will know how to value and commend her well-directed affection, and will join me in wishing that Frederica Vernon may prove more worthy than she has yet done of her mother's tender care.

I have now, my dear sir, written my real sentiments of Lady Susan; you will know from this letter how highly I admire her abilities and esteem her character; but if you are not equally convinced by my full and solemn assurance that your fears have been most idly created, you will deeply mortify and distress me.

I am, etc.,

R. De Courcy

Letter 15

MRS VERNON TO LADY DE COURCY

Churchill

My dear mother,

I return you Reginald's letter, and rejoice with all my heart that my father is made easy by it. Tell him so, with my congratulations; but between ourselves, I must own it has only convinced *me* of my brother's having no *present* intention of marrying Lady Susan – not that he is in no danger of doing so three months hence. He gives a very plausible account of her behaviour at Langford. I wish it may be true, but his intelligence must come from herself, and I am less disposed to believe it than to lament the degree of intimacy subsisting between them implied by the discussion of such a subject.

I am sorry to have incurred his displeasure, but can expect nothing better while he is so very eager in Lady Susan's justification. He is very severe against me, indeed, and yet I hope I have not been hasty in my judgement of her. Poor woman! Though I have reasons enough for my dislike, I can not help pitying her at present, as she is in real distress, and with too much cause. She had this morning a letter from the lady with whom she has placed her daughter, to request that Miss Vernon might be immediately removed, as she had been detected in an attempt to run away. Why, or whither she intended to go, does not appear; but as her situation seems to have been unexceptionable, it is a sad thing and of course highly afflicting to Lady Susan.

Frederica must be as much as sixteen, and ought to know better, but from what her mother insinuates I am afraid she is a perverse girl. She has been sadly neglected, however, and her mother ought to remember it.

Mr Vernon set off for town as soon as she had determined what should be done. He is if possible to prevail on Miss

Summers to let Frederica continue with her, and, if he cannot succeed, to bring her to Churchill for the present, till some other situation can be found for her. Her Ladyship is comforting herself meanwhile by strolling along the shrubbery with Reginald, calling forth all his tender feelings, I suppose, on this distressing occasion. She has been talking a great deal about it to me; she talks vastly well; I am afraid of being ungenerous or I should say she talks too well to feel so very deeply. But I will not look for faults. She may be Reginald's wife. Heaven forbid it! – but why should I be quicker-sighted than anybody else? Mr Vernon declares that he never saw deeper distress than hers, on the receipt of the letter – and is his judgement inferior to mine?

She was very unwilling that Frederica should be allowed to come to Churchill, and justly enough, as it seems a sort of reward to behaviour deserving very differently. But it was impossible to take her anywhere else, and she is not to remain here long.

"It will be absolutely necessary," said she, "as you, my dear sister, must be sensible, to treat my daughter with some severity while she is here – a most painful necessity, but I will endeavour to submit to it. I am afraid I have been too often indulgent, but my poor Frederica's temper could never bear opposition well. You must support and encourage me. You must urge the necessity of reproof, if you see me too lenient."

All this sounds very reasonable. Reginald is so incensed against the poor silly girl! Surely it is not to Lady Susan's credit that he should be so bitter against her daughter; his idea of her must be drawn from the mother's description.

Well, whatever may be his fate, we have the comfort of knowing that we have done our utmost to save him. We must commit the event to an Higher Power. Yours ever, etc.,

Catherine Vernon

Letter 16

LADY SUSAN TO MRS JOHNSON

Churchill

Never, my dearest Alicia, was I so provoked in my life as by a letter this morning from Miss Summers. That horrid girl of mine has been trying to run away. I had not a notion of her being such a little devil before; she seemed to have all the Vernon milkiness; but on receiving the letter in which I declared my intentions about Sir James, she actually attempted to elope; at least, I cannot otherwise account for her doing it. She meant, I suppose, to go to the Clarkes in Staffordshire, for she has no other acquaintance. But she *shall* be punished, she *shall* have him. I have sent Charles to town to make matters up if he can, for I do not by any means want her here. If Miss Summers will not keep her, you must find me out another school, unless we can get her married immediately. Miss S. writes word that she could not get the young lady to assign any cause for her extraordinary conduct, which confirms me in my own private explanation of it.

Frederica is too shy, I think, and too much in awe of me, to tell tales; but if the mildness of her uncle *should* get anything from her, I am not afraid. I trust I shall be able to make my story as good as hers. If I am vain of anything, it is of my eloquence. Consideration and esteem as surely follow command of language as admiration waits on beauty. And here I have opportunity enough for the exercise of my talent, as the chief of my time is spent in conversation. Reginald is never easy unless we are by ourselves, and when the weather is tolerable we pace the shrubbery for hours together. I like him on the whole very well; he is clever and has a good deal to say; but he is sometimes impertinent and troublesome. There is a sort of ridiculous delicacy about him which requires the fullest explanation of whatever he may have heard to my disadvantage, and is never satisfied till he thinks he has ascertained the beginning and end of everything.

This is *one* sort of love – but I confess it does not particularly recommend itself to me. I infinitely prefer the tender and liberal spirit of Manwaring – which, impressed with the deepest conviction of my merit, is satisfied that whatever I do must be right – and look with a degree of contempt on the inquisitive and doubting fancies of that heart which seems always debating on the reasonableness of its emotions. Manwaring is indeed beyond compare superior to Reginald – a superior in everything but the power of being with me. Poor fellow! He is quite distracted by jealousy, which I am not sorry for, as I know no better support of love. He has been teasing me to allow of his coming into this country, and lodging somewhere near me *incog.* – but I forbid anything of the kind. Those women are inexcusable who forget what is due to themselves and the opinion of the world.

S. Vernon

Letter 17

MRS VERNON TO LADY DE COURCY

Churchill

My dear mother,

Mr Vernon returned on Thursday night, bringing his niece with him. Lady Susan had received a line from him by that day's post informing her that Miss Summers had absolutely refused to allow of Miss Vernon's continuance in her academy. We were therefore prepared for her arrival, and expected them impatiently the whole evening. They came while we were at tea, and I never saw any creature look so frightened in my life as Frederica when she entered the room.

Lady Susan, who had been shedding tears before and showing great agitation at the idea of the meeting, received her with perfect self-command and without betraying the least tenderness of spirit. She hardly spoke to her and, on Frederica's bursting into tears as soon as we were seated, took her out of the room and did not return for some time; when she did, her eyes looked very red, and she was as much agitated as before. We saw no more of her daughter.

Poor Reginald was beyond measure concerned to see his fair friend in such distress, and watched her with so much tender solicitude that I, who occasionally caught her observing his countenance with exultation, was quite out of patience. This pathetic representation lasted the whole evening, and so ostentatious and artful a display had entirely convinced me that she did in fact feel nothing.

I am more angry with her than ever since I have seen her daughter. The poor girl looks so unhappy that my heart aches for her. Lady Susan is surely too severe, because Frederica does not seem to have the sort of temper to make severity necessary. She looks perfectly timid, dejected and penitent.

She is very pretty, though not so handsome as her mother, nor at all like her. Her complexion is delicate, but neither so fair, nor so blooming as Lady Susan's – and she has quite the Vernon cast of countenance, the oval face and mild dark eyes, and there is peculiar sweetness in her look when she speaks either to her uncle or me, for as we behave kindly to her, we have of course engaged her gratitude. Her mother has insinuated that her temper is untractable, but I never saw a face less indicative of any evil disposition than hers; and from what I now see of the behaviour of each to the other, the invariable severity of Lady Susan and the silent dejection of Frederica, I am led to believe as heretofore that the former has no real love for her daughter and has never done her justice or treated her affectionately.

I have not yet been able to have any conversation with my niece; she is shy, and I think I can see that some pains are taken to prevent her being much with me. Nothing satisfactory transpires as to her reason for running away. Her kind-hearted uncle, you may be sure, was too fearful of distressing her to ask many questions as they travelled. I wish it had been possible for me to fetch her instead of him; I think I should have discovered the truth in the course of a thirty-mile journey.

The small pianoforte has been removed within these few days, at Lady Susan's request, into her dressing room, and Frederica spends great part of the day there; *practising* it is called, but I seldom hear any noise when I pass that way. What she does with herself there I do not know; there are plenty of books in the room, but it is not every girl who has been running wild the first fifteen years of her life that can or will read. Poor creature! The prospect from her window is not very instructive, for that room overlooks the lawn, you know, with the shrubbery on one side, where she may see her mother walking for an hour together in earnest conversation with Reginald. A girl of Frederica's age must be childish indeed if such things do not strike her. Is it not inexcusable to give such an example to a daughter? Yet Reginald still thinks Lady Susan the best of mothers – still condemns Frederica as a worthless girl! He is convinced that her attempt to run away proceeded from no justifiable cause and had no provocation. I am sure I cannot say that it *had*, but while Miss Summers declares that Miss Vernon showed no sign of obstinacy or perverseness during her whole stay in Wigmore St till she was detected in this scheme, I cannot so readily credit what Lady Susan has made him and wants to make me believe, that it was merely an impatience of restraint and a desire of escaping from the tuition of masters which brought on the plan of an elopement. Oh! Reginald, how is your judgement enslaved! He scarcely dares even allow her to be handsome, and when I speak of her beauty, replies only that her eyes have no brilliancy.

Sometimes he is sure that she is deficient in understanding, and at others that her temper only is in fault. In short, when a person is always to deceive, it is impossible to be consistent. Lady Susan finds it necessary for her own justification that Frederica should be to blame, and probably has sometimes judged it expedient to accuse her of ill nature and sometimes to lament her want of sense. Reginald is only repeating after Her Ladyship.

> I am, etc.,
>
> Catherine Vernon

Letter 18

FROM THE SAME TO THE SAME

Churchill

My dear madam,

I am very glad to find that my description of Frederica Vernon has interested you, for I do believe her truly deserving of our regard, and when I have communicated a notion that has recently struck me, your kind impression in her favour will I am sure be heightened. I cannot help fancying that she is growing partial to my brother, I so very often see her eyes fixed on his face with a remarkable expression of pensive admiration! He is certainly very handsome – and yet more – there is an openness in his manner that must be highly prepossessing, and I am sure she feels it so. Thoughtful and pensive in general, her countenance always brightens with a smile when Reginald says anything amusing; and let the subject be ever so serious that he may be conversing on, I am much mistaken if a syllable of his uttering escapes her.

I want to make him sensible of all this, for we know the power of gratitude on such a heart as his; and could Frederica's artless affection detach him from her mother, we might bless the day which brought her to Churchill. I think, my dear madam, you would not disapprove of her as a daughter. She is extremely young to be sure, has had a wretched education and a dreadful example of levity in her mother, but yet I can pronounce her disposition to be excellent and her natural abilities very good.

Though totally without accomplishment, she is by no means so ignorant as one might expect to find her, being fond of books and spending the chief of her time in reading. Her mother leaves her more to herself now than she *did*, and I have her with me as much as possible, and have taken great pains to overcome her timidity. We are very good friends, and though she never opens her lips before her mother, she talks enough when alone with me to make it clear that if properly treated by Lady Susan she would always appear to much greater advantage. There cannot be a more gentle, affectionate heart, or more obliging manners, when acting without restraint. Her little cousins are all very fond of her.

Yours affectionately,

Catherine Vernon

Letter 19

LADY SUSAN TO MRS JOHNSON

Churchill

You will be eager, I know, to hear something further of Frederica, and perhaps may think me negligent for not writing before. She arrived with her uncle last Thursday fortnight, when of course I lost no time in demanding the reason of her behaviour, and soon found myself to have been perfectly right in attributing it to my own letter. The purport of it frightened her so thoroughly that, with a mixture of true girlish perverseness and folly, without considering that she could not escape from my authority by running away from Wigmore Street, she resolved on getting out of the house and proceeding directly by the stage to her friends the Clarkes, and had really got as far as the length of two streets in her journey when she was fortunately missed, pursued and overtaken.

Such was the first distinguished exploit of Miss Frederica Susanna Vernon, and if we consider that it was achieved at the tender age of sixteen we shall have room for the most flattering prognostics of her future renown. I am excessively provoked, however, at the parade of propriety which prevented Miss Summers from keeping the girl;

and it seems so extraordinary a piece of nicety, considering what are my daughter's family connections, that I can only suppose the lady to be governed by the fear of never getting her money. Be that as it may, however, Frederica is returned on my hands, and having now nothing else to employ her, is busy in pursuing the plan of romance begun at Langford. She is actually falling in love with Reginald De Courcy. To disobey her mother by refusing an unexceptionable offer is not enough; her affections must likewise be given without her mother's approbation. I never saw a girl of her age bid fairer to be the sport of mankind. Her feelings are tolerably lively, and she is so charmingly artless in their display as to afford the most reasonable hope of her being ridiculed and despised by every man who sees her.

Artlessness will never do in love matters, and that girl is born a simpleton who has it either by nature or affectation. I am not yet certain that Reginald sees what she is about; nor is it of much consequence: she is now an object of indifference to him; she would be one of contempt were he to understand her emotions. Her beauty is much admired by the Vernons, but it has no effect on *him*. She is in high favour with her aunt altogether – because she is so little like myself of course. She is exactly the companion for Mrs Vernon, who dearly loves to be first, and to have all the sense and all the wit of the conversation to herself; Frederica will never eclipse her. When she first came, I was at some pains to prevent her seeing much of her aunt, but I have since relaxed, as I believe I may depend on her observing the rules I have laid down for their discourse.

But do not imagine that, with all this lenity, I have for a moment given up my plan of her marriage; no, I am unalterably fixed on that point, though I have not yet quite resolved on the manner of bringing it about. I should not choose to have the business brought forward here, and canvassed by the wise heads of Mr and Mrs Vernon; and I cannot just now afford to go to town. Miss Frederica must therefore wait a little.

Yours ever,
S. Vernon

Letter 20

MRS VERNON TO LADY DE COURCY

Churchill

We have a very unexpected guest with us at present, my dear mother. He arrived yesterday. I heard a carriage at the door as I was sitting with my children while they dined, and supposing I should be wanted, left the nursery soon afterwards and was half-way downstairs when Frederica, as pale as ashes, came running up, and rushed by me into her own room. I instantly followed, and asked her what was the matter. "Oh!" cried she. "He is come, Sir James is come – and what am I to do?" This was no explanation; I begged her to tell me what she meant. At that moment we were interrupted by a knock at the door; it was Reginald, who came by Lady Susan's direction to call Frederica down. "It is Mr De Courcy," said she, colouring violently. "Mama has sent for me, and I must go."

We all three went down together, and I saw my brother examining the terrified face of Frederica with surprise. In the breakfast room we found Lady Susan and a young man of genteel appearance, whom she introduced to me by the name of Sir James Martin – the very person, as you may remember, whom it was said she had been at pains to detach from Miss Manwaring. But the conquest it seems was not designed for herself, or she has since transferred it to her daughter, for Sir James is now desperately in love with Frederica, and with full encouragement from Mama. The poor girl, however, I am sure dislikes him; and though his person and address are very well, he appears both to Mr Vernon and me a very weak young man.

Frederica looked so shy, so confused, when we entered the room, that I felt for her exceedingly. Lady Susan behaved with great attention to her visitor, and yet I thought I could perceive that she had no particular pleasure in seeing him. Sir James talked a good deal, and made many civil excuses to me for the liberty he had taken in coming to Churchill, mixing more frequent laughter with his discourse than the subject required, said many things over and over again and told Lady Susan three times that he had seen Mrs Johnson a few evenings before. He now and then addressed Frederica, but more frequently her mother. The poor girl sat all this time without opening her lips; her eyes cast down, and her colour varying every instant, while Reginald observed all that passed in perfect silence.

At length Lady Susan – weary, I believe, of her situation – proposed walking, and we left the two gentlemen together to put on our pelisses.

As we went upstairs, Lady Susan begged permission to attend me for a few moments in my dressing room, as she was anxious to speak with me in private. I led her thither accordingly, and as soon as the door was closed she said, "I was never more surprised in my life than by Sir James's arrival, and the suddenness of it requires some apology to *you*, my dear sister, though to me as a mother, it is highly flattering. He is so warmly attached to my daughter that he could no longer exist without seeing her. Sir James is a young man of an amiable disposition, and excellent character; a little too much of the *rattle* perhaps, but a year or two will rectify *that*, and he is in other respects so very eligible a match for Frederica that I have always observed his attachment with the greatest pleasure, and am persuaded that you and my brother will give the alliance your hearty approbation. I have never before mentioned the likelihood of its taking place to anyone, because I thought that while Frederica continued at school it had better not be known to exist; but now, as I am convinced that Frederica is too old ever to submit to school confinement, and have therefore begun to consider her union with Sir James as not very distant, I had intended within a few days to acquaint yourself and Mr Vernon with the whole business. I am sure, my dear sister, you will excuse my remaining silent on it so long, and agree with me that such circumstances, while they continue from any cause in suspense, cannot be too cautiously concealed. When you have the happiness of bestowing your sweet little Catherine some years hence on a man, who in connection and character is alike unexceptionable, you will know what I feel now; though – thank Heaven! – you cannot have all my reasons for rejoicing in such an event. Catherine will be amply provided for, and not like my Frederica indebted to a fortunate establishment for the comforts of life."

She concluded by demanding my congratulations. I gave them somewhat awkwardly, I believe; for in fact, the sudden disclosure of so important a matter took from me the power of speaking with any clearness. She thanked me, however, most affectionately for my kind concern in the welfare of herself and her daughter, and then said:

"I am not apt to deal in professions, my dear Mrs Vernon, and I never had the convenient talent of affecting sensations foreign to my heart; and therefore I trust you will believe me when I declare that, much as I had heard in your praise before I knew you, I had no idea that I should ever love you as I now do; and must further say that your friendship towards me is more particularly gratifying, because I have reason to believe that some attempts were made to prejudice you against me. I only wish that they – whoever they are – to whom I am indebted for such kind intentions, could see the terms on which we now are together, and understand the real affection we feel for each other! But I will not detain you any longer. God bless you, for your goodness to me and my girl, and continue to you all your present happiness."

What can one say of such a woman, my dear mother? Such earnestness, such solemnity of expression! And yet I cannot help suspecting the truth of everything she said.

As for Reginald, I believe he does not know what to make of the matter. When Sir James first came, he appeared all astonishment and perplexity. The folly of the young man and the confusion of Frederica entirely engrossed him; and though a little private discourse with Lady Susan has since had its effect, he is still hurt, I am sure, at her allowing of such a man's attentions to her daughter.

Sir James invited himself with great composure to remain here a few days, hoped we would not think it odd, was aware of its being very impertinent, but he took the liberty of a relation, and concluding by wishing, with a laugh, that he might be really one soon. Even Lady Susan seemed a little disconcerted by this forwardness – in her heart, I am persuaded, she sincerely wishes him gone.

But something must be done for this poor girl, if her feelings are such as both her uncle and I believe them to be. She must not be sacrificed to policy or ambition; she must not be even left to suffer from the dread of it. The girl, whose heart can distinguish Reginald De Courcy, deserves, however he may slight her, a better fate than to be Sir James Martin's wife. As soon as I can get her alone, I will discover the real truth, but she seems to wish to avoid me. I hope this does not proceed from anything wrong, and that I shall not find out I have thought too well of her. Her behaviour before Sir James certainly speaks the greatest consciousness and embarrassment; but I see nothing in it more like encouragement.

Adieu, my dear madam,

> Yours, etc.,
>
> Catherine Vernon

Letter 21

MISS VERNON TO MR DE COURCY

Sir,

I hope you will excuse this liberty; I am forced upon it by the greatest distress, or I should be ashamed to trouble you. I am very miserable about Sir James Martin, and have no other way in the world of helping myself but by writing to you, for I am forbidden ever speaking to my uncle or aunt on the subject; and this being the case, I am afraid my applying to you will appear no better than equivocation, and as if I attended only to the letter and not the spirit of Mama's commands, but if you do not take my part, and persuade her to break it off, I shall be half distracted, for I cannot bear him. No human being but you could have any chance of prevailing with her. If you will therefore have the unspeakable great kindness of taking my part with her, and persuading her to send Sir James away, I shall be more obliged to you than it is possible for me to express. I always disliked him from the first – it is not a sudden fancy, I assure you, sir – I always thought him silly and impertinent and disagreeable, and now he is grown worse than ever. I would rather work for my bread than marry him. I do not know how to apologize enough for this letter; I know it is taking so great a liberty; I am aware how dreadfully angry it will make Mama, but I must run the risk. I am, sir, your most humble servant

F.S.V.

Letter 22

LADY SUSAN TO MRS JOHNSON

Churchill

This is insufferable! My dearest friend, I was never so enraged before, and must relieve myself by writing to you, who I know will enter into all my feelings. Who should come on Tuesday but Sir James Martin? Guess my astonishment and vexation – for as you well know, I never wished him to be seen at Churchill. What a pity that you should not have known his intentions! Not content with coming, he actually invited himself to remain here a few days. I could have poisoned him; I made the best of it however, and told my story with great success to Mrs Vernon who, whatever might be her real sentiments, said nothing in opposition to mine. I made a point also of Frederica's behaving civilly to Sir James, and gave her to understand that I was absolutely determined on her marrying him. She said something of her misery, but that was all. I have for some time been more particularly resolved on the match from seeing the rapid increase of her affection for Reginald, and from not feeling perfectly secure that a knowledge of *that* affection might not in the end awaken a return. Contemptible as a regard founded only on compassion must make them both in my eyes, I felt by no means assured that such might not be the consequence. It is true that Reginald had not in any degree grown cool towards me; but yet he had lately mentioned Frederica spontaneously and unnecessarily, and once had said something in praise of her person.

He was all astonishment at the appearance of my visitor; and at first observed Sir James with an attention which I was pleased to see not unmixed with jealousy; but unluckily it was impossible for me really to torment him, as Sir James, though extremely gallant to me, very soon made the whole party understand that his heart was devoted to my daughter.

I had no great difficulty in convincing De Courcy, when we were alone, that I was perfectly justified, all things considered, in desiring the match; and the whole business seemed most comfortably arranged. They could none of them help perceiving that Sir James was no Solomon, but I had positively forbidden Frederica's complaining to Charles Vernon or his wife, and they had therefore no pretence for interference, though my impertinent sister I believe wanted only opportunity for doing so.

Everything, however, was going on calmly and quietly, and though I counted the hours of Sir James's stay, my mind was entirely satisfied with the posture of affairs. Guess then what I must feel at the sudden disturbance of all my schemes, and that too from a quarter whence I had least reason to apprehend it. Reginald came this morning into my dressing room, with a very unusual solemnity of countenance, and after some preface informed me in so many words that he wished to reason with me on the impropriety and unkindness of allowing Sir James Martin to address my daughter, contrary to *her* inclinations. I was all amazement. When I found that he was not to be laughed out of his design, I calmly required an explanation, and begged to know by what he was impelled, and by whom commissioned to reprimand me. He then told me, mixing in this speech a few insolent compliments and ill-timed expressions of tenderness, to which I listened with perfect indifference, that my daughter had acquainted him with some circumstances concerning herself, Sir James and me which gave him great uneasiness.

In short, I found that she had in the first place actually written to him, to request his interference, and that on receiving her letter he had conversed with her on the subject of it, in order to understand the particulars and assure himself of her real wishes!

I have not a doubt but that the girl took this opportunity of making downright love to him; I am convinced of it, from the manner in which he spoke of her. Much good may such love do him! I shall ever despise the man who can be gratified by the passion which he never wished to inspire, nor solicited the avowal of. I shall always detest them both. He can have no true regard for me, or he would not have listened to her; and she, with her little rebellious heart and indelicate feelings to throw herself into the protection of a young man with whom she had scarcely ever exchanged two words before. I am equally confounded at *her* impudence and his credulity. How dared he believe what she told him in my disfavour! Ought he not to have felt assured that I must have unanswerable motives for all that I had done! Where was his reliance on my sense or goodness then; where the resentment which true love would have dictated against the person defaming me, that person, too, a chit, a child, without talent or education, whom he had been always taught to despise?

I was calm for some time, but the greatest degree of forbearance may be overcome – and I hope I was afterwards sufficiently keen. He endeavoured, long endeavoured to soften my resentment, but that woman is a fool indeed who, while insulted by accusation, can be worked on by compliments. At length he left me, as deeply provoked as myself, and he showed his anger *more*. I was quite cool, but he gave way to the most violent indignation. I may therefore expect it will sooner subside; and perhaps his may be vanished for ever, while mine will be found still fresh and implacable.

He is now shut up in his apartment, whither I heard him go on leaving mine. How unpleasant, one would think, must his reflections be! But some people's feelings are incomprehensible. I have not yet tranquillized myself enough to see Frederica. *She* shall not soon forget the occurrences of this day. She shall find that she has poured forth her tender tale of love in vain, and exposed herself for ever to the contempt of the whole world, and the severest resentment of her injured mother.

Yours affectionately,

S. Vernon

Letter 23

MRS VERNON TO LADY DE COURCY

Churchill

Let me congratulate you, my dearest mother. The affair which has given us so much anxiety is drawing to a happy conclusion. Our prospect is most delightful, and since matters have now taken so favourable a turn, I am quite sorry that I ever imparted my apprehensions to you; for the pleasure of learning that the danger is over is perhaps dearly purchased by all that you have previously suffered.

I am so much agitated by delight that I can scarcely hold a pen, but am determined to send you a few lines by James, that you may have some explanation of what must so greatly astonish you, as that Reginald should be returning to Parklands.

I was sitting about half an hour ago with Sir James in the breakfast parlour, when my brother called me out of the room. I instantly saw that something was the matter; his complexion was raised, and he spoke with great emotion. You know his eager manner, my dear madam, when his mind is interested.

"Catherine," said he, "I am going home today. I am sorry to leave you, but I must go. It is a great while since I have seen my father and mother. I am going to send James forward with my hunters immediately; if you have any letter therefore he can take it. I shall not be at home myself till Wednesday or Thursday, as I shall go through London, where I have business. But before I leave you," he continued, speaking in a lower voice and with still greater energy, "I must warn you of one thing. Do not let Frederica Vernon be made unhappy by that Martin. He wants to marry her – her mother promotes the match – but *she* cannot endure the idea of it. Be assured that I speak from the fullest conviction of the truth of what I say. I *know* that Frederica is made wretched by Sir James's continuing here. She is a sweet girl, and deserves a better fate. Send him away immediately. *He* is only a fool – but what her mother can mean, Heaven only knows! Goodbye," he added, shaking my hand with earnestness – "I do not know when you will see me again. But remember what I tell you of Frederica; you must make it your business to see justice done her. She is an amiable girl, and has a very superior mind to what we have ever given her credit for."

He then left me and ran upstairs. I would not try to stop him, for I knew what his feelings must be; the nature of mine, as I listened to him, I need not attempt to describe. For a minute or two I remained in the same spot, overpowered by wonder – of a most agreeable sort indeed; yet it required some consideration to be tranquilly happy.

In about ten minutes after my return to the parlour, Lady Susan entered the room. I concluded of course that she and Reginald had been quarrelling, and looked with anxious curiosity for a confirmation of my belief in her face. Mistress of deceit, however, she appeared perfectly unconcerned, and after chatting on indifferent subjects for a short time, said to me, "I find from Wilson that we are going to lose Mr De Courcy. Is it true that he leaves Churchill this morning?" I replied that it was. "He told us nothing of all this last night," said she laughing, "or even this morning at breakfast. But perhaps he did not know it himself. Young men are often hasty in their resolutions – and not more sudden in forming than unsteady in keeping them. I should not be surprised if he were to change his mind at last, and not go."

She soon afterwards left the room. I trust, however, my dear mother, that we have no reason to fear an alteration of his present plan; things have gone too far. They must have quarrelled, and about Frederica too. Her calmness astonishes me. What delight will be yours in seeing him again, in seeing him still worthy your esteem, still capable of forming your happiness!

When next I write, I shall be able I hope to tell you that Sir James is gone, Lady Susan vanquished and Frederica at peace. We have much to do, but it shall be done. I am all impatience to know how this astonishing change was effected. I finish as I began, with the warmest congratulations.

Yours ever,
Catherine Vernon

Letter 24

FROM THE SAME TO THE SAME

Churchill

Little did I imagine, my dear mother, when I sent off my last letter, that the delightful perturbation of spirits I was then in would undergo so speedy, so melancholy a reverse! I never can sufficiently regret that I wrote to you at all. Yet who could have foreseen what has happened? My dear mother, every hope which but two hours ago made me so happy is vanished. The quarrel between Lady Susan and Reginald is made up, and we are all as we were before. One point only is gained: Sir James Martin is dismissed. What are we now to look forward to? I am indeed disappointed. Reginald was all but gone; his horse was ordered, and almost brought to the door! Who would not have felt safe?

For half an hour I was in momentary expectation of his departure. After I had sent off my letter to you, I went to Mr Vernon and sat with him in his room, talking over the whole matter. I then determined to look for Frederica, whom I had not seen since breakfast. I met her on the stairs and saw that she was crying.

"My dear aunt," said she, "he is going, Mr De Courcy is going, and it is all my fault. I am afraid you will be angry, but indeed I had no idea it would end so."

"My love," replied I, "do not think it necessary to apologize to me on that account. I shall feel myself under an obligation to anyone who is the means of sending my brother home; because (recollecting myself) I know my father wants very much to see him. But what is it that you have done to occasion all this?"

She blushed deeply as she answered, "I was so unhappy about Sir James that I could not help – I have done something very wrong, I know – but you have not an idea of the misery I have been in, and Mama had ordered me never to speak to you or my uncle about it… and…"

"You therefore spoke to my brother, to engage *his* interference," said I, wishing to save her the explanation.

"No – but I wrote to him. I did indeed. I got up this morning before it was light – I was two hours about it – and when my letter was done, I thought I never should have the courage to give it. After breakfast, however, as I was going to my own room, I met him in the passage, and then, as I knew that everything must depend on that moment, I forced myself to give it. He was so good as to take it immediately; I dared not look at him – and ran away directly. I was in such a fright that I could hardly breathe. My dear aunt, you do not know how miserable I have been."

"Frederica," said I, "you ought to have told me all your distresses. You would have found in me a friend always ready to assist you.

Do you think that your uncle and I should not have espoused your cause as warmly as my brother?"

"Indeed I did not doubt your goodness," said she, colouring again, "but I thought that Mr De Courcy could do anything with my mother; but I was mistaken; they have had a dreadful quarrel about it, and he is going. Mama will never forgive me, and I shall be worse off than ever."

"No, you shall not," replied I. "In such a point as this, your mother's prohibition ought not to have prevented your speaking to me on the subject. She has no right to make you unhappy, and she shall *not* do it. Your applying, however, to Reginald can be productive only of good to all parties. I believe it is best as it is. Depend upon it that you shall not be made unhappy any longer."

At that moment, how great was my astonishment at seeing Reginald come out of Lady Susan's dressing room. My heart misgave me instantly. His confusion on seeing me was very evident. Frederica immediately disappeared. "Are you going?" said I. "You will find Mr Vernon in his own room."

"No, Catherine," replied he. "I am *not* going. Will you let me speak to you a moment?"

We went into my room. "I find," continued he, his confusion increasing as he spoke, "that I have been acting with my usual foolish impetuosity. I have entirely misunderstood Lady Susan, and was on the point of leaving the house under a false impression of her conduct. There has been some very great mistake – we have been all mistaken, I fancy. Frederica does not know her mother – Lady Susan means nothing but her good – but Frederica will not make a friend of her. Lady Susan therefore does not always know what will make her daughter happy. Besides, I could have no right to interfere – Miss Vernon was mistaken in applying to me. In short, Catherine, everything has gone wrong – but it is now all happily settled. Lady Susan I believe wishes to speak to you about it, if you are at leisure."

"Certainly," replied I, deeply sighing at the recital of so lame a story. I made no remarks however, for words would have been in vain. Reginald was glad to get away, and I went to Lady Susan, curious indeed to hear her account of it.

"Did not I tell you," said she with a smile, "that your brother would not leave us after all?"

"You did indeed," replied I very gravely, "but I flattered myself that you would be mistaken."

"I should not have hazarded such an opinion," returned she, "if it had not at that moment occurred to me that his resolution of going might be occasioned by a conversation in which we had been this morning engaged, and which had ended very much to his dissatisfaction from our not rightly understanding each other's meaning. This idea struck me at the moment, and I instantly determined that an accidental dispute in which I might probably be as much to blame as himself should not deprive you of your brother. If you remember, I left the room almost immediately. I was resolved to lose no time in clearing up these mistakes as far as I could. The case was this: Frederica had set herself violently against marrying Sir James—"

"And can Your Ladyship wonder that she should?" cried I with some warmth. "Frederica has an excellent understanding, and Sir James has none."

"I am at least very far from regretting it, my dear sister," said she. "On the contrary, I am grateful for so favourable a sign of my daughter's sense. Sir James is certainly under par (his boyish manners make him appear the worse), and had Frederica possessed the penetration, the abilities, which I could have wished in my daughter, or had I ever known her to possess so much as she does, I should not have been anxious for the match."

"It is odd that you alone should be ignorant of your daughter's sense."

"Frederica never does justice to herself; her manners are shy and childish. She is besides afraid of me; she scarcely loves me. During her poor father's life she was a spoilt child; the severity which it has since been necessary for me to show has entirely alienated her affection; neither has she any of that brilliancy of intellect, that genius or vigour of mind which will force itself forward."

"Say rather that she has been unfortunate in her education."

"Heaven knows, my dearest Mrs Vernon, how fully I am aware of *that*; but I would wish to forget every circumstance that might throw blame on the memory of one whose name is sacred with me."

Here she pretended to cry. I was out of patience with her. "But what," said I, "was Your Ladyship going to tell me about your disagreement with my brother?"

"It originated in an action of my daughter's, which equally marks her want of judgement, and the unfortunate dread of me I have been mentioning. She wrote to Mr De Courcy."

"I know she did. You had forbidden her speaking to Mr Vernon or me on the cause of her distress; what could she do therefore but apply to my brother?"

"Good God," she exclaimed, "what an opinion you must have of me! Can you possibly suppose that I was aware of her unhappiness? That it was my object to make my own child miserable, and that I had forbidden her speaking to you on that subject from a fear of your interrupting the diabolical scheme? Do you think me destitute of every honest, every natural feeling? Am I capable of consigning *her* to everlasting misery whose welfare it is my first earthly duty to promote?"

"The idea is horrible. What then was your intention when you insisted on her silence?"

"Of what use, my dear sister, could be any application to you, however the affair might stand? Why should I subject you to entreaties which I refused to attend to myself? Neither for your sake, for hers, nor for my own, could such a thing be desirable. Where my own resolution was taken, I could not wish for the interference, however friendly, of another person. I was mistaken, it is true, but I believed myself to be right."

"But what was this mistake to which Your Ladyship so often alludes? From whence arose so astonishing a misapprehension of your daughter's feelings? Did not you know that she disliked Sir James?"

"I knew that he was not absolutely the man she would have chosen. But I was persuaded that her objections to him did not arise from any perception of his deficiency. You must not question me, however, my dear sister, too minutely on this point," continued she, taking me affectionately by the hand. "I honestly own that there is something to conceal. Frederica makes me very unhappy. Her applying to Mr De Courcy hurt me particularly."

"What is it that you mean to infer," said I, "by this appearance of mystery? If you think your daughter at all attached to Reginald, her objecting to Sir James could not less deserve to be attended to than if the cause of her objecting had been a consciousness of his folly. And why should Your Ladyship at any rate quarrel with my brother for an interference which you must know it was not in his nature to refuse when urged in such a manner?"

"His disposition you know is warm, and he came to expostulate with me, his compassion all alive for this ill-used girl, this heroine in distress! We misunderstood each other. He believed me more to blame than I really was; I considered his interference as less excusable than I now find it. I have a real regard for him, and was beyond expression mortified to find it as I thought so ill bestowed. We were both warm, and of course both to blame. His resolution of leaving Churchill is consistent with his general eagerness; when I understood his intention, however, and at the same time began to think that we had perhaps been equally mistaken in each other's meaning, I resolved to have an explanation before it were too late. For any member of your family I must always feel a degree of affection, and I own it would have sensibly hurt me if my acquaintance with Mr De Courcy had ended so gloomily. I have now only to say further that, as I am convinced of Frederica's having a reasonable dislike to Sir James, I shall instantly inform him that he must give up all hope of her. I reproach myself for having ever, though so innocently, made her unhappy on that score. She shall have all the retribution in my power to make; if she values her own happiness as much as I do, if she judge wisely and command herself as she ought, she may now be easy. Excuse me, my dearest sister, for thus trespassing on your time, but I owed it to my own character; and after this explanation I trust I am in no danger of sinking in your opinion."

I could have said "Not much indeed" – but I left her almost in silence. It was the greatest stretch of forbearance I could practise. I could not have stopped myself, had I begun. Her assurance, her deceit – but I will not allow myself to dwell on them; they will strike you sufficiently. My heart sickens within me.

As soon as I was tolerably composed, I returned to the parlour. Sir James's carriage was at the door, and he, merry as usual, soon afterwards took his leave. How easily does Her Ladyship encourage, or dismiss a lover!

In spite of this release, Frederica still looks unhappy, still fearful perhaps of her mother's anger and, though dreading my brother's departure, jealous, it may be, of his staying. I see how closely she observes him and Lady Susan. Poor girl, I have now no hope for her. There is not a chance of her affection being returned. He thinks very differently of her from what he used to do – he does her some justice – but his reconciliation with her mother precludes every dearer hope.

Prepare, my dear madam, for the worst. The probability of their marrying is surely heightened. He is more securely hers than ever. When that wretched event takes place, Frederica must belong wholly to us.

I am thankful that my last letter will precede this by so little, as every moment that you can be saved from feeling a joy which leads only to disappointment is of consequence.

Yours ever,

Catherine Vernon

Letter 25

LADY SUSAN TO MRS JOHNSON

Churchill

I call on you, dear Alicia, for congratulations. I am again myself – gay and triumphant. When I wrote to you the other day, I was, in truth, in high irritation, and with ample cause. Nay, I know not whether I ought to be quite tranquil now, for I have had more trouble in restoring peace than I ever intended to submit to. This Reginald has a proud spirit of his own! A spirit too, resulting from a fancied sense of superior integrity which is peculiarly insolent. I shall not easily forgive him, I assure you. He was actually on the point of leaving Churchill! I had scarcely concluded my last, when Wilson brought me word of it. I found therefore that something must be done, for I did not choose to have my character at the mercy of a man whose passions were so violent and resentful. It would have been trifling with my reputation to allow of his departing with such an impression in my disfavour; in this light, condescension was necessary.

I sent Wilson to say that I desired to speak with him before he went. He came immediately. The angry emotions which had marked every feature when we last parted were partially subdued. He seemed astonished at the summons, and looked as if half wishing and half fearing to be softened by what I might say.

If my countenance expressed what I aimed at, it was composed and dignified – and yet with a degree of pensiveness which might convince him that I was not quite happy. "I beg your pardon, sir, for the liberty I have taken in sending to you," said I, "but as I have just learnt your intention of leaving this place today, I feel it my duty to entreat that you will not on my account shorten your visit here even an hour. I am perfectly aware that, after what has passed between us, it would ill suit the feelings of either to remain longer in the same house. So very great, so total a change from the intimacy of friendship must render any future intercourse the severest punishment; and your resolution of quitting Churchill is undoubtedly in unison with our situation and with those lively feelings which I know you to possess. But at the same time, it is not for me to suffer such a sacrifice, as it must be, to leave relations to whom you are so much attached and are so dear. My remaining here cannot give that pleasure to Mr and Mrs Vernon which your society must; and my visit has already perhaps been too long. My removal therefore, which must at any rate take place soon, may with perfect convenience be hastened; and I make it my particular request that I may not in any way be instrumental in separating a family so affectionately attached to each other. Where I go is of no consequence to anyone – of very little to myself – but you are of importance to all your connections." Here I concluded, and I hope you will be satisfied with my speech. Its effect on Reginald justifies some portion of vanity, for it was no less favourable than instantaneous. Oh! How delightful it was to watch the variations of his countenance while I spoke, to see the struggle between returning tenderness and the remains of displeasure. There is something agreeable in feelings so easily worked on. Not that I would envy him their possession, nor would for the world have such myself, but they are very convenient when one wishes to influence the passions of another. And yet this Reginald, whom a very few words from me softened at once into the utmost submission, and rendered more tractable, more attached, more devoted than ever, would have left me in the first angry swelling of his proud heart, without deigning to seek an explanation!

Humbled as he now is, I cannot forgive him such an instance of pride, and am doubtful whether I ought not to punish him by dismissing him at once after this our reconciliation, or by marrying and teasing him for ever. But these measures are each too violent to be adopted without some deliberation. At present my thoughts are fluctuating between various schemes. I have many things to compass. I must punish Frederica, and pretty severely too, for her application to Reginald; I must punish him for receiving it so favourably, and for the rest of his conduct. I must torment my sister-in-law for the insolent triumph of her look and manner since Sir James has been dismissed – for in reconciling Reginald to me I was not able to save that ill-fated young man – and I must make myself amends for the humiliations to which I have stooped within these few days. To effect all this I have various plans. I have also an idea of being soon in town and, whatever may be my determination as to the rest, I shall probably put *that* project in execution – for London will be always the fairest field of action, however my views may be directed, and at any rate I shall there be rewarded by your society and a little dissipation for a ten weeks' penance at Churchill.

I believe I owe it to my own character to complete the match between my daughter and Sir James, after having so long intended it. Let me know your opinion on this point. Flexibility of mind, a disposition easily biased by others, is an attribute which you know I am not very desirous of obtaining; nor has Frederica any claim to the indulgence of her whims at the expense of her mother's inclination. Her idle love for Reginald too; it is surely my duty to discourage such romantic nonsense. All things considered therefore, it seems incumbent on me to take her to town and marry her immediately to Sir James.

When my own will is effected contrary to his, I shall have some credit in being on good terms with Reginald, which at present, in fact, I have not, for though he is still in my power I have given up the very article by which our quarrel was produced, and, at best, the honour of victory is doubtful.

Send me your opinion on all these matters, my dear Alicia, and let me know whether you can get lodgings to suit me within a short distance of you.

Your most attached,
S. Vernon

Letter 26

MRS JOHNSON TO LADY SUSAN

Edward St

I am gratified by your reference, and this is my advice: that you come to town yourself without loss of time, but that you leave Frederica behind. It would surely be much more to the purpose to get yourself well established by marrying Mr De Courcy than to irritate him and the rest of his family by making her marry Sir James. You should think more of yourself, and less of your daughter. She is not of a disposition to do you credit in the world, and seems precisely in her proper place, at Churchill with the Vernons; but you are fitted for society, and it is shameful to have you exiled from it. Leave Frederica therefore to punish herself for the plague she has given you, by indulging that romantic tender-heartedness which will always ensure her misery enough; and come yourself to town, as soon as you can.

I have another reason for urging this.

Manwaring came to town last week, and has contrived, in spite of Mr Johnson, to make opportunities of seeing me. He is absolutely miserable about you, and jealous to such a degree of De Courcy that it would be highly unadvisable for them to meet at present; and yet if you do not allow him to see you here, I cannot answer for his not committing some great imprudence – such as going to Churchill for instance, which would be dreadful. Besides, if you take my advice, and resolve to marry De Courcy, it will be indispensably necessary for you to get Manwaring out of the way, and you only can have influence enough to send him back to his wife.

I have still another motive for your coming. Mr Johnson leaves London next Tuesday. He is going for his health to Bath, where if the waters are favourable to his constitution and my wishes, he will be laid up with the gout many weeks. During his absence we shall be able to choose our own society and have true enjoyment.

I would ask you to Edward St but that he once forced from me a kind of promise never to invite you to my house. Nothing but my being in the utmost distress for money could have extorted it from me. I can get you, however, a very nice drawing-room apartment in Upper Seymour St, and we may be always together, there or here, for I consider my promise to Mr Johnson as comprehending only (at least in his absence) your not sleeping in the house.

Poor Manwaring gives me such histories of his wife's jealousy! Silly woman, to expect constancy from so charming a man! But she was always silly – intolerably so – in marrying him at all. She the heiress of a large fortune, he without a shilling! *One* title I know she might have had, besides baronets. Her folly in forming the connection was so great that, though Mr Johnson was her guardian and I do not in general share his feelings, I never can forgive her.

Adieu,

      Yours, Alicia

Letter 27

MRS VERNON TO LADY DE COURCY

Churchill

This letter, my dear mother, will be brought you by Reginald. His long visit is about to be concluded at last, but I fear the separation takes place too late to do us any good. *She* is going to town, to see her particular friend, Mrs Johnson. It was at first her intention that Frederica should accompany her for the benefit of masters, but we overruled her there. Frederica was wretched in the idea of going, and I could not bear to have her at the mercy of her mother. Not all the masters in London could compensate for the ruin of her comfort. I should have feared too for her health, and for everything in short but her principles; *there* I believe she is not to be injured, even by her mother, or all her mother's friends; but with those friends (a very bad set I doubt not), she must have mixed, or have been left in total solitude, and I can hardly tell which would have been worse for her. If she is with her mother, moreover, she must – alas! – in all probability be with Reginald – and that would be the greatest evil of all.

Here we shall in time be at peace. Our regular employments, our books and conversation, with exercise, the children and every domestic pleasure in my power to procure her, will, I trust, gradually overcome this youthful attachment. I should not have a doubt of it were she slighted for any other woman in the world than her own mother.

How long Lady Susan will be in town, or whether she returns here again, I know not. I could not be cordial in my invitation; but if she chooses to come, no want of cordiality on my part will keep her away.

I could not help asking Reginald if he intended being in town this winter, as soon as I found that Her Ladyship's steps would be bent thither; and though he professed himself quite undetermined, there was a something in his look and voice as he spoke which contradicted his words. I have done with lamentation. I look upon the event as so far decided that I resign myself to it in despair. If he leaves you soon for London, everything will be concluded.

Yours affectionately,

Catherine Vernon

Letter 28

MRS JOHNSON TO LADY SUSAN

Edward St

My dearest friend,

I write in the greatest distress; the most unfortunate event has just taken place. Mr Johnson has hit on the most effectual manner of plaguing us all. He had heard, I imagine, by some means or other, that you were soon to be in London, and immediately contrived to have such an attack of the gout as must at least delay his journey to Bath, if not wholly prevent it. I am persuaded the gout is brought on, or kept off at pleasure; it was the same when I wanted to join the Hamiltons to the Lakes; and three years ago when I had a fancy for Bath, nothing could induce him to have a gouty symptom.

I have received yours, and have engaged the lodgings in consequence. I am pleased to find that my letter had so much effect on you, and that De Courcy is certainly your own. Let me hear from you as soon as you arrive, and in particular tell me what you mean to do with Manwaring. It is impossible to say when I shall be able to see you. My confinement must be great. It is such an abominable trick to be ill here, instead of at Bath, that I can scarcely command myself at all. At Bath, his old aunts would have nursed him, but here it all falls upon me – and he bears pain with such patience that I have not the common excuse for losing my temper.

Yours ever,

Alicia

Letter 29

LADY SUSAN TO MRS JOHNSON

Upper Seymour St

My dear Alicia,

There needed not this last fit of the gout to make me detest Mr Johnson; but now the extent of my aversion is not to be estimated. To have you confined, a nurse in his apartment! My dear Alicia, of what a mistake were you guilty in marrying a man of his age! Just old enough to be formal, ungovernable and to have the gout – too old to be agreeable and too young to die.

I arrived last night about five, and had scarcely swallowed my dinner when Manwaring made his appearance. I will not dissemble what real pleasure his sight afforded me, nor how strongly I felt the contrast between his person and manners and those of Reginald, to the infinite disadvantage of the latter. For an hour or two, I was even staggered in my resolution of marrying him – and though this was too idle and nonsensical an idea to remain long on my mind, I do not feel very eager for the conclusion of my marriage, or look forward with much impatience to the time when Reginald, according to our agreement, is to be in town. I shall probably put off his arrival under some pretence or other. He must not come till Manwaring is gone.

I am still doubtful at times as to marriage. If the old man would die, I might not hesitate; but a state of dependence on the caprice of Sir Reginald will not suit the freedom of my spirit; and if I resolve to wait for that event, I shall have excuse enough at present in having been scarcely ten months a widow.

I have not given Manwaring any hint of my intention – or allowed him to consider my acquaintance with Reginald as more than the commonest flirtation – and he is tolerably appeased. Adieu till we meet. I am enchanted with my lodgings.

Yours ever,

S. Vernon

Letter 30

LADY SUSAN TO MR DE COURCY

Upper Seymour St

I have received your letter; and though I do not attempt to conceal that I am gratified by your impatience for the hour of meeting, I yet feel myself under the necessity of delaying that hour beyond the time originally fixed. Do not think me unkind for such an exercise of my power, or accuse me of instability, without first hearing my reasons. In the course of my journey from Churchill, I had ample leisure for reflection on the present state of our affairs, and every review has served to convince me that they require a delicacy and cautiousness of conduct, to which we have hitherto been too little attentive. We have been hurried on by our feelings to a degree of precipitance which ill accords with the claims of our friends, or the opinion of the world. We have been unguarded in forming this hasty engagement; but we must not complete the imprudence by ratifying it while there is so much reason to fear the connection would be opposed by those friends on whom you depend.

It is not for us to blame any expectation on your father's side of your marrying to advantage; where possessions are so extensive as those of your family, the wish of increasing them, if not strictly reasonable, is too common to excite surprise or resentment. He has a right to require a woman of fortune in his daughter-in-law, and I am sometimes quarrelling with myself for suffering you to form a connection so imprudent. But the influence of reason is often acknowledged too late by those who feel like me.

I have now been but a few months a widow; and, however little indebted to my husband's memory for any happiness derived from him during an union of some years, I cannot forget that the indelicacy of so early a second marriage must subject me to the censure of the world, and incur what would be still more insupportable, the displeasure of Mr Vernon. I might perhaps harden myself in time against the injustice of a general reproach; but the loss of *his* valued esteem, I am as you well know, ill fitted to endure; and when to this may be added the consciousness of having injured you with your family, how am I to support myself? With feelings so poignant as mine, the conviction of having divided the son from his parents would make me, even with you, the most miserable of beings.

It will surely therefore be advisable to delay our union, to delay it till appearances are more promising, till affairs have taken a more favourable turn. To assist us in such a resolution, I feel that absence will be necessary. We must not meet. Cruel as this sentence may appear, the necessity of pronouncing it, which can alone reconcile it to myself, will be evident to you when you have considered our situation in the light in which I have found myself imperiously obliged to place it. You may be, you must be well assured that nothing but the strongest conviction of duty could induce me to wound my own feelings by urging a lengthened separation; and of insensibility to yours you will hardly suspect me. Again therefore I say that we ought not, we must not yet meet. By a removal for some months from each other, we shall tranquillize the sisterly fears of Mrs Vernon, who, accustomed herself to the enjoyment of riches, considers fortune as necessary everywhere, and whose sensibilities are not of a nature to comprehend ours.

Let me hear from you soon, very soon. Tell me that you submit to my arguments, and do not reproach me for using such. I cannot bear reproaches. My spirits are not so high as to need being repressed. I must endeavour to seek amusement abroad, and fortunately many of my friends are in town – among them, the Manwarings. You know how sincerely I regard both husband and wife.

> I am ever, faithfully yours,
> S. Vernon

Letter 31

LADY SUSAN TO MRS JOHNSON

Upper Seymour St

My dear friend,

That tormenting creature Reginald is here. My letter, which was intended to keep him longer in the country, has hastened him to town. Much as I wish him away, however, I cannot help being pleased with such a proof of attachment. He is devoted to me heart and soul. He will carry this note himself, which is to serve as an introduction to you, with whom he longs to be acquainted. Allow him to spend the evening with you, that I may be in no danger of his returning here. I have told him that I am not quite well, and must be alone – and should he call again there might be confusion, for it is impossible to be sure of servants. Keep him therefore, I entreat you, in Edward St. You will not find him a heavy companion, and I allow you to flirt with him as much as you like. At the same time do not forget my real interest; say all that you can to convince him that I shall be quite wretched if he remain here; you know my reasons – propriety and so forth. I would urge them more myself, but that I am impatient to be rid of him, as Manwaring comes within half an hour. Adieu.

S.V.

Letter 32

MRS JOHNSON TO LADY SUSAN

Edward St

My dear creature,

I am in agonies, and know not what to do, nor what *you* can do. Mr De Courcy arrived, just when he should not. Mrs Manwaring had that instant entered the house, and forced herself into her guardian's presence, though I did not know a syllable of it till afterwards, for I was out when both she and Reginald came, or I would have sent him away at all events; but *she* was shut up with Mr Johnson, while *he* waited in the drawing room for me. She arrived yesterday in pursuit of her husband; but perhaps you know this already from himself. She came to this house to entreat my husband's interference and, before I could be aware of it, everything that you could wish to be concealed was known to him; and unluckily she had wormed out of Manwaring's servant that he had visited you every day since your being in town, and had just watched him to your door herself! What could I do? Facts are such horrid things! All is by this time known to De Courcy, who is now alone with Mr Johnson. Do not accuse me; indeed, it was impossible to prevent it. Mr Johnson has for some time suspected

De Courcy of intending to marry you, and would speak with him alone, as soon as he knew him to be in the house.

That detestable Mrs Manwaring, who for your comfort had fretted herself thinner and uglier than ever, is still here, and they have been all closeted together. What can be done? If Manwaring is now with you, he had better be gone. At any rate I hope he will plague his wife more than ever. With anxious wishes,

Yours faithfully,
Alicia

Letter 33

LADY SUSAN TO MRS JOHNSON

Upper Seymour St

This *éclaircissement* is rather provoking. How unlucky that you should have been from home! I thought myself sure of you at seven. I am undismayed however. Do not torment yourself with fears on my account. Depend upon it, I can make my own story good with Reginald. Manwaring is just gone; he brought me the news of his wife's arrival. Silly woman! What does she expect by such manoeuvres? Yet, I wish she had stayed quietly at Langford.

Reginald will be a little enraged at first, but by tomorrow's dinner everything will be well again.

Adieu,
S.V.

Letter 34

MR DE COURCY TO LADY SUSAN

Hotel

I write only to bid you farewell. The spell is removed. I see you as you are. Since we parted yesterday, I have received from indisputable authority such an history of you as must bring the most mortifying conviction of the imposition I have been under, and the absolute necessity of an immediate and eternal separation from you. You cannot doubt to what I allude; Langford – Langford – that word will be sufficient. I received my information in Mr Johnson's house, from Mrs Manwaring herself.

You know how I have loved you; you can intimately judge of my present feelings; but I am not so weak as to find indulgence in describing them to a woman who will glory in having excited their anguish, but whose affection they have never been able to gain.

R. De Courcy

Letter 35

LADY SUSAN TO MR DE COURCY

Upper Seymour St

I will not attempt to describe my astonishment on reading the note this moment received from you. I am bewildered in my endeavours to form some rational conjecture of what Mrs Manwaring can have told you to occasion so extraordinary a change in your sentiments. Have I not explained everything to you with respect to myself which could bear a doubtful meaning, and which the ill nature of the world had interpreted to my discredit? What can you now have heard to stagger your esteem for me? Have I ever had a concealment from you? Reginald, you agitate me beyond expression. I cannot suppose that the old story of Mrs Manwaring's jealousy can be revived again or, at least, be *listened* to again. Come to me immediately, and explain what is at present absolutely incomprehensible. Believe me, the single word of *Langford* is not of such potent intelligence as to supersede the necessity of more. If we *are* to part, it will at least be handsome to take your personal leave. But I have little heart to jest; in truth, I am serious enough – for to be sunk, though but an hour, in your opinion is an humiliation to which

I know not how to submit. I shall count every moment till your arrival.

S.V.

Letter 36

MR DE COURCY TO LADY SUSAN

Hotel

Why would you write to me? Why do you require particulars? But since it must be so, I am obliged to declare that all the accounts of your misconduct during the life and since the death of Mr Vernon which had reached me in common with the world in general, and gained my entire belief before I saw you, but which you by the exertion of your perverted abilities had made me resolve to disallow, have been unanswerably proved to me. Nay, more, I am assured that a connection, of which I had never before entertained a thought, has for some time existed, and still continues to exist between you and the man whose family you robbed of its peace, in return for the hospitality with which you were received into it! That you have corresponded with him ever since your leaving Langford – not with his wife – but with him – and that he now visits you every day. Can you, dare you deny it? And all this at the time when I was an encouraged, an accepted lover! From what have I not escaped! I have only to be grateful. Far from me be all complaint, and every sigh of regret. My own folly has endangered me, my preservation I owe to the kindness, the integrity of another. But the unfortunate Mrs Manwaring, whose agonies while she related the past, seemed to threaten her reason – how is *she* to be consoled?

After such a discovery as this, you will scarcely affect further wonder at my meaning in bidding you adieu. My understanding is at length restored, and teaches me no less to abhor the artifices which had subdued me than to despise myself for the weakness on which their strength was founded.

R. De Courcy

Letter 37

LADY SUSAN TO MR DE COURCY

Upper Seymour St

I am satisfied – and will trouble you no more when these few lines are dismissed. The engagement which you were eager to form a fortnight ago is no longer compatible with your views, and I rejoice to find that the prudent advice of your parents has not been given in vain. Your restoration to peace will, I doubt not, speedily follow this act of filial obedience, and I flatter myself with the hope of surviving *my* share in this disappointment.

S.V.

Letter 38

MRS JOHNSON TO LADY SUSAN

Edward St

I am grieved, though I cannot be astonished at your rupture with Mr De Courcy; he has just informed Mr Johnson of it by letter. He leaves London, he says, today. Be assured that I partake in all your feelings, and do not be angry if I say that your intercourse even by letter must soon be given up. It makes me miserable – but Mr Johnson vows that if I persist in the connection he will settle in the country for the rest of his life – and you know it is impossible to submit to such an extremity while any other alternative remains.

You have heard of course that the Manwarings are to part; I am afraid Mrs M. will come home to us again. But she is still so fond of her husband and frets so much about him that perhaps she may not live long.

Miss Manwaring is just come to town to be with her aunt, and they say that she declares she will have Sir James Martin before she leaves London again. If I were you, I would certainly get him myself. I had almost forgot to give you my opinion of De Courcy: I am really delighted with him; he is full as handsome I think as Manwaring, and with such an open, good-humoured countenance that one cannot help loving him at first sight. Mr Johnson and he are the greatest friends in the world. Adieu, my dearest Susan. I wish matters did not go so perversely. That unlucky visit to Langford! But I dare say you did all for the best, and there is no defying destiny.

Your sincerely attached
Alicia

Letter 39

LADY SUSAN TO MRS JOHNSON

Upper Seymour St

My dear Alicia,

I yield to the necessity which parts us. Under such circumstances you could not act otherwise. Our friendship cannot be impaired by it; and in happier times, when your situation is as independent as mine, it will unite us again in the same intimacy as ever. For this I shall impatiently wait; and meanwhile can safely assure you that I never was more at ease, or better satisfied with myself and everything about me, than at the present hour. Your husband I abhor – Reginald I despise – and I am secure of never seeing either again. Have I not reason to rejoice? Manwaring is more devoted to me than *ever*, and were he at liberty, I doubt if I could resist even matrimony offered by *him*. This event, if his wife live with you, it may be in your power to hasten. The violence of her feelings, which must wear her out, may be easily kept in irritation. I rely on your friendship for this. I am now satisfied that I never could have brought myself to marry Reginald; and am equally determined that Frederica never *shall*. Tomorrow I shall fetch her from Churchill, and let Maria Manwaring tremble for the consequence. Frederica shall be Sir James's wife before she quits my house. *She* may whimper, and the Vernons may storm; I regard them not. I am tired of submitting my will to the caprices of others – of resigning my own judgement in deference to those to whom I owe no duty, and for whom I feel no respect. I have given up too much – have been too easily worked on; but Frederica shall now find the difference.

Adieu, dearest of friends. May the next gouty attack be more favourable. And may you always regard me as unalterably yours,

S. Vernon

Letter 40

LADY DE COURCY TO MRS VERNON

Parklands

My dear Catherine,

I have charming news for you, and if I had not sent off my letter this morning, you might have been spared the vexation of knowing of Reginald's being gone to town, for he is returned, Reginald is returned, not to ask our consent to his marrying Lady Susan, but to tell us that they are parted for ever! He has been only an hour in the house, and I have not been able to learn particulars, for he is so very low that I have not the heart to ask questions; but I hope we shall soon know all. This is the most joyful hour he has ever given us since the day of his birth. Nothing is wanting but to have you here, and it is our particular wish and entreaty that you would come to us as soon as you can. You have owed us a visit many long weeks. I hope nothing will make it inconvenient to Mr

Vernon, and pray bring all my grandchildren, and your dear niece is included of course; I long to see her. It has been a sad, heavy winter hitherto, without Reginald, and seeing nobody from Churchill; I never found the season so dreary before, but this happy meeting will make us young again. Frederica runs much in my thoughts, and when Reginald has recovered his usual good spirits (as I trust he soon will), we will try to rob him of his heart once more, and I am full of hopes of seeing their hands joined at no great distance.

Your affectionate mother,

C. De Courcy

Letter 41

MRS VERNON TO LADY DE COURCY

Churchill

My dear madam,

Your letter has surprised me beyond measure. Can it be true that they are really separated – and for ever? I should be overjoyed if I dared depend on it, but after all that I have seen, how can one be secure? And Reginald really with you! My surprise is the greater, because on Wednesday, the very day of his coming to Parklands, we had a most unexpected and unwelcome visit from Lady Susan, looking all cheerfulness and good humour, and seeming more as if she were to marry him when she got back to town than as if parted from him for ever. She stayed nearly two hours, was as affectionate and agreeable as ever, and not a syllable, not a hint was dropped of any disagreement or coolness between them. I asked her whether she had seen my brother since his arrival in town – not as you may suppose with any doubt of the fact – but merely to see how she looked. She immediately answered without any embarrassment that he had been kind enough to call on her on Monday, but she believed he had already returned home – which I was very far from crediting.

67

Your kind invitation is accepted by us with pleasure and, on Thursday next, we and our little ones will be with you. Pray Heaven Reginald may not be in town again by that time!

I wish we could bring dear Frederica too, but I am sorry to add that her mother's errand hither was to fetch her away; and miserable as it made the poor girl, it was impossible to detain her. I was thoroughly unwilling to let her go, and so was her uncle; and all that could be urged, we *did* urge. But Lady Susan declared that, as she was now about to fix herself in town for several months, she could not be easy if her daughter were not with her, for masters, etc. Her manner, to be sure, was very kind and proper – and Mr Vernon believes that Frederica will now be treated with affection. I wish I could think so too!

The poor girl's heart was almost broke at taking leave of us. I charged her to write to me very often, and to remember that, if she were in any distress, we should be always her friends. I took care to see her alone, that I might say all this, and I hope made her a little more comfortable. But I shall not be easy till I can go to town and judge of her situation myself.

I wish there were a better prospect than now appears of the match which the conclusion of your letter declares your expectation of. At present it is not very likely.

Yours, etc.,

Catherine Vernon

Conclusion

This correspondence, by a meeting between some of the parties and a separation between the others, could not, to the great detriment of the Post Office revenue, be continued longer. Very little assistance to the state could be derived from the epistolary intercourse of Mrs Vernon and her niece, for the former soon perceived by the style of Frederica's letters that they were written under her mother's inspection, and therefore deferring all particular enquiry till she could make it personally in town, ceased writing minutely or often.

Having learnt enough in the meanwhile from her open-hearted brother of what had passed between him and Lady Susan to sink the latter lower than ever in her opinion, she was proportionally more anxious to get Frederica removed from such a mother, and placed under her own care; and though with little hope of success, was resolved to leave nothing unattempted that might offer a chance of obtaining her sister-in-law's consent to it. Her anxiety on the subject made her press for an early visit to London; and Mr Vernon, who, as it must have already appeared, lived only to do whatever he was desired, soon found some accommodating business to call him thither. With a heart full of the matter, Mrs Vernon waited on Lady Susan shortly after her arrival in town; and she was met with such an easy and cheerful affection as made her almost turn from her with horror. No remembrance of Reginald, no consciousness of guilt, gave one look of embarrassment. She was in excellent spirits, and seemed eager to show at once, by every possible attention to her brother and sister, her sense of their kindness, and her pleasure in their society.

Frederica was no more altered than Lady Susan; the same restrained manners, the same timid look in the presence of her mother as heretofore, assured her aunt of her situation's being uncomfortable, and confirmed her in the plan of altering it. No unkindness however on the part of Lady Susan appeared. Persecution on the subject of Sir James was entirely at an end – his name merely mentioned to say that he was not in London; and in all her conversation she was solicitous only for the welfare and improvement of her daughter, acknowledging in terms of grateful delight that Frederica was now growing every day more and more what a parent could desire.

Mrs Vernon, surprised and incredulous, knew now what to suspect and, without any change in her own views, only feared greater difficulty in accomplishing them. The first hope of anything better was derived from Lady Susan's asking her whether she thought Frederica looked quite as well as she had done at Churchill, as she must confess herself to have sometimes an anxious doubt of London's perfectly agreeing with her.

Mrs Vernon encouraging the doubt, directly proposed her niece's returning with them into the country. Lady Susan was unable to express her sense of such kindness; yet knew not from a variety of reasons how to part with her daughter; and as, though her own plans were not yet wholly fixed, she trusted it would ere long be in her power to take Frederica into the country herself, concluded by declining entirely to profit by such unexampled attention. Mrs Vernon however persevered in the offer of it, and though Lady Susan continued to resist, her resistance in the course of a few days seemed somewhat less formidable.

The lucky alarm of an influenza decided what might not have been decided quite so soon. Lady Susan's maternal fears were then too much awakened for her to think of anything but Frederica's removal from the risk of infection. Above all disorders in the world, she most dreaded influenza for her daughter's constitution. Frederica returned to Churchill with her uncle and aunt, and three weeks afterwards Lady Susan announced her being married to Sir James Martin.

Mrs Vernon was then convinced of what she had only suspected before, that she might have spared herself all the trouble of urging a removal which Lady Susan had doubtless resolved on from the first. Frederica's visit was nominally for six weeks; but her mother, though inviting her to return in one or two affectionate letters, was very ready to oblige the whole party by consenting to a prolongation of her stay, and in the course of two months ceased to write of her absence, and in the course of two more to write to her at all.

Frederica was therefore fixed in the family of her uncle and aunt till such time as Reginald De Courcy could be talked, flattered and finessed into an affection for her – which, allowing leisure for the conquest of his attachment to her mother, for his abjuring all future attachments and detesting the sex, might be reasonably looked for in the course of a twelvemonth. Three months might have done it in general, but Reginald's feelings were no less lasting than lively.

Whether Lady Susan was, or was not happy in her second choice – I do not see how it can ever be ascertained – for who would take her assurance of it, on either side of the question? The world must judge from probability. She had nothing against her, but her husband and her conscience.

Sir James may seem to have drawn an harder lot than mere folly merited. I leave him therefore to all the pity that anybody can give him. For myself, I confess that *I* can pity only Miss Manwaring, who coming to town and putting herself to an expense in clothes, which impoverished her for two years, on purpose to secure him, was defrauded of her due by a woman ten years older than herself.

FINIS

The Watsons

T HE FIRST WINTER ASSEMBLY in the town of D. in Surrey was to be held on Tuesday October the thirteenth, and it was generally expected to be a very good one; a long list of country families was confidently run over as sure of attending, and sanguine hopes were entertained that the Osbornes themselves would be there.

The Edwards' invitation to the Watsons followed of course. The Edwards were people of fortune who lived in the town and kept their coach; the Watsons inhabited a village about three miles distant, were poor and had no close carriage; and ever since there had been balls in the place, the former were accustomed to invite the latter to dress, dine and sleep at their house, on every monthly return throughout the winter.

On the present occasion, as only two of Mr Watson's children were at home, and one was always necessary as companion to himself, for he was sickly and had lost his wife, one only could profit by the kindness of their friends; Miss Emma Watson, who was very recently returned to her family from the care of an aunt who had brought her up, was to make her first public appearance in the neighbourhood; and her eldest sister, whose delight in a ball was not lessened by ten years' enjoyment, had some merit in cheerfully undertaking to drive her and all her finery in the old chair to D. on the important morning.

As they splashed along the dirty lane, Miss Watson thus instructed and cautioned her inexperienced sister:

"I dare say it will be a very good ball, and among so many officers you will hardly want partners. You will find Mrs Edwards' maid very willing to help you, and I would advise you to ask Mary Edwards's opinion if you are at all at a loss, for she has very good taste. If Mr Edwards does not lose his money at cards, you will stay as late as you can wish for; if he does, he will hurry you home perhaps – but you are sure of some comfortable soup. I hope you will be in good looks. I should not be surprised if you were to be thought one of the prettiest girls in the room; there is a great deal in novelty. Perhaps Tom Musgrave may take notice of you – but I would advise you by all means not to give him any encouragement. He generally pays attention to every new girl, but he is a great flirt and never means anything serious."

"I think I have heard you speak of him before," said Emma. "Who is he?"

"A young man of very good fortune, quite independent, and remarkably agreeable, a universal favourite wherever he goes. Most of the girls hereabouts are in love with him, or have been. I believe I am the only one among them that have escaped with a whole heart, and yet I was the first he paid attention to, when he came into this country, six years ago; and very great attention indeed did he pay me. Some people say that he has never seemed to like any girl so well since, though he is always behaving in a particular way to one or another."

"And how came *your* heart to be the only cold one?" said Emma smiling.

"There was a reason for that," replied Miss Watson, changing colour. "I have not been very well used, Emma, among them; I hope you will have better luck."

"Dear sister, I beg your pardon, if I have unthinkingly given you pain."

"When first we knew Tom Musgrave," continued Miss Watson without seeming to hear her, "I was very much attached to a young man of the name of Purvis, a particular friend of Robert's, who used to be with us a great deal. Everybody thought it would have been a match."

A sigh accompanied these words, which Emma respected in silence – but her sister after a short pause went on: "You will naturally ask why it did not take place, and why he is married to another woman, while I am still single. But you must ask him – not me – you must ask Penelope. Yes Emma, Penelope was at the bottom of it all. She thinks everything fair for a husband; I trusted her, she set him against me, with a view of gaining him herself, and it ended in his discontinuing his visits and soon after marrying somebody else. Penelope makes light of her conduct, but I think such treachery very bad. It has been the ruin of my happiness. I shall never love any man as I loved Purvis. I do not think Tom Musgrave should be named with him in the same day."

"You quite shock me by what you say of Penelope," said Emma. "Could a sister do such a thing? Rivalry, treachery between sisters! I shall be afraid of being acquainted with her – but I hope it was not so. Appearances were against her—"

"You do not know Penelope. There is nothing she would not do to get married – she would as good as tell you so herself. Do not trust her with any secrets of your own, take warning by me, do not trust her; she has her good qualities, but she has no faith, no honour, no scruples, if she can promote her own advantage. I wish with all my heart she was well married. I declare I had rather have her well married than myself."

"Than yourself! Yes, I can suppose so. A heart wounded like yours can have little inclination for matrimony."

"Not much indeed – but you know, we must marry. I could do very well single for my own part – a little company, and a pleasant ball now and then, would be enough for me, if one could be young for ever, but my father cannot provide for us, and it is very bad to grow old and be poor and laughed at. I have lost Purvis, it is true, but very few people marry their first loves. I should not refuse a man because he was not Purvis – not that I can ever quite forgive Penelope."

Emma shook her head in acquiescence.

"Penelope however has had her troubles," continued Miss Watson. "She was sadly disappointed in Tom Musgrave, who afterwards transferred his attentions from me to her, and whom she was very fond of; but he never meant anything serious, and when he had trifled with her long enough, he began to slight her for Margaret, and poor Penelope was very wretched. And since then she has been trying to make some match at Chichester; she won't tell us with whom, but I believe it is a rich old Dr Harding, uncle to the friend she goes to see – and she has taken a vast deal of trouble about him and given up a great deal of time to no purpose as yet. When she went away the other day she said it should be the last time. I suppose you did not know what her particular business was at Chichester – nor guess at the object that could take her away from Stanton just as you were coming home after so many years' absence."

"No indeed, I had not the smallest suspicion of it. I considered her engagement to Mrs Shaw just at that time as very unfortunate for me. I had hoped to find all my sisters at home; to be able to make an immediate friend of each."

"I suspect the doctor to have an attack of the asthma – and that she was hurried away on that account – the Shaws are quite on her side. At least I believe so – but she tells me nothing. She professes to keep her own counsel; she says, and truly enough, that 'too many cooks spoil the broth'."

"I am sorry for her anxieties," said Emma, "but I do not like her plans or her opinions. I shall be afraid of her. She must have too masculine and bold a temper. To be so bent on marriage – to pursue a man merely for the sake of situation – is a sort of thing that shocks me; I cannot understand it. Poverty is a great evil, but to a woman of education and feeling it ought not, it cannot be the greatest. I would rather be a teacher at a school (and I can think of nothing worse) than marry a man I did not like."

"I would rather do anything than be a teacher at a school," said her sister. "I have been at school, Emma, and know what a life they lead you; you never have. I should not like marrying a disagreeable man any more than yourself – but I do not think there *are* very many disagreeable men; I think I could like any good-humoured man with a comfortable income. I suppose my aunt brought you up to be rather refined."

"Indeed, I do not know. My conduct must tell you how I have been brought up. I am no judge of it myself. I cannot compare my aunt's method with any other person's, because I know no other."

"But I can see in a great many things that you are very refined. I have observed it ever since you came home, and I am afraid it will not be for your happiness. Penelope will laugh at you very much."

"*That* will not be for my happiness, I am sure. If my opinions are wrong, I must correct them – if they are above my situation, I must endeavour to conceal them. But I doubt whether ridicule... Has Penelope much wit?"

"Yes – she has great spirits, and never cares what she says."

"Margaret is more gentle, I imagine?"

"Yes – especially in company; she is all gentleness and mildness when anybody is by. But she is a little fretful and perverse among ourselves. Poor creature! She is possessed with the notion of Tom Musgrave's being more seriously in love with her than he ever was with anybody else, and is always expecting him to come to the point. This is the second time within this twelvemonth that she has gone to spend a month with Robert and Jane on purpose to egg him on by her absence – but I am sure she is mistaken, and that he will no more follow her to Croydon now than he did last March. He will never marry unless he can marry somebody very great; Miss Osborne, perhaps, or something in that style."

"Your account of this Tom Musgrave, Elizabeth, gives me very little inclination for his acquaintance."

"You are afraid of him, I do not wonder at you."

"No indeed – I dislike and despise him."

"Dislike and despise Tom Musgrave! No, *that* you never can. I defy you not to be delighted with him if he takes notice of you. I hope he will dance with you – and I dare say he will, unless the Osbornes come with a large party, and then he will not speak to anybody else."

"He seems to have most engaging manners!" said Emma. "Well, we shall see how irresistible Mr Tom Musgrave and I find each other. I suppose I shall know him as soon as I enter the ballroom; he *must* carry some of his charm in his face."

"You will not find him in the ballroom, I can tell you; you will go early that Mrs Edwards may get a good place by the fire, and he never comes till late; and if the Osbornes are coming, he will wait in the passage, and come in with them. I should like to look in upon you, Emma. If it was but a good day with my father, I would wrap myself up, and James should drive me over, as soon as I had made tea for him; and I should be with you by the time the dancing began."

"What! Would you come late at night in this chair?"

"To be sure I would. There, I said you were very refined – and *that's* an instance of it."

Emma for a moment made no answer – at last she said:

"I wish, Elizabeth, you had not made a point of my going to this ball; I wish you were going instead of me. Your pleasure would be greater than mine. I am a stranger here, and know nobody but the Edwardses; my enjoyment therefore must be very doubtful. Yours, among all your acquaintance, would be certain. It is not too late to change. Very little apology could be requisite to the Edwards, who must be more glad of your company than of mine, and I should most readily return to my father; and should not be at all afraid to drive this quiet old creature home. Your clothes I would undertake to find means of sending to you."

"My dearest Emma," cried Elizabeth warmly, "do you think I would do such a thing? Not for the universe – but I shall never forget your good nature in proposing it. You must have a sweet temper indeed – I never met with anything like it! And would you really give up the ball that I might be able to go to it! Believe me, Emma, I am not so selfish as that comes to. No, though I am nine years older than you are, I would not be the means of keeping you from being seen. You are very pretty, and it would be very hard that you should not have as fair a chance as we have all had to make your fortune. No Emma, whoever stays at home this winter, it shan't be you. I am sure I should never have forgiven the person who had kept me from a ball at nineteen."

Emma expressed her gratitude, and for a few minutes they jogged on in silence. Elizabeth first spoke.

"You will take notice who Mary Edwards dances with."

"I will remember her partners if I can – but you know they will be all strangers to me."

"Only observe whether she dances with Captain Hunter more than once; I have my fears in that quarter. Not that her father and mother like officers, but if she does, you know, it is all over with poor Sam. And I have promised to write him word who she dances with."

"Is Sam attached to Miss Edwards?"

"Did not you know that?"

"How should I know it? How should I know in Shropshire what is passing of that nature in Surrey? It is not likely that circumstances of such delicacy should make any part of the scanty communication which passed between you and me for the last fourteen years."

"I wonder I never mentioned it when I wrote. Since you have been at home, I have been so busy with my poor father and our great wash that I have had no leisure to tell you anything – but indeed I concluded you knew it all. He has been very much in love with her these two years, and it is a great disappointment to him that he cannot always get away to our balls – but Mr Curtis won't often spare him, and just now it is a sickly time at Guildford…"

"Do you suppose Miss Edwards inclined to like him?"

"I am afraid not: you know she is an only child, and will have at least ten thousand pounds."

"But she may still like our brother."

"Oh, no! The Edwards look much higher. Her father and mother would never consent to it. Sam is only a surgeon,* you know.

Sometimes I think she does like him. But Mary Edwards is rather prim and reserved; I do not always know what she would be at."

"Unless Sam feels on sure ground with the lady herself, it seems a pity to me that he should be encouraged to think of her at all."

"A young man must think of somebody," said Elizabeth, "and why should not he be as lucky as Robert, who has got a good wife and six thousand pounds?"

"We must not all expect to be individually lucky," replied Emma. "The luck of one member of a family is luck to all."

"Mine is all to come, I am sure," said Elizabeth, giving another sigh to the remembrance of Purvis. "I have been unlucky enough, and I cannot say much for you, as my aunt married again so foolishly. Well – you will have a good ball, I dare say. The next turning will bring us to the turnpike. You may see the church tower over the hedge, and the White Hart is close by it. I shall long to know what you think of Tom Musgrave."

Such were the last audible sounds of Miss Watson's voice, before they passed through the turnpike gate and entered on the pitching of the town – the jumbling and noise of which made further conversation most thoroughly undesirable. The old mare trotted heavily on, wanting no direction of the reins to take the right turning, and making only one blunder, in proposing to stop at the milliner's, before she drew up to Mr Edwards's door. Mr Edwards lived in the best house in the street, and the best in the place, if Mr Tomlinson the banker might be indulged in calling his newly erected house at the end of the town with a shrubbery and sweep in the country. Mr Edwards's house was higher than most of its neighbours with two windows on each side the door, the windows guarded by posts and chain, the door approached by a flight of stone steps.

"Here we are," said Elizabeth – as the carriage ceased moving – "safely arrived – and by the market clock we have been only five and thirty minutes coming – which *I* think is doing pretty well, though it would be nothing for Penelope. Is it not a nice town?

The Edwards have a noble house, you see, and they live quite in style. The door will be opened by a man in livery with a powdered head, I can tell you."

Emma had seen the Edwardses only one morning at Stanton, they were therefore all but strangers to her, and though her spirits were by no means insensible to the expected joys of the evening, she felt a little uncomfortable in the thought of all that was to precede them. Her conversation with Elizabeth too giving her some very unpleasant feelings, with respect to her own family, had made her more open to disagreeable impressions from any other cause and increased her sense of the awkwardness of rushing into intimacy on so slight an acquaintance.

There was nothing in the manners of Mrs or Miss Edwards to give immediate change to these ideas; the mother, though a very friendly woman, had a reserved air, and a great deal of formal civility – and the daughter, a genteel looking girl of twenty-two, with her hair in papers, seemed very naturally to have caught something of the style of the mother who had brought her up. Emma was soon left to know what they could be by Elizabeth's being obliged to hurry away – and some very, very languid remarks on the probable brilliancy of the ball were all that broke at intervals a silence of half an hour before they were joined by the master of the house.

Mr Edwards had a much easier, and more communicative air than the ladies of the family; he was fresh from the street, and he came ready to tell whatever might interest. After a cordial reception of Emma, he turned to his daughter with: "Well Mary, I bring you good news. The Osbornes will certainly be at the ball tonight – horses for two carriages are ordered from the White Hart to be at Osborne Castle by nine…"

"I am glad of it," observed Mrs Edwards, "because their coming gives a credit to our assemblies. The Osbornes being known to have been at the first ball will dispose a great many people to attend the second. It is more than they deserve, for in fact they add nothing to the pleasure of the evening, they come so late, and go so early – but great people have always their charm."

Mr Edwards proceeded to relate every other little article of news which his morning's lounge had supplied him with, and they chatted with greater briskness, till Mrs Edwards's moment for dressing arrived, and the young ladies were carefully recommended to lose no time. Emma was shown to a very comfortable apartment, and as soon as Mrs Edwards's civilities could leave her to herself, the happy occupation, the first bliss of a ball began. The girls, dressing in some measure together, grew unavoidably better acquainted; Emma found in Miss Edwards the show of good sense, a modest unpretending mind and a great wish of obliging – and when they returned to the parlour where Mrs Edwards was sitting respectably attired in one of the two satin gowns which went through the winter, and a new cap from the milliner's, they entered it with much easier feelings and more natural smiles than they had taken away.

Their dress was now to be examined; Mrs Edwards acknowledged herself too old-fashioned to approve of every modern extravagance, however sanctioned – and though complacently viewing her daughter's good looks would give but a qualified admiration; and Mr Edwards, not less satisfied with Mary, paid some compliments of good-humoured gallantry to Emma at her expense. The discussion led to more intimate remarks, and Miss Edwards gently asked Emma if she were not often reckoned very like her youngest brother. Emma thought she could perceive a faint blush accompany the question, and there seemed to be something still more suspicious in the manner in which Mr Edwards took up the subject.

"You are paying Miss Emma no great compliment, I think, Mary," said he hastily. "Mr Sam Watson is a very good sort of young man, and I dare say a very clever surgeon, but his complexion has been rather too much exposed to all weathers to make a likeness to him very flattering."

Mary apologized in some confusion. "She had not thought a strong likeness at all incompatible with very different degrees of beauty. There might be a resemblance in countenance; and the complexion, and even the features be very unlike."

"I know nothing of my brother's beauty," said Emma, "for I have not seen him since he was seven years old – but my father reckons us alike."

"Mr Watson!" cried Mr Edwards. "Well, you astonish *me*. There is not the least likeness in the world: your brother's eyes are grey, yours are brown; he has a long face and a wide mouth – my dear, do you perceive the least resemblance?"

"Not the least. Miss Emma Watson puts me very much in mind of her eldest sister, and sometimes I see a look of Miss Penelope – and once or twice there has been a glance of Mr Robert – but I cannot perceive any likeness to Mr Samuel."

"I see the likeness between her and Miss Watson," replied Mr Edwards, "very strongly – but I am not sensible of the others. I do not think she is like any of the family but Miss Watson; but I am very sure there is no resemblance between her and Sam."

This matter was settled, and they went to dinner.

"Your father, Miss Emma, is one of my oldest friends," said Mr Edwards, as he helped her to wine, when they were drawn round the fire to enjoy their desert. "We must drink to his better health. It is a great concern to me, I assure you, that he should be such an invalid. I know nobody who likes a game of cards in a social way better than he does; and very few people that play a fairer rubber. It is a thousand pities that he should be so deprived of the pleasure. For now we have a quiet little whist club that meets three times a week at the White Hart, and if he could but have his health, how much he would enjoy it."

"I dare say he would, sir – and I wish with all my heart he were equal to it."

"Your club would be better fitted for an invalid," said Mrs Edwards, "if you did not keep it up so late."

This was an old grievance.

"So late, my dear, what are you talking," cried the husband, with sturdy pleasantry. "We are always at home before midnight. They would laugh at Osborne Castle to hear you call *that* late; they are but just rising from dinner at midnight."

"That is nothing to the purpose," retorted the lady calmly. "The Osbornes are to be no rule for us. You had better meet every night and break up two hours sooner."

So far, the subject was very often carried, but Mr and Mrs Edwards were so wise as never to pass that point, and Mr Edwards now turned to something else. He had lived long enough in the idleness of a town to become a little of a gossip, and, having some curiosity to know more of the circumstances of his young guest than had yet reached him, he began with:

"I think, Miss Emma, I remember your aunt very well about thirty years ago; I am pretty sure I danced with her in the old rooms at Bath, the year before I married. She was a very fine woman then – but like other people I suppose she is grown somewhat older since that time. I hope she is likely to be happy in her second choice."

"I hope so, I believe so, sir," said Emma in some agitation.

"Mr Turner had not been dead a great while I think?"

"About two years, sir."

"I forget what her name is now."

"O'Brien."

"Irish! Ah! I remember – and she is gone to settle in Ireland. I do not wonder that you should not wish to go with her into *that* country, Miss Emma – but it must be a great deprivation to her, poor lady! – after bringing you up like a child of her own."

"I was not so ungrateful, sir," said Emma warmly, "as to wish to be anywhere but with her. It did not suit them, it did not suit Captain O'Brien, that I should be of the party."

"Captain!" repeated Mrs Edwards. "The gentleman is in the army then?"

"Yes, ma'am."

"Aye – there is nothing like your officers for captivating the ladies, young or old. There is no resisting a cockade, my dear."

"I hope there is," said Mrs Edwards gravely, with a quick glance at her daughter – and Emma had just recovered from her own perturbation in time to see a blush on Miss Edwards's cheek and, in remembering what Elizabeth had said of Captain Hunter, to wonder and waver between his influence and her brother's.

"Elderly ladies should be careful how they make a second choice," observed Mr Edwards.

"Carefulness – discretion – should not be confined to elderly ladies or to a second choice," added his wife. "It is quite as necessary to young ladies in their first."

"Rather more so, my dear," replied he, "because young ladies are likely to feel the effects of it longer. When an old lady plays the fool, it is not in the course of nature that she should suffer from it many years."

Emma drew her hand across her eyes – and Mrs Edwards on perceiving it changed the subject to one of less anxiety to all.

With nothing to do but to expect the hour of setting off, the afternoon was long to the two young ladies; and though Miss Edwards was rather discomposed at the very early hour which her mother always fixed for going, that early hour itself was watched for with some eagerness. The entrance of the tea things at seven o'clock was some relief – and luckily Mr and Mrs Edwards always drank a dish extraordinary and ate an additional muffin when they were going to sit up late, which lengthened the ceremony almost to the wished-for moment. At a little before eight, the Tomlinsons' carriage was heard to go by, which was the constant signal for Mrs Edwards to order hers to the door; and in a very few minutes the party was transported from the quiet warmth of a snug parlour to the bustle, noise and draughts of air of the broad entrance passage of an inn.

Mrs Edwards, carefully guarding her own dress, while she attended with yet greater solicitude to the proper security of her young charges' shoulders and throats, led the way up the wide staircase, while no sound of a ball but the first scrape of one violin blessed the ears of her followers, and Miss Edwards, on hazarding the anxious enquiry of whether there were many people come yet, was told by the waiter, as she knew she should, that "Mr Tomlinson's family were in the room". In passing along a short gallery to the Assembly Room, brilliant in lights before them, they were accosted by a young man in a morning dress and boots, who was standing in the doorway of a bedchamber, apparently on purpose to see them go by.

"Ah! Mrs Edwards, how do you do? How do you do, Miss Edwards?" he cried, with an easy air. "You are determined to be in good time I see, as usual. The candles are but this moment lit."

"I like to get a good seat by the fire you know, Mr Musgrave," replied Mrs Edwards.

"I am this moment going to dress," said he. "I am waiting for my stupid fellow. We shall have a famous ball; the Osbornes are certainly coming; you may depend upon *that*, for I was with Lord Osborne this morning…"

The party passed on – Mrs Edwards's satin gown swept along the clean floor of the ballroom to the fireplace at the upper end, where one party only were formally seated, while three or four officers were lounging together, passing in and out from the adjoining card-room. A very stiff meeting between these near neighbours ensued – and as soon as they were all duly placed again, Emma, in the low whisper which became the solemn scene, said to Miss Edwards:

"The gentleman we passed in the passage was Mr Musgrave, then? He is reckoned remarkably agreeable, I understand…"

Miss Edwards answered hesitatingly, "Yes… he is very much liked by many people… But *we* are not very intimate."

"He is rich, is not he?"

"He has about eight or nine hundred pounds a year, I believe. He came into possession of it when he was very young, and my father and mother think it has given him rather an unsettled turn. He is no favourite with them."

The cold and empty appearance of the room and the demure air of the small cluster of females at one end of it began soon to give way; the inspiriting sound of other carriages was heard, and continual accessions of portly chaperones, and strings of smartly dressed girls were received, with now and then a fresh gentleman straggler, who, if not enough in love to station himself near any fair creature, seemed glad to escape into the card-room. Among the increasing numbers of military men, one now made his way to Miss Edwards, with an air of *empressement*,* which decidedly said to her companion, "I am Captain Hunter" – and Emma, who could not but watch her at such a moment, saw her looking rather distressed, but by no means displeased, and heard an engagement formed for the two first dances, which made her think her brother Sam's a hopeless case.

Emma in the meanwhile was not unobserved, or unadmired herself. A new face, and a very pretty one, could not be slighted – her name was whispered from one party to another, and no sooner had the signal been given by the orchestra's striking up a favourite air, which seemed to call the young men to their duty and people the centre of the room, than she found herself engaged to dance with a brother officer, introduced by Captain Hunter. Emma Watson was not more than of the middle height – well made and plump, with an air of healthy vigour. Her skin was very brown, but clear, smooth and glowing – which, with a lively eye, a sweet smile and an open countenance, gave beauty to attract and expression to make that beauty improve on acquaintance. Having no reason to be dissatisfied with her partner, the evening began very pleasantly to her; and her feelings perfectly coincided with the reiterated observation of others that it was an excellent ball.

The first two dances were not quite over when the returning sound of carriages, after a long interruption, called general notice, and "the Osbornes are coming, the Osbornes are coming" was repeated round the room. After some minutes of extraordinary bustle without, and watchful curiosity within, the important party, preceded by the attentive master of the inn to open a door which was never shut, made their appearance. They consisted of Lady Osborne, her son Lord Osborne, her daughter Miss Osborne, Miss Carr, her daughter's friend, Mr Howard, formerly tutor to Lord Osborne, now clergyman of the parish in which the castle stood, Mrs Blake, a widow sister who lived with him, her son a fine boy of ten years old and Mr Tom Musgrave – who, probably imprisoned within his own room, had been listening in bitter impatience to the sound of the music for the last half-hour. In their progress up the room, they paused almost immediately behind Emma to receive the compliments of some acquaintance, and she heard Lady Osborne observe that they had made a point of coming early for the gratification of Mrs Blake's little boy, who was uncommonly fond of dancing. Emma looked at them all as they passed – but chiefly and with most interest on Tom Musgrave, who was certainly a genteel, good-looking young man. Of the females, Lady Osborne had by much the finest person – though nearly fifty, she was very handsome, and had all the dignity of rank.

Lord Osborne was a very fine young man; but there was an air of coldness, of carelessness, even of awkwardness about him, which seemed to speak him out of his element in a ballroom. He came in fact only because it was judged expedient for him to please the borough – he was not fond of women's company, and he never danced. Mr Howard was an agreeable-looking man, a little more than thirty.

At the conclusion of the two dances, Emma found herself, she knew not how, seated among the Osborne set; and she was immediately struck with the fine countenance and animated gestures of the little boy, as he was standing before his mother, wondering when they should begin.

"You will not be surprised at Charles's impatience," said Mrs Blake, a lively, pleasant-looking little woman of five- or six-and-thirty, to a lady who was standing near her, "when you know what a partner he is to have. Miss Osborne has been so very kind as to promise to dance the two first dances with him."

"Oh! Yes – we have been engaged this week," cried the boy, "and we are to dance down every couple."

On the other side of Emma, Miss Osborne, Miss Carr and a party of young men were standing engaged in very lively consultation – and soon afterwards she saw the smartest officer of the set walking off to the orchestra to order the dance, while Miss Osborne, passing before her, to her little expecting partner hastily said, "Charles, I beg your pardon for not keeping my engagement, but I am going to dance these two dances with Colonel Beresford. I know you will excuse me, and I will certainly dance with you after tea."

And without staying for an answer, she turned again to Miss Carr, and in another minute was led by Colonel Beresford to begin the set. If the poor little boy's face had in its happiness been interesting to Emma, it was infinitely more so under this sudden reverse; he stood the picture of disappointment, with crimsoned cheeks, quivering lips and eyes bent on the floor. His mother, stifling her own mortification, tried to soothe his with the prospect of Miss Osborne's second promise – but though he contrived to utter with an effort of boyish bravery "Oh! I do not mind it" – it was very evident by the unceasing agitation of his features that he minded it as much as ever. Emma did not think, or reflect – she felt and acted.

"I shall be very happy to dance with you, sir, if you like it," said she, holding out her hand with the most unaffected good humour.

The boy – in one moment restored to all his first delight – looked joyfully at his mother and, stepping forwards with an honest and simple "Thank you, ma'am", was instantly ready to attend his new acquaintance. The thankfulness of Mrs Blake was more diffuse – with a look most expressive of unexpected pleasure and lively gratitude, she turned to her neighbour with repeated and fervent acknowledgements of so great and condescending a kindness to her boy. Emma with perfect truth could assure her that she could not be giving greater pleasure than she felt herself – and Charles being provided with his gloves and charged to keep them on, they joined the set which was now rapidly forming with nearly equal complacency.

It was a partnership which could not be noticed without surprise. It gained her a broad stare from Miss Osborne and Miss Carr as they passed her in the dance.

"Upon my word Charles you are in luck," said the former as she turned him, "you have got a better partner than me" – to which the happy Charles answered, "Yes."

Tom Musgrave, who was dancing with Miss Carr, gave her many inquisitive glances; and after a time Lord Osborne himself came and, under pretence of talking to Charles, stood to look at his partner. Though rather distressed by such observation, Emma could not repent what she had done, so happy had it made both the boy and his mother, the latter of whom was continually making opportunities of addressing her with the warmest civility. Her little partner, she found, though bent chiefly on dancing, was not unwilling to speak, when her questions or remarks gave him anything to say; and she learnt by a sort of inevitable enquiry that he had two brothers and a sister; that they and their mama all lived with his uncle at Wickstead; that his uncle taught him Latin, that he was very fond of riding and had a horse of his own given him by Lord Osborne; and that he had been out once already with Lord Osborne's hounds.

At the end of these dances Emma found they were to drink tea; Miss Edwards gave her a caution to be at hand, in a manner which convinced her of Mrs Edwards's holding it very important to have them both close to her when she moved into the tearoom; and Emma was accordingly on the alert to gain her proper station. It was always the pleasure of the company to have a little bustle and crowd when they thus adjourned for refreshment; the tearoom was a small room within the card-room, and in passing through the latter, where the passage was straightened by tables, Mrs Edwards and her party were for a few moments hemmed in. It happened close by Lady Osborne's cassino* table; Mr Howard, who belonged to it, spoke to his nephew; and Emma, on perceiving herself the object of attention both to Lady Osborne and him, had just turned away her eyes in time to avoid seeming to hear her young companion delightedly whisper aloud, "Oh! Uncle, do look at my partner. She is so pretty!" As they were immediately in motion again, however, Charles was hurried off without being able to receive his uncle's suffrage.

On entering the tearoom, in which two long tables were prepared, Lord Osborne was to be seen quite alone at the end of one, as if retreating as far as he could from the ball, to enjoy his own thoughts and gape without restraint. Charles instantly pointed him out to Emma.

"There's Lord Osborne – let you and I go sit by him."

"No, no," said Emma, laughing, "you must sit with my friends."

Charles was now free enough to hazard a few questions in his turn.

"What o'clock was it?"

"Eleven."

"Eleven! – and I am not at all sleepy. Mama said I should be asleep before ten. Do you think Miss Osborne will keep her word with me when tea is over?"

"Oh yes… I suppose so…" Though she felt that she had no better reason to give than that Miss Osborne had not kept it before.

"When shall you come to Osborne Castle?"

"Never, probably – I am not acquainted with the family."

"But you may come to Wickstead and see Mama, and she can take you to the Castle. There is a monstrous curious stuffed fox there, and a badger – anybody would think they were alive. It is a pity you should not see them."

On rising from tea, there was again a scramble for the pleasure of being first out of the room, which happened to be increased by one or two of the card parties having just broken up and the players being disposed to move exactly the different way. Among these was Mr Howard – his sister leaning on his arm – and no sooner were they within reach of Emma, than Mrs Blake, calling her notice by a friendly touch, said, "Your goodness to Charles, my dear Miss Watson, brings all his family upon you. Give me leave to introduce my brother – Mr Howard."

Emma curtsied, the gentleman bowed – made a hasty request for the honour of her hand in the next two dances, to which as hasty an affirmative was given, and they were immediately impelled in opposite directions. Emma was very well pleased with the circumstances; there was a quietly cheerful, gentlemanlike air in Mr Howard which suited her – and in a few minutes afterwards the value of her engagement increased, when, as she was sitting in the card-room somewhat screened by a door, she heard Lord Osborne, who was lounging on a vacant table near her, call Tom Musgrave towards him and say, "Why do you not dance with that beautiful Emma Watson? I want you to dance with her, and I will come and stand by you."

"I was determining on it this very moment, my Lord; I'll be introduced and dance with her directly."

"Aye do – and if you find she does not want much talking to, you may introduce me by and by."

"Very well my Lord… If she is like her sisters, she will only want to be listened to. I will go this moment. I shall find her in the tearoom. That stiff old Mrs Edwards has never done tea."

Away he went – Lord Osborne after him – and Emma lost no time in hurrying from her corner, exactly the other way, forgetting in her haste that she left Mrs Edwards behind.

"We had quite lost you," said Mrs Edwards, who followed her with Mary, in less than five minutes. "If you prefer this room to the other, there is no reason why you should not be here, but we had better all be together."

Emma was saved the trouble of apologizing, by their being joined at the moment by Tom Musgrave, who, requesting Mrs Edwards aloud to do him the honour of presenting him to Miss Emma Watson, left that good lady without any choice in the business, but that of testifying by the coldness of her manner that she did it unwillingly. The honour of dancing with her was solicited without loss of time – and Emma, however she might like to be thought a beautiful girl by lord and commoner, was so little disposed to favour Tom Musgrave himself that she had considerable satisfaction in avowing her prior engagement.

He was evidently surprised and discomposed. The style of her last partner had probably led him to believe her not overpowered with applications.

"My little friend Charles Blake," he cried, "must not expect to engross you the whole evening. We can never suffer this – it is against the rules of the assembly – and I am sure it will never be patronized by our good friend here, Mrs Edwards; she is by much too nice a judge of decorum to give her licence to such a dangerous particularity."

"I am not going to dance with Master Blake, sir."

The gentleman, a little disconcerted, could only hope he might be more fortunate another time – and seemed unwilling to leave her, though his friend Lord Osborne was waiting in the doorway for the result, as Emma with some amusement perceived – he began to make civil enquiries after her family.

"How comes it that we have not the pleasure of seeing your sisters here this evening? Our assemblies have been used to be so well treated by them that we do not know how to take this neglect."

"My eldest sister is the only one at home – and she could not leave my father."

"Miss Watson the only one at home! You astonish me! It seems but the day before yesterday that I saw them all three in this town. But I am afraid I have been a very sad neighbour of late. I hear dreadful complaints of my negligence wherever I go, and I confess it is a shameful length of time since I was at Stanton. But I shall now endeavour to make myself amends for the past."

Emma's calm curtsy in reply must have struck him as very unlike the encouraging warmth he had been used to receive from her sisters, and gave him probably the novel sensation of doubting his own influence, and of wishing for more attention than she bestowed. The dancing now recommenced; Miss Carr being impatient to *call*, everybody was required to stand up – and Tom Musgrave's curiosity was appeased, on seeing Mr Howard come forward and claim Emma's hand. "That will do as well for me" was Lord Osborne's remark when his friend carried him the news – and he was continually at Howard's elbow during the two dances. The frequency of his appearance there was the only unpleasant part of her engagement, the only objection she could make to Mr Howard. In himself, she thought him as agreeable as he looked; though chatting on the commonest topics, he had a sensible, unaffected way of expressing himself which made them all worth hearing, and she only regretted that he had not been able to make his pupil's manners as unexceptionable as his own.

The two dances seemed very short, and she had her partner's authority for considering them so. At their conclusion the Osbornes and their train were all on the move.

"We are off at last," said His Lordship to Tom. "How much longer do you stay in this heavenly place? Till sunrise?"

"No faith! My Lord, I have had quite enough of it. I assure you – I shall not show myself here again when I have had the honour of attending Lady Osborne to her carriage. I shall retreat in as much secrecy as possible to the most remote corner of the house, where I shall order a barrel of oysters, and be famously snug."

"Let us see you soon at the Castle; and bring me word how she looks by daylight."

Emma and Mrs Blake parted as old acquaintances, and Charles shook her by the hand and wished her "goodbye" at least a dozen times. From Miss Osborne and Miss Carr she received something like a jerking curtsy as they passed her; even Lady Osborne gave her a look of complacency – and His Lordship actually came back after the others were out of the room, to "beg her pardon", and look in the window seat behind her for the gloves which were visibly compressed in his hand.

As Tom Musgrave was seen no more, we may suppose his plan to have succeeded, and imagine him mortifying with his barrel of oysters, in dreary solitude – or gladly assisting the landlady in her bar to make fresh negus for the happy dancers above. Emma could not help missing the party, by whom she had been, though in some respects unpleasantly, distinguished, and the two dances which followed and concluded the ball were rather flat, in comparison with the others. Mr Edwards having played with good luck, they were some of the last in the room.

"Here we are, back again, I declare…" said Emma sorrowfully, as she walked into the dining room, where the table was prepared, and the neat upper maid was lighting the candles. "My dear Miss Edwards – how soon it is at an end! I wish it could come all over again!…"

A great deal of kind pleasure was expressed in her having enjoyed the evening so much – and Mr Edwards was as warm as herself in praise of the fullness, brilliancy and spirit of the meeting, though as he had been fixed the whole time at the same table in the same room, with only one change of chairs, it might have seemed a matter scarcely perceived. But he had won four rubbers out of five, and everything went well. His daughter felt the advantage of this gratified state of mind, in the course of the remarks and retrospections which now ensued, over the welcome soup.

"How came you not to dance with either of the Mr Tomlinsons, Mary?" said her mother.

"I was always engaged when they asked me."

"I thought you were to have stood up with Mr James the last two dances; Mrs Tomlinson told me he was gone to ask you – and I had heard you say two minutes before that you were not engaged."

"Yes... but... there was a mistake... I had misunderstood... I did not know I was engaged... I thought it had been for the two dances after, if we stayed so long – but Captain Hunter assured me it was for those very two..."

"So you ended with Captain Hunter Mary, did you?' said her father. "And who did you begin with?"

"Captain Hunter" was repeated, in a very humble tone.

"Hum! That is being constant, however. But who else did you dance with?"

"Mr Norton, and Mr Styles."

"And who are they?"

"Mr Norton is a cousin of Captain Hunter's."

"And who is Mr Styles?"

"One of his particular friends."

"All in the same regiment," added Mrs Edwards. "Mary was surrounded by redcoats the whole evening. I should have been better pleased to see her dancing with some of our old neighbours, I confess..."

"Yes, yes, we must not neglect our old neighbours... But if these soldiers are quicker than other people in a ballroom, what are young ladies to do?"

"I think there is no occasion for their engaging themselves so many dances beforehand, Mr Edwards."

"No – perhaps not – but I remember, my dear, when you and I did the same."

Mrs Edwards said no more, and Mary breathed again. A great deal of good-humoured pleasantry followed – and Emma went to bed in charming spirits, her head full of Osbornes, Blakes and Howards.

The next morning brought a great many visitors. It was the way of the place always to call on Mrs Edwards on the morning after a ball, and this neighbourly inclination was increased in the present instance by a general spirit of curiosity on Emma's account, as everybody wanted to look again at the girl who had been admired the night before by Lord Osborne.

Many were the eyes, and various the degrees of approbation with which she was examined. Some saw no fault, and some no beauty. With some her brown skin was the annihilation of every grace, and others could never be persuaded that she were half so handsome as Elizabeth Watson had been ten years ago. The morning passed quietly away in discussing the merits of the ball with all this succession of company – and Emma was at once astonished by finding it two o'clock, and considering that she had heard nothing of her father's chair. After this discovery she had walked twice to the window to examine the street, and was on the point of asking leave to ring the bell and make enquiries when the light sound of a carriage driving up to the door set her heart at ease. She stepped again to the window – but instead of the convenient but very un-smart family equipage perceived a neat curricle. Mr Musgrave was shortly afterwards announced – and Mrs Edwards put on her very stiffest look at the sound. Not at all dismayed, however, by her chilling air, he paid his compliments to each of the ladies with no unbecoming ease, and, continuing to address Emma, presented her a note, which he had the honour of bringing her from her sister; but to which he must observe that a verbal postscript from himself would be requisite.

The note, which Emma was beginning to read rather *before* Mrs Edwards had entreated her to use no ceremony, contained a few lines from Elizabeth importing that their father, in consequence of being unusually well, had taken the sudden resolution of attending the visitation that day, and that, as his road lay quite wide from R., it was impossible for her to come home till the following morning, unless the Edwardses would send her, which was hardly to be expected, or she could meet with any chance conveyance, or did not mind walking so far.

She had scarcely run her eye through the whole, before she found herself obliged to listen to Tom Musgrave's further account. "I received that note from the fair hands of Miss Watson only ten minutes ago," said he. "I met her in the village of Stanton, whither my good stars prompted me to turn my horses' heads – she was at that moment in quest of a person to employ on the errand, and I was fortunate enough to convince her that she could not find a more willing or speedy messenger than myself – remember, I say nothing of my disinterestedness. My reward is to be the indulgence of conveying you to Stanton in my curricle. Though they are not written down, I bring your sister's orders for the same..."

Emma felt distressed; she did not like the proposal – she did not wish to be on terms of intimacy with the proposer – and yet, fearful of encroaching on the Edwardses, as well as wishing to go home herself, she was at a loss how entirely to decline what he offered – Mrs Edwards continued silent, either not understanding the case, or waiting to see how the young lady's inclination lay. Emma thanked him – but professed herself very unwilling to give him so much trouble. "The trouble was, of course, honour, pleasure, delight. What had he or his horses to do?" Still she hesitated. "She believed she must beg leave to decline his assistance – she was rather afraid of the sort of carriage... The distance was not beyond a walk..." Mrs Edwards was silent no longer. She enquired into the particulars – and then said:

"We shall be extremely happy, Miss Emma, if you can give us the pleasure of your company until tomorrow – but if you cannot conveniently do so, our carriage is quite at your service, and Mary will be pleased with the opportunity of seeing your sister."

This was precisely what Emma had longed for, and she accepted the offer most thankfully, acknowledging that as Elizabeth was entirely alone, it was her wish to return home to dinner. The plan was warmly opposed by their visitor.

"I cannot suffer it indeed. I must not be deprived of the happiness of escorting you. I assure you there is not a possibility of fear with my horses. You might guide them yourself. *Your sisters* all know how quiet they are; they have none of them the smallest scruple in trusting themselves with me, even on a racecourse.

– Believe me..." he added, lowering his voice. "*You* are quite safe; the danger is only *mine*."

Emma was not more disposed to oblige him for all this.

"And as to Mrs Edwards's carriage being used the day after a ball, it is a thing quite out of rule, I assure you – never heard of before – the old coachman will look as black as his horses – won't he, Miss Edwards?"

No notice was taken. The ladies were silently firm, and the gentleman found himself obliged to submit.

"What a famous ball we had last night!" he cried, after a short pause. "How long did you keep it up, after the Osbornes and I went away?"

"We had two dances more."

"It is making it too much of a fatigue I think, to stay so late. I suppose your set was not a very full one."

"Yes, quite as full as ever, except the Osbornes. There seemed no vacancy anywhere – and everybody danced with uncommon spirit to the very last."

Emma said this – though against her conscience.

"Indeed! Perhaps I might have looked in upon you again, if I had been aware of as much – for I am rather fond of dancing than not. Miss Osborne is a charming girl, is not she?"

"I do not think her handsome," replied Emma, to whom all this was chiefly addressed.

"Perhaps she is not critically handsome, but her manners are delightful. And Fanny Carr is a most interesting little creature. You can imagine nothing more *naive* and *piquante*. And what do you think of *Lord Osborne*, Miss Watson?"

"That he would be handsome even, though he were not a lord – and perhaps – better bred; more desirous of pleasing, and showing himself pleased in a right place—"

"Upon my word, you are severe upon my friend! I assure you Lord Osborne is a very good fellow—"

"I do not dispute his virtues – but I do not like his careless air—"

"If it were not a breach of confidence," replied Tom with an important look, "perhaps I might be able to win a more favourable opinion of poor Osborne…"

Emma gave him no encouragement, and he was obliged to keep his friend's secret. He was also obliged to put an end to his visit – for Mrs Edwards having ordered her carriage, there was no time to be lost on Emma's side in preparing for it. Miss Edwards accompanied her home but, as it was dinner hour at Stanton, stayed with them only a few minutes.

"Now, my dear Emma," said Miss Watson, as soon as they were alone, "you must talk to me all the rest of the day, without stopping, or I shall not be satisfied. But first of all Nanny shall bring in the dinner. Poor thing! You will not dine as you did yesterday, for we have nothing but some fried beef. How nice Mary Edwards looks in her new pelisse! And now tell me how you like them all, and what I am to say to Sam. I have begun my letter; Jack Stokes is to call for it tomorrow, for his uncle is going within a mile of Guildford the next day…"

Nanny brought in the dinner. "We will wait upon ourselves," continued Elizabeth, "and then we shall lose no time. And so, you would not come home with Tom Musgrave?"

"No. You had said so much against him that I could not wish either for the obligation, or the intimacy which the use of his carriage must have created. I should not even have liked the appearance of it."

"You did very right; though I wonder at your forbearance, and I do not think I could have done it myself. He seemed so eager to fetch you that I could not say no, though it rather went against me to be throwing you together, so well as I knew his tricks – but I did long to see you, and it was a clever way of getting you home; besides, it won't do to be too nice. Nobody could have thought of the Edwardses letting you have their coach – after the horses being out so late. But what am I to say to Sam?"

"If you are guided by me, you will not encourage him to think of Miss Edwards. The father is decidedly against him, the mother shows him no favour, and I doubt his having any interest with Mary. She danced twice with Captain Hunter, and I think shows him in general as much encouragement as is consistent with her disposition, and the circumstances she is placed in. She once mentioned Sam, and certainly with a little confusion – but that was perhaps merely owing to the consciousness of his liking her, which may very probably have come to her knowledge."

"Oh! Dear yes – she has heard enough of that from us all. Poor Sam! He is out of luck as well as other people. For the life of me, Emma, I cannot help feeling for those that are crossed in love. Well – now begin, and give me an account of everything as it happened."

Emma obeyed her – and Elizabeth listened with very little inter-ruption till she heard of Mr Howard as a partner.

"Dance with Mr Howard – good Heavens! You don't say so! Why – he is quite one of the great and grand ones – did not you find him very high?"

"His manners are of a kind to give *me* much more ease and confidence than Tom Musgrave's."

"Well – go on. I should have been frightened out of my wits to have had anything to do with the Osbornes' set."

Emma concluded her narration.

"And so, you really did not dance with Tom Musgrave at all? But you must have liked him, you must have been struck with him altogether."

"I do *not* like him, Elizabeth. I allow his person and air to be good – and that his manners to a certain point – his address, rather – is pleasing. But I see nothing else to admire in him. On the contrary, he seems very vain, very conceited, absurdly anxious for distinction and absolutely contemptible in some of the measures he takes for becoming so. There is a ridiculousness about him that entertains me – but his company gives me no other agreeable emotion."

"My dearest Emma! You are like nobody else in the world. It is well Margaret is not by. You do not offend *me*, though I hardly know how to believe you. But Margaret would never forgive such words."

"I wish Margaret could have heard him profess his ignorance of her being out of the country; he declared it seemed only two days since he had seen her."

"Aye – that is just like him, and yet this is the man she *will* fancy so desperately in love with her. He is no favourite of mine, as you well know, Emma – but you must think him agreeable. Can you lay your hand on your heart, and say you do not?"

"Indeed I can, both hands; and spread to their widest extent."

"I should like to know the man you *do* think agreeable."

"His name is Howard."

"Howard! Dear me. I cannot think of *him*, but as playing cards with Lady Osborne, and looking proud. I must own however that it *is* a relief to me to find you can speak as you do of Tom Musgrave; my heart did misgive me that you would like him too well. You talked so stoutly beforehand that I was sadly afraid your brag would be punished. I only hope it will last – and that he will not come on to pay you much attention; it is a hard thing for a woman to stand against the flattering ways of a man when he is bent upon pleasing her."

As their quietly sociable little meal concluded, Miss Watson could not help observing how comfortably it had passed. "It is so delightful to me," said she, "to have things going on in peace and good humour. Nobody can tell how much I hate quarrelling. Now, though we have had nothing but fried beef, how good it has all seemed. I wish everybody were as easily satisfied as you – but poor Margaret is very snappish, and Penelope owns she had rather have quarrelling going on than nothing at all."

Mr Watson returned in the evening, not the worse for the exertion of the day, and consequently pleased with what he had done, and glad to talk of it over his own fireside.

Emma had not foreseen any interest to herself in the occurrences of a visitation – but when she heard Mr Howard spoken of as the preacher, and as having given them an excellent sermon, she could not help listening with a quicker ear.

"I do not know when I have heard a discourse more to my mind," continued Mr Watson, "or one better delivered. He reads extremely well, with great propriety and in a very impressive manner; and at the same time, without any theatrical grimace or violence. I own, I do not like much action in the pulpit – I do not like the studied air and artificial inflexions of voice which your very popular and most admired preachers generally have. A simple delivery is much better calculated to inspire devotion, and shows a much better taste. Mr Howard read like a scholar and a gentleman."

"And what had you for dinner, sir?' said his eldest daughter.

He related the dishes and told what he had ate himself. "Upon the whole," he added, "I have had a very comfortable day; my old friends were quite surprised to see me amongst them – and I must say that everybody paid me great attention, and seemed to feel for me as an invalid. They would make me sit near the fire, and as the partridges were pretty high Dr Richards would have them sent away to the other end of the table, that they might not offend Mr Watson – which I thought very kind of him. But what pleased me as much as anything was Mr Howard's attention. There is a pretty steep flight of steps up to the room we dine in – which do not quite agree with my gouty foot – and Mr Howard walked by me from the bottom to the top, and would make me take his arm. It struck me as very becoming in so young a man, but I am sure I had no claim to expect it; for I never saw him before in my life. By and by, he enquired after one of my daughters, but I do not know which. I suppose you know among yourselves."

* * *

On the third day after the ball, as Nanny at five minutes before three was beginning to bustle into the parlour with the tray and the knife case, she was suddenly called to the front door by the sound of as smart a rap as the end of a riding whip would give – and though charged by Miss Watson to let nobody in, returned in half a minute, with a look of awkward dismay, to hold the parlour door open for Lord Osborne and Tom Musgrave.

The surprise of the young ladies may be imagined. No visitors would have been welcome at such a moment; but such visitors as these – such a one as Lord Osborne at least, a nobleman and a stranger, was really distressing. He looked a little embarrassed himself – as, on being introduced by his easy, voluble friend, he muttered something of doing himself the honour of waiting on Mr Watson. Though Emma could not but take the compliment of the visit to herself, she was very far from enjoying it. She felt all the inconsistency of such an acquaintance with the very humble style in which they were obliged to live; and, having in her aunt's family been used to many of the elegancies of life, was fully sensible of all that must be open to the ridicule of richer people in her present home.

Of the pain of such feelings, Elizabeth knew very little; her simpler mind or juster reason saved her from such mortification – and though shrinking under a general sense of inferiority, she felt no particular shame. Mr Watson, as the gentlemen had already heard from Nanny, was not well enough to be downstairs. With much concern they took their seats – Lord Osborne near Emma, and the convenient Mr Musgrave, in high spirits at his own importance, on the other side of the fireplace with Elizabeth. *He* was at no loss for words – but when Lord Osborne had hoped that Emma had not caught cold at the ball, he had nothing more to say for some time, and could only gratify his eye by occasional glances at his fair neighbour.

Emma was not inclined to give herself much trouble for his entertainment – and, after hard labour of mind, he produced the remark of its being a very fine day, and followed it up with the question of: "Have you been walking this morning?"

"No, my lord. We thought it too dirty."

"You should wear half-boots." After another pause: "Nothing sets off a neat ankle more than a half-boot; nankeen galoshed with black looks very well. Do not you like half-boots?"

"Yes – but unless they are so stout as so injure their beauty, they are not fit for country walking."

"Ladies should ride in dirty weather. Do you ride?"

"No, my lord."

"I wonder every lady does not. A woman never looks better than on horseback."

"But every woman may not have the inclination, or the means."

"If they knew how much it became them, they would all have the inclination, and I fancy, Miss Watson – when once they had the inclination, the means would soon follow."

"Your Lordship thinks we always have our own way. *That* is a point on which ladies and gentlemen have long disagreed. But without pretending to decide it, I may say that there are some circumstances which even *women* cannot control. Female economy will do a great deal, my lord, but it cannot turn a small income into a large one."

Lord Osborne was silenced. Her manner had been neither sententious nor sarcastic, but there was a something in its mild seriousness, as well as in the words themselves which made His Lordship think – and when he addressed again, it was with a degree of considerate propriety, totally unlike the half-awkward, half-fearless style of his former remarks. It was a new thing with him to wish to please a woman; it was the first time that he had ever felt what was due to a woman in Emma's situation. But as he wanted neither sense nor a good disposition, he did not feel it without effect.

"You have not been long in this country, I understand," said he in the tone of a gentleman. "I hope you are pleased with it."

He was rewarded by a gracious answer, and a more liberal full view of her face than she had yet bestowed. Unused to exert himself, and happy in contemplating her, he then sat in silence for some minutes longer, while Tom Musgrave was chattering to Elizabeth, till they were interrupted by Nanny's approach, who, half-opening the door and putting in her head, said,

"Please, ma'am, Master wants to know why he be'nt to have his dinner."

The gentlemen, who had hitherto disregarded every symptom, however positive, of the nearness of that meal, now jumped up with apologies, while Elizabeth briskly called after Nanny "to tell Betty to take up the fowls".

"I am sorry it happens so," she added, turning good-humouredly towards Musgrave, "but you know what early hours we keep."

Tom had nothing to say for himself, he knew it very well, and such honest simplicity, such shameless truth rather bewildered him. Lord Osborne's parting compliments took some time, his inclination for speech seeming to increase with the shortness of the term for indulgence. He recommended exercise in defiance of dirt – spoke again in praise of half-boots – begged that his sister might be allowed to send Emma the name of her shoemaker – and concluded with saying, "My hounds will be hunting this country next week – I believe they will throw off at Stanton Wood on Wednesday at nine o'clock. I mention this in hopes of your being drawn out to see what's going on. If the morning's tolerable, pray do us the honour of giving us your good wishes in person."

The sisters looked on each other with astonishment, when their visitors had withdrawn.

"Here's an unaccountable honour!" cried Elizabeth at last. "Who would have thought of Lord Osborne's coming to Stanton. He is very handsome – but Tom Musgrave looks all to nothing the smartest and most fashionable man of the two. I am glad he did not say anything to me; I would not have had to talk to such a great man for the world. Tom was very agreeable, was not he? But did you hear him ask where Miss Penelope and Miss Margaret were when he first came in? It put me out of patience. I am glad

Nanny had not laid the cloth, however, it would have looked so awkward – just the tray did not signify..."

To say that Emma was not flattered by Lord Osborne's visit would be to assert a very unlikely thing, and describe a very odd young lady; but the gratification was by no means unalloyed; his coming was a sort of notice which might please her vanity, but did not suit her pride, and she would rather have known that he wished the visit without presuming to make it than have seen him at Stanton. Among other unsatisfactory feelings it once occurred to her to wonder why Mr Howard had not taken the same privilege of coming, and accompanied His Lordship – but she was willing to suppose that he had either known nothing about it, or had declined any share in a measure which carried quite as much impertinence in its form as good breeding.

Mr Watson was very far from being delighted when he heard what had passed – a little peevish under immediate pain, and ill-disposed to be pleased, he only replied, "Phoo! Phoo! What occasion could there be for Lord Osborne's coming? I have lived here fourteen years without being noticed by any of the family. It is some foolery of that idle fellow Tom Musgrave. I cannot return the visit – I would not if I could." And when Tom Musgrave was met with again, he was commissioned with a message of excuse to Osborne Castle, on the too sufficient plea of Mr Watson's infirm state of health.

A week or ten days rolled quietly away after this visit before any new bustle arose to interrupt even for half a day the tranquil and affectionate intercourse of the two sisters, whose mutual regard was increasing with the intimate knowledge of each other which such intercourse produced. The first circumstance to break in on this serenity was the receipt of a letter from Croydon to announce the speedy return of Margaret, and a visit of two or three days from Mr and Mrs Robert Watson, who undertook to bring her home and wished to see their sister Emma.

It was an expectation to fill the thoughts of the sisters at Stanton, and to busy the hours of one of them at least – for as Jane had been a woman of fortune, the preparations for her entertainment were considerable, and as Elizabeth had at all times more goodwill than method in her guidance of the house, she could make no change without a bustle.

An absence of fourteen years had made all her brothers and sisters strangers to Emma, but in her expectation of Margaret there was more than the awkwardness of such an alienation; she had heard things which made her dread her return; and the day which brought the party to Stanton seemed to her the probable conclusion of almost all that had been comfortable in the house.

Robert Watson was an attorney at Croydon, in a good way of business; very well satisfied with himself for the same, and for having married the only daughter of the attorney to whom he had been the clerk, with a fortune of six thousand pounds. Mrs Robert was not less pleased with herself for having had that six thousand pounds, and for being now in possession of a very smart house in Croydon, where she gave genteel parties, and wore fine clothes. In her person there was nothing remarkable; her manners were pert and conceited. Margaret was not without beauty; she had a slight, pretty figure, and rather wanted countenance than good features; but the sharp and anxious expression of her face made her beauty in general little felt. On meeting her long-absent sister, as on every occasion of show, her manner was all affection and her voice all gentleness; continual smiles and a very slow articulation being her constant resort when determined on pleasing.

She was now so "delighted to see dear, dear Emma" that she could hardly speak a word in a minute. "I am sure we shall be great friends," she observed, with much sentiment, as they were sitting together. Emma scarcely knew how to answer such a proposition – and the manner in which it was spoken she could not attempt to equal. Mrs Robert Watson eyed her with much familiar curiosity and triumphant compassion – the loss of the aunt's fortune was uppermost in her mind at the moment of meeting – and she could not but feel how much better it was to be the daughter of a gentleman of property in Croydon than the niece of an old woman who threw herself away on an Irish captain.

Robert was carelessly kind, as became a prosperous man and a brother; more intent on settling with the post boy, inveighing against the exorbitant advance in posting and pondering over a doubtful half-crown, than on welcoming a sister who was no longer likely to have any property for him to get the direction of.

"Your road through the village is infamous, Elizabeth," said he, "worse than ever it was. By Heaven! I would indite it if I lived near you. Who is the surveyor now?"

There was a little niece at Croydon, to be fondly enquired after by the kind-hearted Elizabeth, who regretted very much her not being of the party.

"You are very good," replied her mother, "and I assure you it went very hard with Augusta to have us come away without her. I was forced to say we were only going to church and promise to come back for her directly. But you know it would not do to bring her without her maid, and I am as particular as ever in having her properly attended to."

"Sweet little darling!" cried Margaret. "It quite broke my heart to leave her—"

"Then why was you in such a hurry to run away from her?" cried Mrs Robert. "You are a sad, shabby girl. I have been quarrelling with you all the way we came, have not I? Such a visit as this, I never heard of! You know how glad we are to have any of you with us – if it be for months together. And I am sorry" (with a witty smile) "we have not been able to make Croydon agreeable this autumn."

"My dearest Jane – do not overpower me with your raillery. You know what inducements I had to bring me home – spare me, I entreat you – I am no match for your arch sallies."

"Well, I only beg you will not set your neighbours against the place. Perhaps Emma may be tempted to go back with us, and stay till Christmas, if you don't put in your word."

Emma was greatly obliged.

"I assure you we have very good society at Croydon. I do not much attend the balls: they are rather too mixed – but our parties are very select and good. I had seven tables last week in my drawing room. Are you fond of the country? How do you like Stanton?"

"Very much," replied Emma, who thought a comprehensive answer most to the purpose. She saw that her sister-in-law despised her immediately. Mrs Robert Watson was indeed wondering what sort of a home Emma could possibly have been used to in Shropshire, and setting it down as certain that her aunt could never have had six thousand pounds.

"How charming Emma is!" whispered Margaret to Mrs Robert in her most languishing tone. Emma was quite distressed by such behaviour – and she did not like it better when she heard Margaret five minutes afterwards say to Elizabeth in a sharp, quick accent totally unlike the first:

"Have you heard from Penelope since she went to Chichester? I had a letter the other day. I don't fancy she is likely to make anything of it. I fancy she'll come back 'Miss Penelope' as she went."

Such, she feared, would be Margaret's common voice, when the novelty of her own appearance were over; the tone of artificial sensibility was not recommended by the idea. The ladies were invited upstairs to prepare for dinner.

"I hope you will find things tolerably comfortable, Jane," said Elizabeth as she opened the door of the spare bedchamber.

"My good creature," replied Jane, "use no ceremony with me, I entreat you. I am one of those who always take things as they find them. I hope I can put up with a small apartment for two or three nights, without making a piece of work. I always wish to be treated quite *en famille* when I come to see you – and now I do hope you have not been getting a great dinner for us. Remember we never eat suppers."

"I suppose," said Margaret rather quickly to Emma, "you and I are to be together; Elizabeth always takes care to have a room to herself."

"No – Elizabeth gives me half hers."

"Oh!" (in a softened voice, and rather mortified to find she was not ill used). "I am sorry I am not to have the pleasure of your company – especially as it makes me nervous to be much alone."

Emma was the first of the females in the parlour again; on entering it she found her brother alone.

"So, Emma," said he, "you are quite the stranger at home. It must seem odd enough to you to be here. A pretty piece of work your Aunt Turner has made of it! By Heaven! A woman should never be trusted with money. I always said she ought to have settled something on you as soon as her husband died."

"But that would have been trusting *me* with money," replied Emma, "and *I* am a woman too."

"It might have been secured to your future use, without your having any power over it now. What a blow it must have been upon you! – to find yourself, instead of heiress of eight or nine thousand pounds, sent back a weight upon your family, without a sixpence. I hope the old woman will smart for it."

"Do not speak disrespectfully of her – she was very good to me; and if she has made an imprudent choice, she will suffer more from it herself than *I* can possibly do."

"I do not mean to distress you, but you know everybody must think her an old fool. I thought Turner had been reckoned an extraordinary sensible, clever man. How the devil came he to make such a will?"

"My uncle's sense is not at all impeached in my opinion, by his attachment to my aunt. She had been an excellent wife to him. The most liberal and enlightened minds are always the most confiding. The event has been unfortunate, but my uncle's memory is if possible endeared to me by such a proof of tender respect for my aunt."

"That's odd sort of talking! He might have provided decently for his widow, without leaving everything that he had to dispose of, or any part of it at her mercy."

"My aunt may have erred" – said Emma warmly – "she *has* erred – but my uncle's conduct was faultless. I was her own niece, and he left to herself the power and the pleasure of providing for me."

"But unluckily she had left the pleasure of providing for you to your father, and without the power. That's the long and the short of the business. After keeping you at a distance from your family for such a length of time as must do away all natural affection among us, and breeding you up (I suppose) in a superior style, you are returned upon their hands without a sixpence."

"You know," replied Emma, struggling with her tears, "my uncle's melancholy state of health. He was a greater invalid than my father. He could not leave home."

"I do not mean to make you cry," said Robert, rather softened – and after a short silence, by way of changing the subject, he added. "I am just come from my father's room, he seems very indifferent. It will be a sad breakup when he dies. Pity, you can none of you get married! You must come to Croydon as well as the rest, and see what you can do there. I believe if Margaret had had a thousand or fifteen hundred pounds, there was a young man who would have thought of her."

Emma was glad when they were joined by the others; it was better to look at her sister-in-law's finery than listen to Robert, who had equally irritated and grieved her. Mrs Robert exactly as smart as she had been at her own party, came in with apologies for her dress. "I would not make you wait," said she, "so I put on the first thing I met with. I am afraid I am a sad figure. My dear Mr Watson" (to her husband) "you have not put any fresh powder in your hair."

"No – I do not intend it. I think there is powder enough in my hair for my wife and sisters."

"Indeed, you ought to make some alteration in your dress before dinner when you are out visiting, though you do not at home."

"Nonsense."

"It is very odd you should not like to do what other gentlemen do. Mr Marshall and Mr Hemmings change their dress every day of their lives before dinner. And what was the use of my putting up your last new coat if you are never to wear it."

"Do be satisfied with being fine yourself, and leave your husband alone."

To put an end to this altercation, and soften the evident vexation of her sister-in-law, Emma (though in no spirits to make such nonsense easy) began to admire her gown. It produced immediate complacency.

"Do you like it?" said she. "I am very happy. It has been excessively admired; but I sometimes think the pattern too large. I shall wear one tomorrow that I think you will prefer to this. Have you seen the one I gave Margaret?"

Dinner came, and except when Mrs Robert looked at her husband's head, she continued gay and flippant, chiding Elizabeth for the profusion on the table, and absolutely protesting against the entrance of the roast turkey – which formed the only exception to "You see your dinner". "I do beg and entreat that no turkey may be seen today. I am really frightened out of my wits with the number of dishes we have already. Let us have no turkey, I beseech you."

"My dear," replied Elizabeth, "the turkey is roasted, and it may just as well come in as stay in the kitchen. Besides, if it is cut, I am in hopes my father may be tempted to eat a bit, for it is rather a favourite dish."

"You may have it in my dear, but I assure you I shan't touch it."

Mr Watson had not been well enough to join the party at dinner, but was prevailed on to come down and drink tea with them.

"I wish we may be able to have a game of cards tonight," said Elizabeth to Mrs Robert, after seeing her father comfortably seated in his armchair.

"Not on my account, my dear, I beg. You know I am no card-player. I think a snug chat infinitely better. I always say cards are very well sometimes, to break a formal circle, but one never wants them among friends."

"I was thinking of its being something to amuse my father," answered Elizabeth, "if it was not disagreeable to you. He says his head won't bear whist – but perhaps if we make a round game he may be tempted to sit down with us."

"By all means, my dear creature. I am quite at your service. Only do not oblige me to choose the game, that's all. Speculation is the only round game at Croydon now, but I can play anything. When there is only one or two of you at home, you must be quite at a loss to amuse him – why do not you get him to play at cribbage? Margaret and I have played at cribbage most nights that we have not been engaged."

A sound like a distant carriage was at this moment caught; everybody listened; it became more decided; it certainly drew nearer. It was an unusual sound in Stanton at any time of the day, for the village was on no very public road, and contained no gentleman's family but the rector's. The wheels rapidly approached – in two minutes the general expectation was answered; they stopped beyond a doubt at the garden gate of the parsonage.

"Who could it be? It was certainly a post-chaise. Penelope was the only creature to be thought of. She might perhaps have met with some unexpected opportunity of returning."

A pause of suspense ensued. Steps were distinguished, first along the paved footway which led under the windows of the house to the front door, and then within the passage. They were the steps of a man. It could not be Penelope. It must be Samuel.

The door opened, and displayed Tom Musgrave in the wrap of a traveller. He had been in London and was now on his way home, and he had come half a mile out of his road merely to call for ten minutes at Stanton. He loved to take people by surprise, with sudden visits at extraordinary seasons; and in the present instance had had the additional motive of being able to tell the Miss Watsons, whom he depended on finding sitting quietly employed after tea, that he was going home to an eight o'clock dinner.

As it happened however, he did not give more surprise than he received, when instead of being shown into the usual little sitting room, the door of the best parlour a foot larger each way than the other was thrown open, and he beheld a circle of smart people whom he could not immediately recognize arranged with all the honours of visiting round the fire, and Miss Watson sitting at the best Pembroke table, with the best tea things before her. He stood for a few seconds in silent amazement.

"Musgrave!" ejaculated Margaret in a tender voice.

He recollected himself, and came forward, delighted to find such a circle of friends and blessing his good fortune for the unlooked-for indulgence. He shook hands with Robert, bowed and smiled to the ladies and did everything very prettily; but as to any particularity of address or emotion towards Margaret, Emma, who closely observed him, perceived nothing that did not justify Elizabeth's opinions, though Margaret's modest smiles imported that she meant to take the visit to herself.

He was persuaded without much difficulty to throw off his greatcoat and drink tea with them. "For whether he dined at eight or nine," as he observed, "was a matter of very little consequence" – and without seeming to seek, he did not turn away from the chair close to Margaret which she was assiduous in providing him. She had thus secured him from her sisters – but it was not immediately in her power to preserve him from her brother's claims, for as he came avowedly from London, and had left it only four hours ago, the last current report as to public news and the general opinion of the day must be understood before Robert could let his attention be yielded to the less national and important demands of the women.

At last, however, he was at liberty to hear Margaret's soft address, as she spoke her fears of his having had a most terrible, cold, dark, dreadful journey.

"Indeed, you should not have set out so late."

"I could not be earlier," he replied. "I was detained chatting at the Bedford by a friend. All hours are alike to me. How long have you been in the country, Miss Margaret?"

"We came only this morning. My kind brother and sister brought me home this very morning – 'tis singular, is not it?"

"You were gone a great while, were not you? A fortnight I suppose?"

"*You* may call a fortnight a great while, Mr Musgrave," said Mrs Robert smartly, "but *we* think a month very little. I assure you we bring her home at the end of a month, much against our will."

"A month! Have you really been gone a month! 'Tis amazing how time flies."

"You may imagine," said Margaret in a sort of whisper, "what are my sensations at finding myself once more at Stanton. You know what a sad visitor I make. And I was so excessively impatient to see Emma; I dreaded the meeting, and at the same time longed for it. Do you not comprehend the sort of feeling?"

"Not at all," cried he aloud. "I could never dread a meeting with Miss Emma Watson – or any of her sisters."

It was lucky that he added that finish.

"Were you speaking to me?' said Emma, who had caught her own name.

"Not absolutely," he answered, "but I was thinking of you – as many at a greater distance are probably doing at this moment. Fine open weather, Miss Emma! Charming season for hunting."

"Emma is delightful, is not she?" whispered Margaret. "I have found her more than answer my warmest hopes. Did you ever see anything more perfectly beautiful? I think even you must be a convert to a brown complexion."

He hesitated; Margaret was fair herself, and he did not particularly want to compliment her; but Miss Osborne and Miss Carr were likewise fair, and his devotion to them carried the day.

"Your sister's complexion," said he at last, "is as fine as a dark complexion can be, but I still profess my preference of a white skin. You have seen Miss Osborne? She is my model for a truly feminine complexion, and she is very fair."

"Is she fairer than me?"

Tom made no reply.

"Upon my honour, ladies," said he, giving a glance over his own person, "I am highly indebted to your condescension for admitting me in such *déshabillé* into your drawing room. I really did not consider how unfit I was to be here or I hope I should have kept my distance. Lady Osborne would tell me that I were growing as careless as her son, if she saw me in this condition."

The ladies were not wanting in civil returns; and Robert Watson, stealing a view of his own head in an opposite glass, said with equal civility:

"You cannot be more in *déshabillé* than myself. We got here so late that I had not time even to put a little fresh powder in my hair."

Emma could not help entering into what she supposed her sister-in-law's feelings at that moment.

When the tea things were removed, Tom began to talk of his carriage – but the old card table being set out, and the fish and counters with a tolerably clean pack brought forward from the buffet by Miss Watson, the general voice was so urgent with him to join their party that he agreed to allow himself another quarter of an hour. Even Emma was pleased that he would stay, for she was beginning to feel that a family party might be the worst of all parties; and the others were delighted.

"What's your game?" cried he, as they stood round the table.

"Speculation I believe," said Elizabeth. "My sister recommends it, and I fancy we all like it. I know *you* do, Tom."

"It is the only round game played at Croydon now," said Mrs Robert. "We never think of any other. I am glad it is a favourite with you."

"Oh, me!" cried Tom. "Whatever you decide on will be a favourite with *me*. I have had some pleasant hours at speculation in my time – but I have not been in the way of it now for a long while.

Vingt-un is the game at Osborne Castle; I have played nothing but vingt-un of late. You would be astonished to hear the noise we make there. The fine old lofty drawing room rings again. Lady Osborne sometimes declares she cannot hear herself speak. Lord Osborne enjoys it famously – he makes the best dealer without exception that I ever beheld – such quickness and spirit! – he lets nobody dream over their cards – I wish you could see him overdraw himself on both his own cards – it is worth anything in the world!"

"Dear me!" cried Margaret. "Why should not we play at vingt-un? I think it is a much better game than speculation. I cannot say I am very fond of speculation."

Mrs Robert offered not another word in support of the game. She was quite vanquished, and the fashions of Osborne Castle carried it over the fashions of Croydon.

"Do you see much of the parsonage family at the Castle, Mr Musgrave?" asked Emma, as they were taking their seats.

"Oh! Yes – they are almost always there. Mrs Blake is a nice little good-humoured woman; she and I are sworn friends; and Howard's a very gentleman-like, good sort of fellow! You are not forgotten, I assure you, by any of the party. I fancy you must have a little cheek-glowing now and then Miss Emma. Were you not rather warm last Saturday about nine or ten o'clock in the evening? I will tell you how it was. I see you are dying to know. Says Howard to Lord Osborne—"

At this interesting moment he was called on by the others to regulate the game and determine some disputable point; and his attention was so totally engaged in the business and afterwards by the course of the game as never to revert to what he had been saying before; and Emma, though suffering a good deal from curiosity, dared not remind him.

He proved a very useful addition to their table; without him, it would have been a party of such very near relations as could have felt little interest, and perhaps maintained little complaisance, but his presence gave variety and secured good manners. He was in fact excellently qualified to shine at a round game, and few situations made him appear to greater advantage. He played with spirit, and had a great deal to say and, though with no wit himself, could sometimes make use of wit in an absent friend; and had a lively way of retailing a commonplace, or saying a mere nothing, that had great effect at a card table. The ways and good jokes of Osborne Castle were now added to his ordinary means of entertainment; he repeated the smart sayings of one lady, detailed the oversights of another and indulged them even with a copy of Lord Osborne's style of overdrawing himself on both cards.

The clock struck nine, while he was thus agreeably occupied; and when Nanny came in with her master's basin of gruel, he had the pleasure of observing to Mr Watson that he should leave him at supper while he went home to dinner himself. The carriage was ordered to the door – and no entreaties for his staying longer could now avail – for he well knew that if he stayed he must sit down to supper in less than ten minutes – which to a man whose heart had long been fixed on calling his next meal a dinner was quite insupportable.

On finding him determined to go, Margaret began to wink and nod at Elizabeth to ask him to dinner for the following day; and Elizabeth, at last not able to resist hints which her own hospitable, social temper more than half seconded, gave the invitation.

"Would he give Robert the meeting, they should be very happy."

"With the greatest pleasure" was his first reply. In a moment afterwards: "That is, if I can possibly get here in time – but I shoot with Lady Osborne, and therefore must not engage. You will not think of me unless you see me."

And so, he departed, delighted with the uncertainty in which he had left it.

* * *

Margaret, in the joy of her heart under circumstances which she chose to consider as peculiarly propitious, would willingly have made a confidante of Emma when they were alone for a short time the next morning; and had proceeded so far as to say:

"The young man who was here last night, my dear Emma, and returns today, is more interesting to me than perhaps you may be aware" – but Emma, pretending to understand nothing extraordinary in the words, made some very inapplicable reply and, jumping up, ran away from a subject which was odious to her feelings.

As Margaret would not allow a doubt to be repeated of Musgrave's coming to dinner, preparations were made for his entertainment much exceeding what had been deemed necessary the day before; and taking the office of superintendence entirely from her sister, she was half the morning in the kitchen herself directing and scolding. After a great deal of indifferent cooking and anxious suspense, however, they were obliged to sit down without their guest. Tom Musgrave never came, and Margaret was at no pains to conceal her vexation under the disappointment, or repress the peevishness of her temper.

The peace of the party for the remainder of that day, and the whole of the next, which comprised the length of Robert and Jane's visit, was continually invaded by her fretful displeasure and querulous attacks. Elizabeth was the usual object of both. Margaret had just respect enough for her brother and sister's opinion to behave properly by *them*, but Elizabeth and the maids could never do anything right – and Emma, whom she seemed no longer to think about, found the continuance of the gentle voice beyond her calculation short. Eager to be as little among them as possible, Emma was delighted with the alternative of sitting above, with her father, and warmly entreated to be his constant companion each evening – and as Elizabeth loved company of any kind too well not to prefer being below, at all risks, as she had rather talk of Croydon to Jane, with every interruption of Margaret's perverseness, than sit with only her father, who frequently could not endure talking at all, the affair was so settled, as soon as she could be persuaded to believe it no sacrifice on her sister's part.

To Emma, the change was most acceptable, and delightful. Her father, if ill, required little more than gentleness and silence; and, being a man of sense and education, was, if able to converse, a welcome companion.

In *his* chamber, Emma was at peace from the dreadful mortifications of an unequal society and family discord – from the immediate endurance of hard-hearted prosperity, low-minded conceit and wrong-headed folly, engrafted on an untoward disposition. She still suffered from them in the contemplation of their existence, in memory and in prospect, but for the moment, she ceased to be tortured by their effects. She was at leisure, she could read and think – though her situation was hardly such as to make reflection very soothing. The evils arising from the loss of her uncle were neither trifling, nor likely to lessen; and when thought had been freely indulged, in contrasting the past and the present, the employment of mind, the dissipation of unpleasant ideas which only reading could produce made her thankfully turn to a book.

The change in her home society and style of life in consequence of the death of one friend and the imprudence of another had indeed been striking. From being the first object of hope and solicitude of an uncle who had formed her mind with the care of a parent, and of tenderness to an aunt whose amiable temper had delighted to give her every indulgence, from being the life and spirit of a house where all had been comfort and elegance, and the expected heiress of an easy independence, she was become of importance to no one, a burden on those whose affection she could not expect, an addition in an house already overstocked, surrounded by inferior minds with little chance of domestic comfort and as little hope of future support. It was well for her that she was naturally cheerful – for the change was such as might have plunged weak spirits in despondence.

She was very much pressed by Robert and Jane to return with them to Croydon, and had some difficulty in getting a refusal accepted, as they thought too highly of their own kindness and situation to suppose the offer could appear in a less advantageous light to anybody else. Elizabeth gave them her interest, though evidently against her own, in privately urging Emma to go.

"You do not know what you refuse, Emma" said she, "nor what you have to bear at home. I would advise you by all means to accept the invitation; there is always something lively going on at Croydon, you will be in company almost every day and Robert and Jane will be very kind to you. As for me, I shall be no worse off without you than I have been used to be; but poor Margaret's disagreeable ways are new to you, and they would vex you more than you think for, if you stay at home."

Emma was of course uninfluenced, except to greater esteem for Elizabeth, by such representations – and the visitors departed without her.*

Sanditon

Chapter 1

A GENTLEMAN AND LADY travelling from Tonbridge towards that part of the Sussex coast which lies between Hastings and Eastbourne, being induced by business to quit the high road and attempt a very rough lane, were overturned in toiling up its long ascent half rock, half sand. The accident happened just beyond the only gentleman's house near the lane – a house which their driver, on first being required to take that direction, had conceived to be necessarily their object, and had with most unwilling looks been constrained to pass by. He had grumbled and shaken his shoulders so much indeed, and pitied and cut his horses so sharply, that he might have been open to the suspicion of overturning them on purpose (especially as the carriage was not his master's own) if the road had not indisputably become considerably worse than before, as soon as the premises of the said house were left behind – expressing with a most intelligent portentous countenance that beyond it no wheels but cart wheels could safely proceed. The severity of the fall was broken by their slow pace and the narrowness of the lane and, the gentleman having scrambled out and helped his companion, they neither of them at first felt more than shaken or bruised. But the gentleman had in the course of the extrication sprained his foot – and, soon becoming sensible of it, was obliged in a few moments to cut short both his remonstrance to the driver and his congratulations to his wife and himself – and sit down on the bank, unable to stand.

"There is something wrong here," said he – putting his hand to his ankle – "but never mind, my dear" – looking up at her with a smile – "it could not have happened, you know, in a better place. Good out of evil. The very thing perhaps to be wished for. We shall soon get relief. *There*, I fancy, lies my cure" – pointing to the neat-looking end of a cottage, which was seen romantically situated among wood on a high eminence at some little distance. "Does not *that* promise to be the very place?"

His wife fervently hoped it was – but stood, terrified and anxious, neither able to do or suggest anything – and receiving her first real comfort from the sight of several persons now coming to their assistance. The accident had been discerned from a hayfield adjoining the house they had passed – and the persons who approached were a well-looking, hale, gentlemanlike man of middle age, the proprietor of the place, who happened to be among his haymakers at the time, and three or four of the ablest of them summoned to attend their master – to say nothing of all the rest of the field, men, women and children – not very far off.

Mr Heywood – such was the name of the said proprietor – advanced with a very civil salutation – much concern for the accident – some surprise at anybody's attempting that road in a carriage – and ready offers of assistance. His courtesies were received with good breeding and gratitude, and while one or two of the men lent their help to the driver in getting the carriage upright again, the traveller said, "You are extremely obliging, sir, and I take you at your word. The injury to my leg is, I dare say, very trifling, but it is always best in these cases to have a surgeon's opinion without loss of time; and as the road does not seem at present in a favourable state for my getting up to his house myself, I will thank you to send off one of these good people for the surgeon."

"The surgeon, sir!" replied Mr Heywood. "I am afraid you will find no surgeon at hand here, but I dare say we shall do very well without him."

"Nay sir, if *he* is not in the way, his partner will do just as well – or rather better. I would rather see his partner indeed – I would prefer the attendance of his partner. One of these good people can be with him in three minutes I am sure. I need not ask whether I see the house" – looking towards the cottage – "for, excepting your own, we have passed none in this place which can be the abode of a gentleman."

Mr Heywood looked very much astonished – and replied, "What, sir! Are you expecting to find a surgeon in that cottage? We have neither surgeon nor partner in the parish I assure you."

"Excuse me, sir," replied the other. "I am sorry to have the appearance of contradicting you – but though from the extent of the parish or some other cause you may not be aware of the fact. Stay. Can I be mistaken in the place? Is not this Willingden?"

"Yes, sir, this is certainly Willingden."

"Then sir, I can bring proof of your having a surgeon in the parish – whether you may know it or not. Here, sir" – taking out his pocket book – "if you will do me the favour of casting your eye over these advertisements, which I cut out myself from the *Morning Post* and the *Kentish Gazette*, only yesterday morning in London – I think you will be convinced that I am not speaking at random. You will find it an advertisement, sir, of the dissolution of a partnership in the medical line – in your own parish – extensive business – undeniable character – respectable references – wishing to form a separate establishment – you will find it at full length sir" – offering him the two little oblong extracts.

"Sir" – said Mr Heywood with a good-humoured smile – "if you were to show me all the newspapers that are printed in one week throughout the kingdom, you would not persuade me of there being a surgeon in Willingden – for having lived here ever since I was born, man and boy fifty-seven years, I think I must have known of such a person, at least I may venture to say that he has not *much business*. To be sure, if gentlemen were to be often attempting this lane in post-chaises, it might not be a bad speculation for a surgeon to get a house at the top of the hill. But as to that cottage, I can assure you sir that it is, in fact (in spite of its spruce air at this distance), as indifferent a double tenement as any in the parish, and that my shepherd lives at one end and three old women at the other."

He took the pieces of paper as he spoke – and, having looked them over, added: "I believe I can explain it, sir. Your mistake is in the place. There are two Willingdens in this country – and your advertisement refers to the other – which is Great Willingden, or Willingden Abbots, and lies seven miles off, on the other side of Battle – quite down in the Weald. And *we*, sir" – speaking rather proudly – "are not in the Weald."

"Not *down* in the Weald I am sure, sir," replied the traveller pleasantly. "It took us half an hour to climb your hill. Well, sir, I dare say it is as you say, and I have made an abominably stupid blunder. All done in a moment – the advertisements did not catch my eye till the last half-hour of our being in town – when everything was in the hurry and confusion which always attend a short stay there. One is never able to complete anything in the way of business, you know, till the carriage is at the door – and accordingly satisfying myself with a brief enquiry, and finding we were actually to pass within a mile or two of a *Willingden*, I sought no further... My dear" – to his wife – "I am very sorry to have brought you into this scrape. But do not be alarmed about my leg. It gives me no pain while I am quiet – and as soon as these good people have succeeded in setting the carriage to rights and turning the horses round, the best thing we can do will be to measure back our steps into the turnpike road and proceed to Hailsham, and so home, without attempting anything further. Two hours take us home from Hailsham. And when once at home, we have our remedy at hand you know. A little of our own bracing sea air will soon set me on my feet again. Depend upon it, my dear, it is exactly a case for the sea. Saline air and immersion will be the very thing. My sensations tell me so already."

In a most friendly manner Mr Heywood here interposed, entreating them not think of proceeding till the ankle had been examined, and some refreshment taken, and very cordially pressing them to make use of his house for both purposes.

CHAPTER I

"We are always well stocked," said he, "with all the common remedies for sprains and bruises – and I will answer for the pleasure it will give my wife and daughters to be of service to you and this lady in every way in their power."

A twinge or two, in trying to move his foot, disposed the traveller to think rather more as he had done at first of the benefit of immediate assistance – and consulting his wife in the few words of "Well, my dear, I believe it will be better for us" – turned again to Mr Heywood – and said, "Before we accept your hospitality, sir – and in order to do away with any unfavourable impression which the sort of wild-goose chase you find me in may have given rise to – allow me to tell you who we are. My name is Parker – Mr Parker of Sanditon – this lady, my wife Mrs Parker. We are on our road home from London. My name, perhaps – though I am by no means the first of my family holding landed property in the parish of Sanditon, may be unknown at this distance from the coast – but Sanditon itself – everybody has heard of Sanditon – the favourite – for a young and rising bathing place, certainly the favourite spot of all that are to be found along the coast of Sussex; the most favoured by nature, and promising to be the most chosen by man."

"Yes – I have heard of Sanditon," replied Mr Heywood. "Every five years, one hears of some new place or other starting up by the sea, and growing the fashion. How they can half of them be filled is the wonder! *Where* people can be found with money or time to go to them! Bad things for a country – sure to raise the price of provisions and make the poor good for nothing – as I dare say you find, sir."

"Not at all, sir, not at all," cried Mr Parker eagerly. "Quite the contrary, I assure you. A common idea – but a mistaken one. It may apply to your large, overgrown places, like Brighton, or Worthing, or Eastbourne – but not to a small village like Sanditon, precluded by its size from experiencing any of the evils of civilization, while the growth of the place, the buildings, the nursery grounds, the

131

demand for everything, and the sure resort of the very best company, whose regular, steady, private families of thorough gentility and character, who are a blessing everywhere, excited the industry of the poor and diffuse comfort and improvement among them of every sort. No, sir, I assure you, Sanditon is not a place—"

"I do not mean to take exceptions to *any* place in particular, sir," answered Mr Heywood. "I only think our coast is too full of them altogether. But had we not better try to get you—"

"Our coast too full," repeated Mr Parker. "On that point perhaps we may not totally disagree – at least there are *enough*. Our coast is abundant enough; it demands no more. Everybody's taste and everybody's finances may be suited – and those good people who are trying to add to the number are in my opinion excessively absurd, and must soon find themselves the dupes of their own fallacious calculations. Such a place as Sanditon, sir, I may say was wanted, was called for. Nature had marked it out – had spoken in most intelligible characters. The finest, purest sea breeze on the coast – acknowledged to be so – excellent bathing – fine hard sand – deep water ten yards from the shore – no mud – no weeds – no slimy rocks. Never was there a place more palpably designed by nature for the resort of the invalid – the very spot which thousands seemed in need of. The most desirable distance from London! One complete, measured mile nearer than Eastbourne. Only conceive, sir, the advantage of saving a whole mile in a long journey. But Brinshore, sir, which I dare say you have in your eye – the attempts of two or three speculating people about Brinshore, this last year, to raise that paltry hamlet, lying, as it does between a stagnant marsh, a bleak moor and the constant effluvia of a ridge of putrifying seaweed, can end in nothing but their own disappointment. What in the name of common sense is to *recommend* Brinshore? A most insalubrious air – roads proverbially detestable – water brackish beyond example, impossible to get a good dish of tea within three miles of the place – and as for the soil, it is so cold and ungrateful that it can hardly be made to yield a cabbage. Depend upon it, sir, that this is a faithful description of Brinshore – not in the smallest degree exaggerated – and if you have heard it differently spoke of—"

"Sir, I never heard it spoken of in my life before," said Mr Heywood. "I did not know there was such a place in the world."

"You did not! There, my dear" – turning with exultation to his wife – "you see how it is. So much for the celebrity of Brinshore! This gentleman did not know there was such a place in the world. Why, in truth, sir, I fancy we may apply to Brinshore that line of the poet Cowper in his description of the religious cottager, as opposed to Voltaire: 'She never heard of half a mile from home'.*

"With all my heart, sir – apply any verses you like to it. But I want to see something applied to your leg – and I am sure by your lady's countenance that she is quite of my opinion and thinks it a pity to lose any more time – and here come my girls to speak for themselves and their mother." (Two or three genteel-looking young women, followed by as many maidservants, were now seen issuing from the house.) "I began to wonder the bustle should not have reached *them*. A thing of this kind soon makes a stir in a lonely place like ours. Now, sir, let us see how you can be best conveyed into the house."

The young ladies approached and said everything that was proper to recommend their father's offers; and in an unaffected manner calculated to make the strangers easy. And as Mrs Parker was exceedingly anxious for relief – and her husband by this time not much less disposed for it – a very few civil scruples were enough – especially as the carriage, being now set up, was discovered to have received such injury on the fallen side as to be unfit for present use. Mr Parker was therefore carried into the house, and his carriage wheeled off to a vacant barn.

Chapter 2

THE ACQUAINTANCE, thus oddly begun, was neither short nor unimportant. For a whole fortnight the travellers were fixed at Willingden, Mr Parker's sprain proving too serious for him to move sooner. He had fallen into very good hands. The Heywoods were a thoroughly respectable family, and every possible attention was paid in the kindest and most unpretending manner to both husband and wife. *He* was waited on and nursed, and *she* cheered and comforted with unremitting kindness – and as every office of hospitality and friendliness was received as it ought – as there was not more goodwill on one side than gratitude on the other – nor any deficiency of generally pleasant manners on either – they grew to like each other in the course of that fortnight exceedingly well.

Mr Parker's character and history were soon unfolded. All that he understood of himself he readily told, for he was very open-hearted – and where he might be himself in the dark, his conversation was still giving information to such of the Heywoods as could observe. By such he was perceived to be an enthusiast – on the subject of Sanditon, a complete enthusiast. Sanditon – the success of Sanditon as a small, fashionable bathing place was the object for which he seemed to live. A very few years ago, and it had been a quiet village of no pretensions; but some natural advantages in its position and some accidental circumstances having suggested to himself and the other principal landholder the probability of its becoming a profitable speculation, they had engaged in it, and planned and built, and praised and puffed, and raised it to a something of young renown – and Mr Parker could now think of very little besides.

The facts which, in more direct communication, he laid before them were that he was about five-and-thirty – had been married – very happily married seven years – and had four sweet children at home; that he was of a respectable family, and easy though not large fortune; no profession – succeeding as eldest son to the property which two or three generations had been holding and accumulating before him; that he had two brothers and two sisters – all single and all independent – the eldest of the two former indeed, by collateral inheritance, quite as well provided for as himself.

His object in quitting the high road to hunt for an advertising surgeon was also plainly stated; it had not proceeded from any intention of spraining his ankle or doing himself any other injury for the good of such surgeon – nor (as Mr Heywood had been apt to suppose) from any design of entering into partnership with him – it was merely in consequence of a wish to establish some medical man at Sanditon, which the nature of the advertisement induced him to expect to accomplish in Willingden. He was convinced that the advantage of a medical man at hand would very materially promote the rise and prosperity of the place – would in fact tend to bring a prodigious influx – nothing else was wanting. He had *strong* reason to believe that *one* family had been deterred last year from trying Sanditon on that account – and probably very many more – and his own sisters, who were sad invalids, and whom he was very anxious to get to Sanditon this summer, could hardly be expected to hazard themselves in a place where they could not have immediate medical advice.

Upon the whole, Mr Parker was evidently an amiable family man, fond of wife, children, brothers and sisters – and generally kind-hearted; liberal, gentlemanlike, easy to please; of a sanguine turn of mind, with more imagination than judgement. And Mrs Parker was as evidently a gentle, amiable, sweet-tempered woman, the properest wife in the world for a man of strong understanding, but not of capacity to supply the cooler reflection which her own husband sometimes needed, and so entirely waiting to be guided on every occasion that whether he were risking his fortune or spraining his ankle she remained equally useless.

Sanditon was a second wife and four children to him – hardly less dear – and certainly more engrossing. He could talk of it for ever. It had indeed the highest claims – not only those of birthplace, property and home – it was his mine, his lottery, his speculation and his hobby horse; his occupation, his hope and his futurity. He was extremely desirous of drawing his good friends at Willingden thither; and his endeavours in the cause were as grateful and disinterested as they were warm.

He wanted to secure the promise of a visit – to get as many of the family as his own house would contain to follow him to Sanditon as soon as possible – and healthy as they all undeniably were – foresaw that every one of them would be benefited by the sea. He held it indeed as certain that no person could be really well, no person (however upheld for the present by fortuitous aids of exercise and spirits in a semblance of health) could be really in a state of secure and permanent health without spending at least six weeks by the sea every year. The sea air and sea bathing together were nearly infallible, one or the other of them being a match for every disorder, of the stomach, the lungs or the blood; they were antispasmodic, antipulmonary, antiseptic, antibilious and antirheumatic. Nobody could catch cold by the sea, nobody wanted appetite by the sea, nobody wanted spirits, nobody wanted strength. They were healing, softening, relaxing – fortifying and bracing – seemingly just as was wanted – sometimes one, sometimes the other. If the sea breeze failed, the sea bath was the certain corrective – and where bathing disagreed, the sea breeze alone was evidently designed by nature for the cure.

His eloquence, however, could not prevail. Mr and Mrs Heywood never left home. Marrying early and having a very numerous family, their movements had long been limited to one small circle; and they were older in habits than in age. Excepting two journeys to London in the year to receive his dividends, Mr Heywood went no farther than his feet or his well-tried old horse could carry him, and Mrs Heywood's adventurings were only now and then to visit her neighbours in the old coach which had been new when they were married and fresh-lined on their eldest son's coming of age ten years ago. They had a very pretty property – enough, had their family been of reasonable limits, to have allowed them a very gentlemanlike share of luxuries and change – enough for them to have indulged in a new carriage and better roads, an occasional month at Tunbridge Wells, and symptoms of the gout and a winter at Bath – but the maintenance, education and fitting out of fourteen children demanded a very quiet, settled, careful course of life – and obliged them to be stationary and healthy at Willingden.

What prudence had at first enjoined was now rendered pleasant by habit. They never left home, and they had a gratification in saying so. But very far from wishing their children to do the same, they were glad to promote *their* getting out into the world as much as possible. *They* stayed at home, that their children *might* get out – and, while making that home extremely comfortable, welcomed every change from it which could give useful connections or respectable acquaintance to sons or daughters. When Mr and Mrs Parker therefore ceased from soliciting a family visit, and bounded their views to carrying back one daughter with them, no difficulties were started. It was general pleasure and consent.

Their invitation was to Miss Charlotte Heywood, a very pleasing young woman of two-and-twenty, the eldest of the daughters at home, and the one who under her mother's directions had been particularly useful and obliging to them; who had attended them most and knew them best. Charlotte was to go, with excellent health, to bathe and be better if she could – to receive every possible pleasure which Sanditon could be made to supply by the gratitude of those she went with – and to buy new parasols, new gloves and new brooches for her sisters and herself at the library which Mr Parker was anxiously wishing to support.

All that Mr Heywood himself could be persuaded to promise was that he would send everyone to Sanditon who asked his advice, and that nothing should ever induce him (as far as the future could be answered for) to spend even five shillings at Brinshore.

Chapter 3

EVERY NEIGHBOURHOOD should have a great lady. The great lady of Sanditon was Lady Denham; and in their journey from Willingden to the coast, Mr Parker gave Charlotte a more detailed account of her than had been called for before. She had been necessarily often mentioned at Willingden – for, being his colleague in speculation, Sanditon itself could not be talked of long without the introduction of Lady Denham, and that she was a very rich old lady, who had buried two husbands, who knew the value of money, was very much looked up to and had a poor cousin living with her, were facts already well known, but some further particulars of her history and her character served to lighten the tediousness of a long hill, or a heavy bit of road, and to give the visiting young lady a suitable knowledge of the person with whom she might now expect to be daily associating.

Lady Denham had been a rich Miss Brereton, born to wealth but not to education. Her first husband had been a Mr Hollis, a man of considerable property in the country, of which a large share of the parish of Sanditon, with manor and mansion house, made a part. He had been an elderly man when she married him – her own age about thirty. Her motives for such a match could be little understood at the distance of forty years, but she had so well nursed and pleased Mr Hollis that at his death he left her everything – all his estates, and all at her disposal. After a widowhood of some years, she had been induced to marry again. The late Sir Harry Denham, of Denham Park in the neighbourhood of Sanditon, had succeeded in removing her and her large income to his own domains, but he could not succeed in the views of permanently enriching his family, which were attributed to him. She had been too wary to put anything out of her own power – and when on Sir Harry's decease she returned again to her own house at Sanditon, she was said to have made this boast to a friend, "that though she had *got* nothing but her title from the family, still she had *given* nothing for it".

For the title it was to be supposed that she had married – and Mr Parker acknowledged there being just such a degree of value for it apparent now as to give her conduct that natural explanation. "There is at times," said he, "a little self-importance – but it is not offensive – and there are moments, there are points, when her love of money is carried greatly too far. But she is a good-natured woman, a very good-natured woman – a very obliging, friendly neighbour; a cheerful, independent, valuable character – and her faults may be entirely imputed to her want of education. She has good natural sense, but quite uncultivated. She has a fine, active mind, as well as a fine healthy frame for a woman of seventy, and enters into the improvement of Sanditon with a spirit truly admirable – though now and then a littleness *will* appear. She cannot look forward quite as I would have her – and takes alarm at a trifling present expense, without considering what returns it *will* make her in a year or two. That is – we think *differently*, we now and then see things *differently*, Miss Heywood. Those who tell their own story you know must be listened to with caution. When you see us in contact, you will judge for yourself."

Lady Denham was indeed a great lady beyond the common wants of society – for she had many thousands a year to bequeath, and three distinct sets of people to be courted by; her own relations, who might very reasonably wish for her original thirty thousand pounds among them, the legal heirs of Mr Hollis, who must hope to be more indebted to *her* sense of justice than he had allowed them to be to his, and those members of the Denham family whom her second husband had hoped to make a good bargain for. By all of these, or by branches of them, she had no doubt been long, and still continued to be, well attacked – and of these three divisions, Mr Parker did not hesitate to say that Mr Hollis's kindred were the *least* in favour and Sir Harry Denham's the *most*. The former, he believed, had done themselves irremediable harm by expressions of very unwise and unjustifiable resentment at the time of Mr Hollis's death – the latter, to the advantage of being the remnant of a connection which she certainly valued, joined those of having been known to her from their childhood, and of being always at hand to preserve their interest by reasonable attention. Sir Edward, the present baronet, nephew to Sir Harry, resided constantly at Denham Park; and Mr Parker had little doubt that he and his sister Miss Denham, who lived with him, would be principally remembered in her will. He sincerely hoped it. Miss Denham had a very small provision – and her brother was a poor man for his rank in society.

"He is a warm friend to Sanditon," said Mr Parker, "and his hand would be as liberal as his heart, had he the power. He would be a noble coadjutor! As it is, he does what he can – and is running up a tasteful little cottage *orné*,* on a strip of waste ground Lady Denham has granted him, which I have no doubt we shall have many a candidate for, before the end even of this season."

Till within the last twelvemonth, Mr Parker had considered Sir Edward as standing without a rival, as having the fairest chance of succeeding to the greater part of all that she had to give – but there was now another person's claims to be taken into account, those of the young female relation whom Lady Denham had been induced to receive into her family. After having always protested against any such addition, and long and often enjoyed the repeated defeats she had given to every attempt of her relations to introduce this young lady, or that young lady as a companion at Sanditon House, she had brought back with her from London last Michaelmas a Miss Brereton, who bid fair by her merits to vie in favour with Sir Edward, and to secure for herself and her family that share of the accumulated property which they had certainly the best right to inherit.

Mr Parker spoke warmly of Clara Brereton, and the interest of his story increased very much with the introduction of such a character. Charlotte listened with more than amusement now; it was solicitude and enjoyment, as she heard her described to be lovely, amiable, gentle, unassuming, conducting herself uniformly with great good sense and evidently gaining by her innate worth on the affections of her patroness. Beauty, sweetness, poverty and dependence do not want the imagination of a man to operate upon. With due exceptions – woman feels for woman very promptly and compassionately. He gave the particulars which had led to Clara's admission at Sanditon as no bad exemplification of that mixture of character, that union of littleness with kindness, with good sense, with even liberality, which he saw in Lady Denham.

After having avoided London for many years, principally on account of these very cousins, who were continually writing, inviting and tormenting her, and whom she was determined to keep at a distance, she had been obliged to go there last Michaelmas with the certainty of being detained at least a fortnight. She had gone to an hotel – living by her own account as prudently as possible, to defy the reputed expensiveness of such a home, and at the end of three days calling for her bill, that she might judge of her state. Its amount was such as determined her on not staying another hour in the house, and she was preparing, in all the anger and perturbation which a belief of very gross imposition *there*, and an ignorance of where to go for better usage, to leave the hotel at all hazards, when the cousins, the politic and lucky cousins, who seemed always to have a spy on her, introduced themselves at this important moment and, learning her situation, persuaded her to accept such a home for the rest of her stay as their humbler house in a very inferior part of London could offer.

She went; was delighted with her welcome and the hospitality and attention she received from everybody; found her good cousins the Breretons beyond her expectation worthy people; and finally was impelled by a personal knowledge of their narrow income and pecuniary difficulties to invite one of the girls of the family to pass the winter with her. The invitation was to one for six months – with the probability of another being then to take her place – but in *selecting* the one, Lady Denham had shown the good part of her character – for passing by the actual *daughters* of the house, she had chosen Clara, a niece – more helpless and more pitiable of course than any – a dependant on poverty – an additional burthen on an encumbered circle – and one who had been so low in every worldly view, as with all natural endowments and powers, to have been preparing for a situation little better than a nursery maid.

Clara had returned with her – and by her good sense and merit had now, to all appearance, secured a very strong hold in Lady Denham's regard. The six months had long been over – and not a syllable was breathed of any change, or exchange. She was a general favourite; the influence of her steady conduct and mild, gentle temper was felt by everybody. The prejudices which had met her at first in some quarters were all dissipated. She was felt to be worthy of trust – to be the very companion who would guide and soften Lady Denham – who would enlarge her mind and open her hand. She was as thoroughly amiable as she was lovely – and since having had the advantage of their Sanditon breezes, that loveliness was complete.

Chapter 4

"AND WHOSE VERY SNUG-LOOKING PLACE is this?" said Charlotte, as in a sheltered dip within two miles of the sea, they passed close by a moderate-sized house, well fenced and planted, and rich in the garden, orchard and meadows which are the best embellishments of such a dwelling. "It seems to have as many comforts about it as Willingden."

"Ah!" said Mr Parker. "This is my old house – the house of my forefathers – the house where I and all my brothers and sisters were born and bred – and where my own three eldest children were born – where Mrs Parker and I lived till within the last two years – till our new house was finished. I am glad you are pleased with it. It is an honest old place – and Hillier keeps it in very good order. I have given it up, you know, to the man who occupies the chief of my land. *He* gets a better house by it – and I a rather better situation! One other hill brings us to Sanditon – modern Sanditon – a beautiful spot. Our ancestors, you know, always built in a hole. Here were we, pent down in this little contracted nook, without air or view, only one mile and three quarters from the noblest expanse of ocean between the south foreland and the land's end, and without the smallest advantage from it. You will not think I have made a bad exchange when we reach Trafalgar House – which, by the by, I almost wish I had not named Trafalgar – for Waterloo is more the thing now. However, Waterloo is in reserve – and if we have encouragement enough this year for a little crescent to be ventured on (as I trust we shall), then we shall be able to call it Waterloo Crescent – and the name joined to the form of the building, which always takes, will give us the command of lodgers. In a good season we should have more applications than we could attend to."

"It was always a very comfortable house," said Mrs Parker – looking at it through the back window with something like the fondness of regret. "And such a nice garden – such an excellent garden."

"Yes, my love, but that we may be said to carry with us. *It* supplies us, as before, with all the fruit and vegetables we want; and we have in fact all the comfort of an excellent kitchen garden, without the constant eyesore of its formalities; or the yearly nuisance of its decaying vegetation. Who can endure a cabbage bed in October?"

"Oh, dear – yes. We are quite as well off for garden stuff as ever we were – for if it is forgot to be brought at any time, we can always buy what we want at Sanditon House. The gardener there is glad enough to supply us. But it was a nice place for the children to run about in. So shady in summer!"

"My dear, we shall have shade enough on the hill and more than enough in the course of a very few years – the growth of my plantations is a general astonishment. In the meanwhile we have the canvas awning, which gives us the most complete comfort within doors – and you can get a parasol at Whitby's for little Mary at any time, or a large bonnet at Jebb's – and as for the boys, I must say I would rather *them* run about in the sunshine than not. I am sure we agree, my dear, in wishing our boys to be as hardy as possible."

"Yes, indeed, I am sure we do – and I will get Mary a little parasol, which will make her as proud as can be. How grave she will walk about with it, and fancy herself quite a little woman. Oh! I have not the smallest doubt of our being a great deal better off where we are now. If we any of us want to bathe, we have not a quarter of a mile to go. But you know" – still looking back – "one loves to look at an old friend, at a place where one has been happy. The Hilliers did not seem to feel the storms last winter at all. I remember seeing Mrs Hillier after one of those dreadful nights, when we had been literally rocked in our bed, and she did not seem at all aware of the wind being anything more than common."

"Yes, yes – that's likely enough. We have all the grandeur of the storm, with less real danger, because the wind meeting with nothing to oppose or confine it around our house simply rages and passes on – while down in this gutter – nothing is known of the state of the air, below the tops of the trees – and the inhabitants may be taken totally unawares by one of those dreadful currents which do more mischief in a valley, when they *do* arise, than an open country ever experiences in the heaviest gale. But my dear love – as to garden stuff – you were saying that any accidental omission is supplied in a moment by Lady Denham's gardener – but it occurs to me that we ought to go elsewhere upon such occasions – and that old Stringer and his son have a higher claim. I encouraged him to set up – and am afraid he does not do very well – that is, there has not been time enough yet. He *will* do very well beyond a doubt – but at first it is uphill work; and therefore we must give him what help we can – and when any vegetables or fruit happen to be wanted – and it will not be amiss to have them often wanted, to have something or other forgotten most days – just to have a nominal supply you know, that poor old Andrew may not lose his daily job – but in fact to buy the chief of our consumption of the Stringers."

"Very well, my love, that can easily be done – and cook will be satisfied – which will be a great comfort, for she is always complaining of old Andrew now, and says he never brings her what she wants. There – now the old house is quite left behind. What is it your brother says about its being a hospital?"

"Oh, my dear Mary, merely a joke of his. He pretends to advise me to make a hospital of it. He pretends to laugh at my improvements. Sidney says anything, you know. He has always said what he chose of and to us all. Most families have such a member among them, I believe, Miss Heywood. There is a someone in most families privileged by superior abilities or spirits to say anything. In ours, it is Sidney, who is a very clever young man – and with great powers of pleasing. He lives too much in the world to be settled; that is his only fault. He is here and there and everywhere. I wish we may get him to Sanditon. I should like to have you acquainted with him. And it would be a fine thing for the place! Such a young man as Sidney, with his neat equipage and fashionable air – you and I, Mary, know what effect it might have: many a respectable family, many a careful mother, many a pretty daughter might it secure us, to the prejudice of Eastbourne and Hastings."

They were now approaching the church and the real village of Sanditon, which stood at the foot of the hill they were afterwards to ascend – a hill whose side was covered with the woods and enclosures of Sanditon House and whose height ended in an open down where the new buildings might soon be looked for. A branch only of the valley, winding more obliquely towards the sea, gave a passage to an inconsiderable stream, and formed at its mouth a third habitable division in a small cluster of fishermen's houses.

The village contained little more than cottages, but the spirit of the day had been caught, as Mr Parker observed with delight to

Charlotte, and two or three of the best of them were smartened up with a white curtain and "Lodgings to let" – and farther on, in the little green court of an old farmhouse, two females in elegant white were actually to be seen with their books and camp stools – and in turning the corner of the baker's shop, the sound of a harp might be heard through the upper casement.

Such sights and sounds were highly blissful to Mr Parker. Not that he had any personal concern in the success of the village itself; for considering it as too remote from the beach, he had done nothing there – but it was a most valuable proof of the increasing fashion of the place altogether. If the *village* could attract, the hill might be nearly full. He anticipated an amazing season. At the same time last year (late in July), there had not been a single lodger in the village! Nor did he remember any during the whole summer, excepting one family of children who came from London for sea air after the whooping cough, and whose mother would not let them be nearer the shore for fear of their tumbling in.

"Civilization, civilization indeed!" cried Mr Parker, delighted. "Look, my dear Mary. Look at William Heeley's windows. Blue shoes, and nankeen boots! Who would have expected such a sight at a shoemaker's in old Sanditon! This is new within the month. There was no blue shoe when we passed this way a month ago. Glorious indeed! Well, I think I *have* done something in my day. Now, for our hill, our health-breathing hill…"

In ascending, they passed the lodge gates of Sanditon House, and saw the top of the house itself among its groves. It was the last building of former days in that line of the parish. A little higher up, the modern began; and, in crossing the down, a Prospect House, a Bellevue Cottage and a Denham Place were to be looked at by Charlotte with the calmness of amused curiosity, and by Mr Parker with the eager eye which hoped to see scarcely any empty houses. More bills at the window than he had calculated on – and a smaller show of company on the hill – fewer carriages, fewer walkers. He had fancied it just the time of day for them to be all returning from their airings to dinner – but the sands and the Terrace always attracted some – and the tide must be flowing – about half-tide now.

He longed to be on the sands, the cliffs, at his own house and everywhere out of his house at once. His spirits rose with the very sight of the sea, and he could almost feel his ankle getting stronger already. Trafalgar House, on the most elevated spot on the down, was a light, elegant building, standing in a small lawn with a very young plantation round it, about a hundred yards from the brow of a steep but not very lofty cliff – and the nearest to it, of every building, excepting one short row of smart-looking houses called the Terrace, with a broad walk in front, aspiring to be the Mall of the place. In this row were the best milliner's shop and the library – a little detached from it, the hotel and billiard room – here began the descent to the beach, and to the bathing machines – and this was therefore the favourite spot for beauty and fashion.

At Trafalgar House, rising at a little distance behind the Terrace, the travellers were safely set down, and all was happiness and joy between Papa and Mama and their children; while Charlotte, having received possession of her apartment, found amusement enough in standing at her ample Venetian window, and looking over the miscellaneous foreground of unfinished buildings, waving linen and tops of houses, to the sea, dancing and sparkling in sunshine and freshness.

Chapter 5

WHEN THEY MET BEFORE DINNER, Mr Parker was looking over letters.

"Not a line from Sidney!" said he. "He is an idle fellow. I sent him an account of my accident from Willingden, and thought he would have vouchsafed me an answer. But perhaps it implies that he is coming himself. I trust it may. But here is a letter from one of my sisters. *They* never fail me. Women are the only correspondents to be depended on. Now, Mary" – smiling at his wife – "before I open it, what shall we guess as to the state of health of those it comes from – or rather what would Sidney say if he were here? Sidney is a saucy fellow, Miss Heywood. And you must know, he will have it there is a good deal of imagination in my two sisters' complaints – but it really is not so – or very little. They have wretched health, as you have heard us say frequently, and are subject to a variety of very serious disorders. Indeed, I do not believe they know what a day's health is – and at the same time, they are such excellent useful women and have so much energy of character that, where any good is to be done, they force themselves on exertions which, to those who do not thoroughly know them, have an extraordinary appearance. But there is really no affectation about them. They have only weaker constitutions and stronger minds than are often met with, either separate or together. And our youngest brother who lives with them, and who is not much above twenty, I am sorry to say, is almost as great an invalid as themselves. He is so delicate that he can engage in no profession. Sidney laughs at him – but it really is no joke – though Sidney often makes me laugh at them all in spite of myself. Now, if he were here, I know he would be offering odds that either Susan, Diana or Arthur would appear by this letter to have been at the point of death within the last month."

Having run his eye over the letter, he shook his head and began: "No chance of seeing them at Sanditon I am sorry to say. A very indifferent account of them indeed. Seriously, a very indifferent account – Mary, you will be quite sorry to hear how ill they have been and are. Miss Heywood, if you will give me leave, I will read Miss Diana's letter aloud. I like to have my friends acquainted with each other – and I am afraid this is the only sort of acquaintance I shall have the means of accomplishing between you. And I can have no scruple on Diana's account – for her letters show her exactly as she is, the most active, friendly, warm-hearted being in existence, and therefore must give a good impression."

He read:

"*My dear Tom, we were all much grieved at your accident, and if you had not described yourself as fallen into such very good hands, I should have been with you at all hazards the day after the receipt of your letter, though it found me suffering under a more severe attack than usual of my old grievance, spasmodic bile, and hardly able to crawl from my bed to the sofa. But how were you treated? Send me more particulars in your next. If indeed a simple sprain, as you denominate it, nothing would have been so judicious as friction, friction by the hand alone, supposing it could be applied* instantly. *Two years ago I happened to be calling on Mrs Sheldon when her coachman sprained his foot as he was cleaning the carriage and could hardly limp into the house – but by the immediate use of friction alone steadily persevered in (and I rubbed his ankle with my own hand for six hours without intermission), he was well in three days. Many thanks, my dear Tom, for the kindness with respect to us, which had so large a share in bringing on your accident. But pray never run into peril again, in looking for an apothecary on our account, for had you the most experienced man in his line settled at Sanditon, it would be no recommendation to us. We have entirely done with the whole medical tribe. We have consulted physician after physician in vain, till we are quite convinced that they can do nothing for us and that we must trust to our own knowledge of our own wretched constitutions for any relief. But if you think it advisable for the interest of the* place, *to get a medical man there, I will undertake the commission with pleasure, and have no doubt of succeeding. I could soon put the necessary irons in the fire. As for getting to Sanditon myself, it is quite an impossibility. I grieve to say that I dare not attempt it, but my feelings tell me* too plainly that in my present state, the sea air would probably be the death of me. And neither of my dear companions will leave me, or I would promote their going down to you for a fortnight. But in truth I doubt whether Susan's nerves would be equal to the effort. She has been suffering much from the headache, and six leeches a day for ten days together relieved her so little that we thought it right to change our measures – and, being convinced on examination that much of the evil lay in her gum, I persuaded her to attack the disorder there. She has accordingly had three teeth drawn, and is decidedly better, but her nerves are a good deal deranged. She can only speak in a whisper – and fainted away twice this morning on poor Arthur's trying to suppress a cough. He, I am happy to say is tolerably well – though more languid than I like – and I fear for his liver. I have heard nothing of Sidney since your being together in town, but conclude his scheme to the Isle of Wight has not taken place, or we should have seen him in his way. Most sincerely do we wish you a good season at Sanditon, and though we cannot contribute to your beau monde in person, we are doing our utmost to send you company worth having; and think we may safely reckon on securing you two large families, one a rich West Indian* from Surrey, the other, a most respectable girls' boarding school, or academy, from Camberwell. I will not tell you how many people I have employed in the business – wheel within wheel. But success more than repays. Yours most affectionately…"

"Well…" said Mr Parker as he finished. "Though I dare say Sidney might find something extremely entertaining in this letter and make us laugh for half an hour together, I declare I by myself can see nothing in it but either what is very pitiable or very creditable. With all their sufferings, you perceive how much they are occupied in promoting the good of others! So anxious for Sanditon! Two large families – one, for Prospect House probably, the other, for

Number 2, Denham Place – or the end house of the Terrace – and extra beds at the hotel. I told you my sisters were excellent women, Miss Heywood."

"And I am sure they must be very extraordinary ones," said Charlotte. "I am astonished at the cheerful style of the letter, considering the state in which both sisters appear to be. Three teeth drawn at once! Frightful! Your sister Diana seems almost as ill as possible, but those three teeth of your sister Susan's are more distressing than all the rest."

"Oh, they are so used to the operation – to every operation – and have such fortitude!"

"Your sisters know what they are about, I dare say, but their measures seem to touch on extremes. I feel that in any illness I should be so anxious for professional advice, so very little venturesome for myself, or anybody I loved! But then, we have been so healthy a family that I can be no judge of what the habit of self-doctoring may do."

"Why, to own the truth," said Mrs Parker, "I *do* think the Miss Parkers carry it too far sometimes – and so do you my love, you know. You often think they would be better if they would leave themselves more alone – and especially Arthur. I know you think it a great pity they should give *him* such a turn for being ill."

"Well, well – my dear Mary – I grant you, it *is* unfortunate for poor Arthur that at his time of life he should be encouraged to give way to indisposition. It is bad; it is bad that he should be fancying himself too sickly for any profession – and sit down at one-and-twenty, on the interest of his own little fortune, without any idea of attempting to improve it, or of engaging in any occupation that may be of use to himself or others. But let us talk of pleasanter things. These two large families are just what we wanted. But – here is something at hand, pleasanter still – Morgan, with his 'Dinner on table'."

Chapter 6

T HE PARTY WERE VERY SOON moving after dinner. Mr
Parker could not be satisfied without an early visit to the
library, and the library subscription book, and Charlotte was glad
to see as much, and as quickly as possible, where all was new.
They were out in the very quietest part of a watering-place day,
when the important business of dinner or of sitting after dinner
was going on in almost every inhabited lodging; here and there a
solitary elderly man might be seen, who was forced to move early
and walk for health – but in general, it was a thorough pause of
company, it was emptiness and tranquillity on the Terrace, the
cliffs and the sands.

The shops were deserted – the straw hats and pendant lace
seemed left to their fate both within the house and without, and
Mrs Whitby at the library was sitting in her inner room, reading
one of her own novels, for want of employment. The list of sub-
scribers was but commonplace. The Lady Denham, Miss Brereton,
Mr and Mrs Parker, Sir Edward Denham and Miss Denham,
whose names might be said to lead off the season, were followed
by nothing better than – Mrs Mathews – Miss Mathews, Miss E.
Mathews, Miss H. Mathews – Dr and Mrs Brown – Mr Richard
Pratt – Lieutenant Smith R.N., Captain Little – Limehouse – Mrs
Jane Fisher. Miss Fisher, Miss Scroggs – Revd Mr Hanking. Mr
Beard – solicitor, Grays Inn – Mrs Davis and Miss Merryweather.

Mr Parker could not but feel that the list was not only without
distinction, but less numerous than he had hoped. It was but
July, however, and August and September were the months – and
besides, the promised large families from Surrey and Camberwell
were an ever-ready consolation.

Mrs Whitby came forward without delay from her literary
recess, delighted to see Mr Parker again, whose manners recommended him to everybody, and they were fully occupied in their
various civilities and the communications, while Charlotte, having
added her name to the list as the first offering to the success of

the season, was busy in some immediate purchases for the further good of everybody as soon as Miss Whitby could be hurried down from her toilette, with all her glossy curls and smart trinkets, to wait on her.

The library, of course, afforded everything; all the useless things in the world that could not be done without, and among so many pretty temptations, and with so much goodwill for Mr Parker to encourage expenditure, Charlotte began to feel that she must check herself – or rather she reflected that at two-and-twenty there could be no excuse for her doing otherwise – and that it would not do for her to be spending all her money the very first evening. She took up a book; it happened to be a volume of *Camilla*.* She had not Camilla's youth, and had no intention of having her distress – so she turned from the drawers of rings and brooches, repressed further solicitation and paid for what she bought.

For her particular gratification, they were then to take a turn on the cliff – but as they quitted the library, they were met by two ladies whose arrival made an alteration necessary, Lady Denham and Miss Brereton. They had been to Trafalgar House, and been directed thence to the library, and though Lady Denham was a great deal too active to regard the walk of a mile as anything requiring rest, and talked of going home again directly, the Parkers knew that to be pressed into their house, and obliged to take her tea with them, would suit her best – and therefore the stroll on the cliff gave way to an immediate return home.

"No, no," said Her Ladyship. "I will not have you hurry your tea on my account. I know you like your tea late. My early hours are not to put my neighbours to inconvenience. No, no, Miss Clara and I will get back to our own tea. We came out with no other thought. We wanted just to see you and make sure of your being really come – but we get back to our own tea."

She went on however towards Trafalgar House and took possession of the drawing room very quietly – without seeming to hear a word of Mrs Parker's orders to the servant, as they entered, to bring tea directly. Charlotte was fully consoled for the loss of her walk by finding herself in company with those whom the conversation of the morning had given her a great curiosity to see. She observed them well. Lady Denham was of middle height, stout, upright and alert in her motions, with a shrewd eye and self-satisfied air – but not an unagreeable countenance – and though her manner was rather downright and abrupt, as of a person who valued herself on being free-spoken, there was a good humour and cordiality about her – a civility and readiness to be acquainted with Charlotte herself and a heartiness of welcome towards her old friends which was inspiring the goodwill she seemed to feel – and as for Miss Brereton, her appearance so completely justified Mr Parker's praise that Charlotte thought she had never beheld a more lovely or more interesting young woman.

Elegantly tall, regularly handsome, with great delicacy of complexion and soft-blue eyes, a sweetly modest and yet naturally graceful address, Charlotte could see in her only the most perfect representation of whatever heroine might be most beautiful and bewitching in all the numerous volumes they had left behind them on Mrs Whitby's shelves. Perhaps it might be partly owing to her having just issued from a circulating library – but she could not separate the idea of a complete heroine from Clara Brereton. Her situation with Lady Denham so very much in favour of it! She seemed placed with her on purpose to be ill used. Such poverty and dependence, joined to such beauty and merit, seemed to leave no choice in the business.

These feelings were not the result of any spirit of romance in Charlotte herself. No, she was a very sober-minded young lady, sufficiently well read in novels to supply her imagination with amusement, but not at all unreasonably influenced by them; and while she pleased herself the first five minutes with fancying the persecutions which *ought to* be the lot of the interesting Clara, especially in the form of the most barbarous conduct on Lady Denham's side, she found no reluctance to admit from subsequent observation that they appeared to be on very comfortable terms. She could see nothing worse in Lady Denham than the sort of old-fashioned formality of always calling her *Miss Clara* – nor anything objectionable in the degree of observance and attention which Clara paid. On one side it seemed protecting kindness, on the other grateful and affectionate respect.

The conversation turned entirely upon Sanditon, its present number of visitants and the changes of a good season. It was evident that Lady Denham had more anxiety, more fears of loss than her coadjutor. She wanted to have the place fill faster, and seemed to have more harassing apprehensions of the lodgings being in some instances underlet. Miss Diana Parker's two large families were not forgotten.

"Very good, very good," said Her Ladyship. "A West Indy family and a school. That sounds well. That will bring money."

"No people spend more freely, I believe, than West Indians," observed Mr Parker.

"Aye – so I have heard – and because they have full purses, fancy themselves equal, maybe, to your old country families. But then, they who scatter their money so freely never think of whether they may not be doing mischief of raising the price of things – and I have heard that's very much the case with your West Injines – and if they come among us to raise the price of our necessaries of life, we shall not much thank them, Mr Parker."

"My dear madam, they can only raise the price of consumable articles by such an extraordinary demand for them and such a diffusion of money among us as must do us more good than harm. Our butchers and bakers and traders in general cannot get rich without bringing prosperity to us. If *they* do not gain, our rents must be insecure – and in proportion to their profit must be ours eventually in the increased value of our houses."

"Oh, well! But I should not like to have butcher's meat raised, though – and I shall keep it down as long as I can. Aye – that young lady smiles I see – I dare say she thinks me an odd sort of a creature – but *she* will come to care about such matters herself in time. Yes, yes, my dear, depend upon it, you will be thinking of the price of butcher's meat in time – though you may not happen to have quite such a servants' hall full to feed as I have. And I do believe *those* are the best off that have fewest servants. I am not a woman of parade, as all the world knows, and if it was not for what I owe to poor Mr Hollis's memory, I should never keep up Sanditon House as I do – it is not for my own pleasure. Well, Mr Parker – and the other is a boarding school, a French boarding school, is it? No harm in that. They'll stay their six weeks. And out of such a number who knows but what some may be consumptive and want asses' milk – and I have two milch asses at this present time. But perhaps the little misses may hurt the furniture. I hope they will have a good sharp governess to look after them."

Poor Mr Parker got no more credit from Lady Denham than he had from his sisters for the object which had taken him to Willingden.

"Lord! My dear sir," she cried, "how could you think of such a thing? I am very sorry you met with your accident, but upon my word you deserved it. Going after a doctor! Why, what should we do with a doctor here? It would be only encouraging our servants and the poor to fancy themselves ill, if there was a doctor at hand. Oh, pray, let us have none of the tribe at Sanditon. We go on very well as we are. There is the sea and the downs and my milch asses – and I have told Mrs Whitby that if anybody enquires for a chamber horse they may be supplied at a fair rate (poor Mr Hollis's chamber horse, as good as new) – and what can people want for more? Here have I lived seventy good years in the world and never took physic above twice – and never saw the face of a doctor in all my life, on my *own* account. And I verily believe if my poor dear Sir Harry had never seen one neither, he would have been alive now. Ten fees, one after another, did the man take who sent *him* out of the world. I beseech you, Mr Parker, no doctors here."

The tea things were brought in.

"Oh, my dear Mrs Parker – you should not indeed – why would you do so? I was just upon the point of wishing you good evening. But since you are so very neighbourly, I believe Miss Clara and I must stay."

Chapter 7

THE POPULARITY OF THE PARKERS brought them some visitors the very next morning – amongst them, Sir Edward Denham and his sister, who, having been at Sanditon House, drove on to pay their compliments; and the duty of letter-writing being accomplished, Charlotte was settled with Mrs Parker in the drawing room in time to see them all.

The Denhams were the only ones to excite particular attention. Charlotte was glad to complete her knowledge of the family by an introduction to them, and found them, the better half at least (for while single, the *gentleman* may sometimes be thought the better half of the pair), not unworthy notice. Miss Denham was a fine young woman, but cold and reserved, giving the idea of one who felt her consequence with pride and her poverty with discontent, and who was immediately gnawed by the want of a handsomer equipage than the simple gig in which they travelled, and which their groom was leading about still in her sight. Sir Edward was much her superior in air and manner – certainly handsome, but yet more to be remarked for his very good address and wish of paying attention and giving pleasure. He came into the room remarkably well, talked much – and very much to Charlotte, by whom he chanced to be placed – and she soon perceived that he had a fine countenance, a most pleasing gentleness of voice and a great deal of conversation. She liked him. Sober-minded as she was, she thought him agreeable, and did not quarrel with the suspicion of his finding her equally so, which would arise from his evidently disregarding his sister's motion to go, and persisting in his station and his discourse. I make no apologies for my heroine's vanity. If there are young ladies in the world at her time of life more dull of fancy and more careless of pleasing, I know them not, and never wish to know them.

At last, from the low French windows of the drawing room which commanded the road and all the paths across the down, Charlotte and Sir Edward, as they sat, could not but observe Lady Denham and Miss Brereton walking by – and there was instantly a slight change in Sir Edward's countenance – with an anxious glance after them as they proceeded – followed by an early proposal to his sister – not merely for moving, but for walking on together to the Terrace – which altogether gave a hasty turn to Charlotte's fancy, cured her of her half-hour's fever and placed her in a more capable state of judging, when Sir Edward was gone, of *how* agreeable he had actually been. "Perhaps there was a good deal in his air and address, and his title did him no harm."

She was very soon in his company again. The first object of the Parkers, when their house was cleared of morning visitors, was to get out themselves; the Terrace was the attraction to all; everybody who walked must begin with the Terrace, and there, seated on one of the two green benches by the gravel walk, they found the united Denham party – but though united in the gross, very distinctly divided again – the two superior ladies being at one end of the bench, and Sir Edward and Miss Brereton at the other. Charlotte's first glance told her that Sir Edward's air was that of a lover. There could be no doubt of his devotion to Clara. How Clara received it was less obvious – but she was inclined to think not very favourably; for though sitting thus apart with him (which probably she might not have been able to prevent), her air was calm and grave.

That the young lady at the other end of the bench was doing penance was indubitable. The difference in Miss Denham's countenance, the change from Miss Denham sitting in cold grandeur in Mrs Parker's drawing room to be kept from silence by the efforts of others, to Miss Denham at Lady Denham's elbow, listening and talking with smiling attention or solicitous eagerness, was very striking – and very amusing – or very melancholy, just as satire or morality might prevail. Miss Denham's character was pretty well decided with Charlotte. Sir Edward's required longer observation. He surprised her by quitting Clara immediately on their all joining and agreeing to walk, and by addressing his attentions entirely to herself.

Stationing himself close by her, he seemed to mean to detach her as much as possible from the rest of the party and to give her the whole of his conversation. He began, in a tone of great taste and feeling, to talk of the sea and the seashore – and ran with energy through all the usual phrases employed in praise of their sublimity, and descriptive of the *undescribable* emotions they excite in the mind of sensibility. The terrific grandeur of the ocean in a storm, its glassy surface in a calm, its gulls and its samphire, and the deep fathoms of its abysses, its quick vicissitudes, its direful deceptions, its mariners tempting it in sunshine and overwhelmed by the sudden tempest, all were eagerly and fluently touched – rather commonplace, perhaps, but doing very well from the lips of a handsome Sir Edward – and she could not but think him a man of feeling – till he began to stagger her with the number of his quotations, and the bewilderment of some of his sentences.

"Do you remember," said he, "Scott's beautiful lines on the sea? – Oh, what a description they convey! They are never out of my thoughts when I walk here. That man who can read them unmoved must have the nerves of an assassin! Heaven defend me from meeting such a man unarmed."

"What description do you mean?" said Charlotte. "I remember none at this moment, of the sea, in either of Scott's poems."

"Do you not indeed? Nor can I exactly recall the beginning at this moment. But – you cannot have forgotten his description of woman:

"Oh! Woman in our hours of ease..."

"Delicious! Delicious! Had he written nothing more, he would have been immortal. And then again, that unequalled, unrivalled address to parental affection:

"Some feelings are to mortals given
With less of earth in them than heaven",* etc.

"But while we are on the subject of poetry, what think you, Miss Heywood of Burns's lines to his Mary? Oh, there is pathos to madden one! If ever there was a man who *felt*, it was Burns. Montgomery has all the fire of poetry, Wordsworth has the true soul of it – Campbell in his 'Pleasures of Hope' has touched the extreme of our sensations: "Like angels' visits, few and far between."* Can you conceive anything more subduing, more melting, more fraught with the deep sublime than that line? But Burns – I confess my sense of his pre-eminence, Miss Heywood. If Scott *has* a fault, it is the want of passion. Tender, elegant, descriptive – but *tame*. The man who cannot do justice to the attributes of woman is my contempt. Sometimes indeed a flash of feeling seems to irradiate him – as in the lines we were speaking of – "Oh! Woman in our hours of ease". But Burns is always on fire. His soul was the altar in which lovely woman sat enshrined, his spirit truly breathed the immortal incense which is her due."

"I have read several of Burns's poems with great delight," said Charlotte as soon as she had time to speak, "but I am not poetic enough to separate a man's poetry entirely from his character, – and poor Burns's known irregularities greatly interrupt my enjoyment of his lines. I have difficulty in depending on the *truth* of his feelings as a lover. I have not faith in the *sincerity* of the affections of a man of his description. He felt and he wrote and he forgot."

"Oh, no, no!" exclaimed Sir Edward in an ecstasy. "He was all ardour and truth! His genius and his susceptibilities might lead him into some aberrations – but who is perfect? It were hyper-criticism, it were pseudo-philosophy to expect from the soul of high-toned genius the grovellings of a common mind. The coruscations of talent, elicited by impassioned feeling in the breast of man, are perhaps incompatible with some of the prosaic decencies of life – nor can you, loveliest Miss Heywood" – speaking with an air of deep sentiment – "nor can any woman be a fair judge of what a man may be propelled to say, write or do, by the sovereign impulses of illimitable ardour."

This was very fine – but, if Charlotte understood it at all, not very moral – and being moreover by no means pleased with his extraordinary style of compliment, she gravely answered, "I really know nothing of the matter. This is a charming day. The wind I fancy must be southerly."

"Happy, happy wind, to engage Miss Heywood's thoughts!"

She began to think him downright silly. His choosing to walk with her, she had learnt to understand. It was done to pique Miss Brereton. She had read it in an anxious glance or two on his side – but why he should talk so much nonsense, unless he could do no better, was unintelligible. He seemed very sentimental, very full of some feelings or other, and very much addicted to all the newest-fashioned hard words – had not a very clear brain, she presumed, and talked a good deal by rote. The future might explain him further – but when there was a proposition for going into the library she felt that she had had quite enough of Sir Edward for one morning, and very gladly accepted Lady Denham's invitation of remaining on the Terrace with her.

The others all left them, Sir Edward with looks of very gallant despair in tearing himself away, and they united their agreeableness – that is, Lady Denham, like a true great lady, talked and talked only of her own concerns, and Charlotte listened – amused in considering the contrast between her two companions. Certainly, there was no strain of doubtful sentiment, nor any phrase of difficult interpretation in Lady Denham's discourse. Taking hold of Charlotte's arm with the ease of one who felt that any notice from her was an honour, and communicative from the influence of the same conscious importance or a natural love of talking, she immediately said in a tone of great satisfaction – and with a look of arch sagacity: "Miss Esther wants me to invite her and her brother to spend a week with me at Sanditon House, as I did last summer. But I shan't. She has been trying to get round me every way, with her praise of this, and her praise of that; but I saw what she was about – I saw through it all. I am not very easily taken in, my dear."

Charlotte could think of nothing more harmless to be said than the simple enquiry of "Sir Edward and Miss Denham?"

"Yes, my dear. *My young folks*, as I call them sometimes, for I take them very much by the hand. I had them with me last summer about this time, for a week, from Monday to Monday, and very delighted and thankful they were. For they are very good young people, my dear. I would not have you think that I *only* notice them for poor dear Sir Harry's sake. No, no: they are very deserving themselves, or trust me, they would not be so much in *my* company. I am not the woman to help anybody blindfold. I always take care to know what I am about and who I have to deal with before I stir a finger. I do not think I was ever overreached in my life, and that is a good deal for a woman to say that has been married twice. Poor dear Sir Harry (between ourselves) thought at first to have got more. But" – with a bit of a sigh – "he is gone, and we must not find fault with the dead. Nobody could live happier together than us – and he was a very honourable man, quite the gentleman of ancient family. And when he died, I gave Sir Edward his gold watch."

She said this with a look at her companion which implied its right to produce a great impression – and, seeing no rapturous astonishment in Charlotte's countenance, added quickly: "He did not bequeath it to his nephew, my dear – it was no bequest. It was not in the will. He only told me, and *that* but once, that he should wish his nephew to have his watch; but it need not have been binding, if I had not chose it."

"Very kind indeed! Very handsome!" said Charlotte, absolutely forced to affect admiration.

"Yes, my dear – and it is not the *only* kind thing I have done by him. I have been a very liberal friend to Sir Edward. And poor young man, he needs it bad enough; for though I am only the *dowager*, my dear, and he is the *heir*, things do not stand between us in the way they commonly do between those two parties. Not a shilling do I receive from the Denham estate. Sir Edward has no payments to make *me*. He don't stand uppermost, believe me. It is I that help *him*."

"Indeed! He is a very fine young man – particularly elegant in his address."

This was said chiefly for the sake of saying something – but Charlotte directly saw that it was laying her open to suspicion by Lady Denham's giving a shrewd glance at her and replying: "Yes, yes, he is very well to look at – and it is to be hoped that some lady of large fortune will think so – for Sir Edward *must* marry for money. He and I often talk that matter over. A handsome young fellow like him will go smirking and smiling about and paying girls compliments, but he knows he *must* marry for money. And Sir Edward is a very steady young man in the main, and has got very good notions."

"Sir Edward Denham," said Charlotte, "with such personal advantages may be almost sure of getting a woman of fortune, if he chooses it."

This glorious sentiment seemed quite to remove suspicion.

"Aye, my dear – that's very sensibly said," cried Lady Denham. "And if we could but get a young heiress to Sanditon! But heiresses are monstrous scarce! I do not think we have had an heiress here, or even a co-heiress, since Sanditon has been a public place. Families come after families, but as far as I can learn it is not one in an hundred of them that have any real property, landed or funded. An income perhaps, but no property. Clergymen may be, or lawyers from town, or half-pay officers, or widows with only a jointure. And what good can such people do anybody? Except just as they take our empty houses – and (between ourselves) I think they are great fools for not staying at home. Now, if we could get a young heiress to be sent here for her health (and if she was ordered to drink asses' milk I could supply her), and, as soon as she got well, have her fall in love with Sir Edward!"

"That would be very fortunate indeed."

"And Miss Esther must marry somebody of fortune too – she must get a rich husband. Ah! Young ladies that have no money are very much to be pitied!... But" – after a short pause – "if Miss Esther thinks to talk me into inviting them to come and stay at Sanditon House, she will find herself mistaken. Matters are altered with me since last summer, you know. I have Miss Clara with me now, which makes a great difference."

She spoke this so seriously that Charlotte instantly saw in it the evidence of real penetration and prepared for some fuller remarks – but it was followed only by "I have no fancy for having my house as full as an hotel. I should not choose to have my two housemaids' time taken up all the morning, in dusting out bedrooms. They have Miss Clara's room to put to rights as well as my own every day. If they had hard places, they would want higher wages."

For objections of this nature, Charlotte was not prepared, and she found it so impossible even to affect sympathy that she could say nothing. Lady Denham soon added, with great glee: "And besides all this, my dear, am I to be filling my house to the prejudice of Sanditon? If people want to be by the sea, why don't they take lodgings? Here are a great many empty houses – three on this very Terrace; no fewer than three lodging papers staring us in the face at this very moment, Numbers 3, 4 and 8. 8, the corner house, may be too large for them, but either of the two others are nice little snug houses, very fit for a young gentleman and his sister. And so, my dear, the next time Miss Esther begins talking about the dampness of Denham Park and the good bathing always does her, I shall advise them to come and take one of these lodgings for a fortnight. Don't you think that will be very fair? Charity begins at home, you know."

Charlotte's feelings were divided between amusement and indignation – but indignation had the larger and the increasing share. She kept her countenance and she kept a civil silence. She could not carry her forbearance further; but, without attempting to listen longer, and only conscious that Lady Denham was still talking on in the same way, allowed her thoughts to form themselves into such a meditation as this:

"She is thoroughly mean. I had not expected anything so bad. Mr Parker spoke too mildly of her. His judgement is evidently not to be trusted. His own good nature misleads him. He is too kind-hearted to see clearly. I must judge for myself. And their very *connection* prejudices him. He has persuaded her to engage in the same speculation – and because their object in that line is the same, he fancies she feels like him in others. But she is very, very mean. I can see no good in her. Poor Miss Brereton! And she makes everybody mean about her. This poor Sir Edward and his sister – how far nature meant them to be respectable I cannot tell, but they are *obliged* to be mean in their servility to her. And I am mean too, in giving her my attention, with the appearance of coinciding with her. Thus it is, when rich people are sordid."

Chapter 8

THE TWO LADIES CONTINUED walking together till rejoined by the others, who as they issued from the library were followed by a young Whitby running off with five volumes under his arm to Sir Edward's gig – and Sir Edward, approaching Charlotte, said, "You may perceive what has been our occupation. My sister wanted my counsel in the selection of some books. We have many leisure hours, and read a great deal. I am no indiscriminate novel-reader. The mere trash of the common circulating library I hold in the highest contempt. You will never hear me advocating those puerile emanations which detail nothing but discordant principles incapable of amalgamation, or those vapid tissues of ordinary occurrences from which no useful deductions can be drawn. In vain may we put them into a literary alembic; we distil nothing which can add to science. You understand me, I am sure?"

"I am not quite certain that I do. But if you will describe the sort of novels which you *do* approve, I dare say it will give me a clearer idea."

"Most willingly, fair questioner. The novels which I approve are such as display human nature with grandeur – such as show her in the sublimities of intense feeling – such as exhibit the progress of strong passion from the first germ of incipient susceptibility to the utmost energies of reason half-dethroned – where we see the strong spark of woman's captivations elicit such fire in the soul of man as leads him (though at the risk of some aberration from the strict line of primitive obligations) to hazard all, dare all, achieve all, to obtain her. Such are the works which I peruse with delight and, I hope I may say, with amelioration. They hold forth the most splendid portraitures of high conceptions, unbounded views, illimitable ardour, indomptable decision – and even when the event is plainly anti-prosperous to the high-toned machinations of the prime character, the potent, pervading hero of the story, it leaves us full of generous emotions for him; – our hearts are paralysed. 'Twere pseudo-philosophy to assert that we do not feel more enwrapped by the brilliancy of his career than by the tranquil and morbid virtues of any opposing character. Our approbation of the latter is but eleemosynary. These are the novels which enlarge the primitive capabilities of the heart, and which it cannot impugn the sense or be any dereliction of the character of the most anti-puerile man to be conversant with."

"If I understand you aright," said Charlotte, "our taste in novels is not at all the same."

And here they were obliged to part – Miss Denham being too much tired of them all to stay any longer.

The truth was that Sir Edward, whom circumstances had confined very much to one spot, had read more sentimental novels than agreed with him. His fancy had been early caught by all the impassioned and most exceptionable parts of Richardson's;* and such authors as have since appeared to tread in Richardson's steps, so far as man's determined pursuit of woman in defiance of every feeling and convenience is concerned, had since occupied the greater part of his literary hours and formed his character. With a perversity of judgement, which must be attributed to his not having by nature a very strong head, the graces, the spirit, the sagacity and the perseverance of the villain of the story outweighed all his absurdities and all his atrocities with Sir Edward. With him, such conduct was genius, fire and feeling. It interested and inflamed him; and he was always more anxious for its success and mourned over its discomfitures with more tenderness than could ever have been contemplated by the authors.

Though he owed many of his ideas to this sort of reading, it were unjust to say that he read nothing else, or that his language were not formed on a more general knowledge of modern literature. He read all the essays, letters, tours and criticisms of the day – and with the same ill luck which made him derive only false principles from the lessons of morality, and incentives to vice from the history of its overthrow, he gathered only hard words and involved sentences from the style of our most approved writers.

Sir Edward's great object in life was to be seductive. With such personal advantages as he knew himself to possess, and such talents as he did also give himself credit for, he regarded it as his duty. He felt that he was formed to be a dangerous man – quite in the line of the Lovelaces.* The very name of Sir Edward, he thought, carried some degree of fascination with it. To be generally gallant and assiduous about the fair, to make fine speeches to every pretty girl, was but the inferior part of the character he had to play. Miss Heywood, or any other young woman with any pretensions to beauty, he was entitled (according to his own view of society) to approach with high compliment and rhapsody on the slightest acquaintance; but it was Clara alone on whom he had serious designs; it was Clara whom he meant to seduce.

Her seduction was quite determined on. Her situation in every way called for it. She was his rival in Lady Denham's favour; she was young, lovely and dependent. He had very early seen the necessity of the case, and had now been long trying with cautious assiduity to make an impression on her heart, and to undermine her principles. Clara saw through him, and had not the least intention of being seduced – but she bore with him patiently enough to confirm the sort of attachment which her personal charms had raised. A greater degree of discouragement indeed would not have affected Sir Edward. He was armed against the highest pitch of disdain or aversion. If she could not be won by affection, he must carry her off. He knew his business. Already had he had many musings on the subject. If he *were* constrained so to act, he must naturally wish to strike out something new, to exceed those who had gone before him – and he felt a strong curiosity to ascertain whether the neighbourhood of Timbuctoo might not afford some solitary house adapted for Clara's reception – but the expense – alas! – of measures in that masterly style was ill suited to his purse, and prudence obliged him to prefer the quietest sort of ruin and disgrace for the object of his affections to the more renowned.

Chapter 9

ONE DAY, SOON AFTER CHARLOTTE'S ARRIVAL at Sanditon, she had the pleasure of seeing, just as she ascended from the sands to the Terrace, a gentleman's carriage with post horses standing at the door of the hotel, as very lately arrived, and by the quantity of luggage taking off,

bringing, it might be hoped, some respectable family determined on a long residence.

Delighted to have such good news for Mr and Mrs Parker, who
had both gone home some time before, she proceeded for Trafalgar
House with as much alacrity as could remain, after having been
contending for the last two hours with a very fine wind blowing
directly onshore; but she had not reached the little lawn when
she saw a lady walking nimbly behind her at no great distance;
and convinced that it could be no acquaintance of her own, she
resolved to hurry on and get into the house if possible before her.
But the stranger's pace did not allow this to be accomplished.
Charlotte was on the steps and had rung, but the door was not
opened, when the other crossed the lawn – and when the servant
appeared, they were just equally ready for entering the house.

The ease of the lady, her "How do you do, Morgan?" and
Morgan's looks on seeing her were a moment's astonishment;
but another moment brought Mr Parker into the hall to welcome
the sister he had seen from the drawing room; and Charlotte was
soon introduced to Miss Diana Parker. There was a great deal of
surprise but still more pleasure in seeing her. Nothing could be
kinder than her reception from both husband and wife. "How
did she come? And with whom? And they were so glad to find
her equal to the journey! And that she was to belong to *them* was
taken as a thing of course."

Miss Diana Parker was about four-and-thirty, of middling height
and slender; delicate-looking rather than sickly; with an agreeable face and a very animated eye; her manners resembling her
brother's in their ease and frankness, though with more decision
and less mildness in her tone. She began an account of herself
without delay. Thanking them for their invitation, but "*that* was
quite out of the question, for they were all three come and meant
to get into lodgings and make some stay".

"All three come! What! Susan and Arthur! Susan able to come
too! This was better and better."

"Yes – we are actually all come. Quite unavoidable. Nothing else to be done. You shall hear all about it. But my dear Mary, send for the children – I long to see them."

"And how has Susan borne the journey? And how is Arthur? And why do we not see him here with you?"

"Susan has borne it wonderfully. She had not a wink of sleep either the night before we set out or last night at Chichester, and as this is not so common with her as with *me*, I have had a thousand fears for her – but she has kept up wonderfully – had no hysterics of consequence till we came within sight of poor old Sanditon – and the attack was not very violent – nearly over by the time we reached your hotel, so that we got her out of the carriage extremely well, with only Mr Woodcock's assistance – and when I left her she was directing the disposal of the luggage and helping old Sam uncord the trunks. She desired her best love, with a thousand regrets at being so poor a creature that she could not come with me. And as for poor Arthur, he would not have been unwilling himself, but there is so much wind that I did not think he could safely venture – for I am *sure* there is lumbago hanging about him – and so I helped him on with his greatcoat and sent him off to the Terrace to take us lodgings. Miss Heywood must have seen our carriage standing at the hotel. I knew Miss Heywood the moment I saw her before me on the down. My dear Tom, I am so glad to see you walk so well. Let me feel your ankle. That's right; all right and clean. The play of your sinews a *very* little affected – barely perceptible. Well, now for the explanation of my being here. I told you in my letter of the two considerable families I was hoping to secure for you – the West Indians and the seminary."

Here Mr Parker drew his chair still nearer to his sister, and took her hand again most affectionately as he answered, "Yes, yes – how active and how kind you have been!"

"The West Indians," she continued, "whom I look upon as the *most* desirable of the two – as the best of the good – prove to be a Mrs Griffiths and her family. I know them only through others.

You must have heard me mention Miss Capper, the particular friend of *my* very particular friend Fanny Noyce; now, Miss Capper is extremely intimate with a Mrs Darling, who is on terms of constant correspondence with Mrs Griffiths herself. Only a *short* chain, you see, between us, and not a link wanting. Mrs Griffiths meant to go to the sea for her young people's benefit, had fixed on the coast of Sussex, but was undecided as to the where, wanted something private and wrote to ask the opinion of her friend, Mrs Darling. Miss Capper happened to be staying with Mrs Darling when Mrs Griffiths's letter arrived, and was consulted on the question; *she* wrote the same day to Fanny Noyce and mentioned it to her – and Fanny, all alive for *us*, instantly took up her pen and forwarded the circumstance to me, except as to *names* – which have but lately transpired. There was but *one* thing for *me* to do. I answered Fanny's letter by the same post and pressed for the recommendation of Sanditon. Fanny had feared your having no house large enough to receive such a family. But I seem to be spinning out my story to an endless length. You see how it was all managed. I had the pleasure of hearing soon afterwards, by the same simple link of connection, that Sanditon *had been* recommended by Mrs Darling, and that the West Indians were very much disposed to go thither. This was the state of the case when I wrote to you – but two days ago – yes, the day before yesterday – I heard again from Fanny Noyce, saying that *she* had heard from Miss Capper, who by a letter from Mrs Darling understood that Mrs Griffiths had expressed herself in a letter to Mrs Darling more doubtingly on the subject of Sanditon. Am I clear? I would be anything rather than not clear."

"Oh, perfectly, perfectly. Well?"

"The reason of this hesitation was her having no connections in the place, and no means of ascertaining that she should have good accommodations on arriving there; and she was particularly careful and scrupulous on all those matters, more on account of a certain Miss Lambe, a young lady (probably a niece) under her care than on her own account, or her daughters'. Miss Lambe has an immense fortune – richer than all the rest – and very delicate health. One sees clearly enough by all this the *sort* of woman Mrs Griffiths must be: as helpless and indolent as wealth and a hot climate are apt to make us. But we are not born to equal energy. What was to be done? I had a few moments' indecision – whether to offer to write to you, or to Mrs Whitby, to secure them a house – but neither pleased me. I hate to employ others when I am equal to act myself; and my conscience told me that this was an occasion which called for me. Here was a family of helpless invalids whom I might essentially serve. I sounded Susan – the same thought had occurred to her. Arthur made no difficulties. Our plan was arranged immediately, we were off yesterday morning at six, left Chichester at the same hour today – and here we are."

"Excellent! Excellent!" cried Mr Parker. "Diana, you are une-qualled in serving your friends and doing good to all the world. I know nobody like you. Mary, my love, is not she a wonderful creature? Well, and now, what house do you design to engage for them? What is the size of their family?"

"I do not at all know," replied his sister, "have not the least idea – never heard any particulars – but I am very sure that the largest house at Sanditon cannot be *too* large. They are more likely to want a second. I shall take only one, however, and that but for a week certain. Miss Heywood, I astonish you. I see by your looks that you are not used to such quick measures."

The words "Unaccountable officiousness! Activity run mad!" had just passed through Charlotte's mind, but a civil answer was easy.

"I dare say I do look surprised," said she, "because these are very great exertions, and I know what invalids both you and your sister are.

"Invalids indeed. I trust there are not three people in England who have so sad a right to that appellation! But my dear Miss Heywood, we are sent into this world to be as extensively useful as possible and, where some degree of strength of mind is given, it is not a feeble body which will excuse us or incline us to excuse ourselves. The world is pretty much divided between the weak of mind and the strong; between those who can act and those who cannot, and it is the bounden duty of the capable to let no opportunity of being useful escape them. My sister's complaints and mine are happily not often of a nature to threaten existence *immediately* – and as long as we *can* exert ourselves to be of use to others, I am convinced that the body is the better for the refreshment the mind receives in doing its duty. While I have been travelling with this object in view, I have been perfectly well."

The entrance of the children ended this little panegyric on her own disposition – and after having noticed and caressed them all, she prepared to go.

"Cannot you dine with us? Is not it possible to prevail on you to dine with us?" was then the cry; and that being absolutely negatived, it was "And when shall we see you again? And how can we be of use to you?" – and Mr Parker warmly offered his assistance in taking the house for Mrs Griffiths.

"I will come to you the moment I have dined," said he, "and we will go about together."

But this was immediately declined.

"No, my dear Tom, upon no account in the world shall you stir a step on any business of mine. Your ankle wants rest. I see by the position of your foot that you have used it too much already. No, I shall go about my house-taking directly. Our dinner is not ordered till six – and by that time I hope to have completed it. It is now only half-past four. As to seeing *me* again today, I cannot answer for it. The others will be at the hotel all the evening and delighted to see you at any time, but as soon as I get back I shall hear what Arthur has done about our own lodgings, and probably the moment dinner is over shall be out again on business relative to them, for we hope to get into some lodgings or other and be settled after breakfast tomorrow. I have not much confidence in poor Arthur's skill for lodging-taking, but he seemed to like the commission."

"I think you are doing too much," said Mr Parker. "You will knock yourself up. You should not move again after dinner."

"No, indeed you should not," cried his wife, "for dinner is such a mere *name* with you all that it can do you no good. I know what your appetites are."

"My appetite is very much mended, I assure you, lately. I have been taking some bitters of my own decocting which have done wonders. Susan never eats, I grant you – and just at present I shall want nothing; I never eat for about a week after a journey – but as for Arthur, he is only too much disposed for food. We are often obliged to check him."

"But you have not told me anything of the *other* family coming to Sanditon," said Mr Parker as he walked with her to the door of the house. "The Camberwell Seminary; have we a good chance of *them*?"

"Oh, certain – quite certain. I had forgotten them for the moment, but I had a letter three days ago from my friend Mrs Charles Dupuis which assured me of Camberwell. Camberwell will be here to a certainty, and very soon. *That* good woman (I do not know her name), not being so wealthy and independent as Mrs Griffiths, can travel and choose for herself. I will tell you how I got at *her*. Mrs Charles Dupuis lives almost next door to a lady who has a relation lately settled at Clapham who actually attends the seminary and gives lessons on eloquence and belles-lettres to some of the girls. I got this man a hare from one of Sidney's friends, and he recommended Sanditon – without *my* appearing, however – Mrs Charles Dupuis managed it all."

Chapter 10

I T WAS NOT A WEEK SINCE Miss Diana Parker had been told by her feelings that the sea air would probably, in her present state, be the death of her, and now she was at Sanditon, intending to make some stay and without appearing to have the slightest recollection of having written or felt any such thing. It was impossible for Charlotte not to suspect a good deal of fancy in such an extraordinary state of health. Disorders and recoveries so very much out of the common way seemed more like the amusement of eager minds in want of employment than of actual afflictions and relief. The Parkers were, no doubt, a family of imagination and quick feelings, and while the eldest brother found vent for his superfluity of sensation as a projector, the sisters were perhaps driven to dissipate theirs in the invention of odd complaints.

The *whole* of their mental vivacity was evidently not so employed; part was laid out in a zeal for being useful. It should seem that they must either be very busy for the good of others, or else extremely ill themselves. Some natural delicacy of constitution, in fact, with an unfortunate turn for medicine, especially quack medicine, had given them an early tendency at various times to various disorders; the rest of their sufferings was from fancy, the love of distinction and the love of the wonderful. They had charitable hearts and many amiable feelings – but a spirit of restless activity, and the glory of doing more than anybody else had their share in every exertion of benevolence – and there was vanity in all they did, as well as in all they endured.

Mr and Mrs Parker spent a great part of the evening at the hotel, but Charlotte had only two or three views of Miss Diana posting over the down after a house for this lady whom she had never seen, and who had never employed her. She was not made acquainted with the others till the following day, when, being removed into lodgings and all the party continuing quite well, their brother and sister and herself were entreated to drink tea with them.

They were in one of the Terrace houses – and she found them arranged for the evening in a small neat drawing room, with a beautiful view of the sea if they had chosen it – but though it had been a very fair English summer day, not only was there no open window, but the sofa and the table, and the establishment in general, was all at the other end of the room by a brisk fire. Miss Parker, whom, remembering the three teeth drawn in one day, Charlotte approached with a peculiar degree of respectful compassion, was not very unlike her sister in person or manner – though more thin and worn by illness and medicine, more relaxed in air and more subdued in voice. She talked, however, the whole evening as incessantly as Diana – and, excepting that she sat with salts in her hand, took drops two or three times from one out of several phials already at home on the mantelpiece and made a great many odd faces and contortions, Charlotte could perceive no symptoms of illness which she, in the boldness of her own good health, would not have undertaken to cure by putting out the fire, opening the window and disposing of the drops and the salts by means of one or the other. She had very considerable curiosity to see Mr Arthur Parker; and having fancied him a very puny, delicate-looking young man, was astonished to find him quite as tall as his brother, and a great deal stouter – broad-made and lusty – and with no other look of an invalid than a sodden complexion.

Diana was evidently the chief of the family; principal mover and actor – she had been on her feet the whole morning, on Mrs Griffiths's business or their own, and was still the most alert of the three. Susan had only superintended their final removal from the hotel, bringing two heavy boxes herself, and Arthur had found the air so cold that he had merely walked from one house to the other as nimbly as he could – and boasted much of sitting by the fire till he had cooked up a very good one. Diana, whose exercise had been too domestic to admit of calculation, but who, by her own account, had not once sat down during the space of seven hours, confessed herself a little tired. She had been too success-ful, however, for much fatigue; for not only had she, by walking and talking down a thousand difficulties, at last secured a proper house at eight guineas per week for Mrs Griffiths, she had also opened so many treaties with cooks, housemaids, washerwomen and bathing women that Mrs Griffiths would have little more to do on her arrival than to wave her hand and collect them around her for choice. Her concluding effort in the cause had been a few polite lines of information to Mrs Griffiths herself – time not allowing for the circuitous train of intelligence which had been hitherto kept up – and she was now regaling in the delight of opening the first trenches of an acquaintance with such a powerful discharge of unexpected obligation.

Mr and Mrs Parker and Charlotte had seen two post-chaises crossing the down to the hotel as they were setting off – a joyful sight – and full of speculation. The Miss Parkers and Arthur had also seen something; they could distinguish from their window that there *was* an arrival at the hotel, but not its amount. Their visitors answered for two hack chaises. Could it be the Camberwell Seminary? Mr Parker was confident of another new family.

When they were all finally seated, after some removals to look at the sea and the hotel, Charlotte's place was by Arthur, who was sitting next to the fire with a degree of enjoyment which gave a good deal of merit to his civility in wishing her to take his chair. There was nothing dubious in her manner of declining it, and he sat down again with much satisfaction. She drew back her chair to have all the advantage of his person as a screen, and was very thankful for every inch of back and shoulders beyond her preconceived idea. Arthur was heavy in eye as well as figure, but by no means indisposed to talk; and while the other four were chiefly engaged together, he evidently felt it no penance to have a fine young woman next to him, requiring in common politeness some attention – as his brother, who felt the decided want of some motive for action, some powerful object of animation for him, observed with considerable pleasure.

Such was the influence of youth and bloom that he began even to make a sort of apology for having a fire. "We should not have had one at home," said he, "but the sea air is always damp. I am not afraid of anything so much as damp."

"I am so fortunate," said Charlotte, "as never to know whether the air is damp or dry. It has always some property that is wholesome and invigorating to me."

"I like the air too, as well as anybody can," replied Arthur. "I am very fond of standing at an open window when there is no wind – but, unluckily, a damp air does not like *me*. It gives me the rheumatism. You are not rheumatic, I suppose?"

"Not at all."

"That's a great blessing. But perhaps you are nervous?"

"No, I believe not. I have no idea that I am."

"I am very nervous. To say the truth, nerves are the worst part of my complaints in *my* opinion. My sisters think me bilious, but I doubt it."

"You are quite in the right to doubt it as long as you possibly can, I am sure."

"If I were bilious," he continued, "you know, wine would disagree with me, but it always does me good. The more wine I drink (in moderation), the better I am. I am always best of an evening. If you had seen me today before dinner, you would have thought me a very poor creature."

Charlotte could believe it. She kept her countenance, however, and said, "As far as I can understand what nervous complaints are, I have a great idea of the efficacy of air and exercise for them – daily, regular exercise – and I should recommend rather more of it to *you* than I suspect you are in the habit of taking."

"Oh, I am very fond of exercise myself," he replied, "and I mean to walk a great deal while I am here, if the weather is temperate. I shall be out every morning before breakfast and take several turns upon the Terrace, and you will often see me at Trafalgar House."

"But you do not call a walk to Trafalgar House much exercise?"

"Not as to mere distance, but the hill is so steep! Walking up that hill, in the middle of the day, would throw me into such a perspiration! You would see me all in a bath by the time I got there! I am very subject to perspiration, and there cannot be a surer sign of nervousness."

They were now advancing so deep in physics that Charlotte viewed the entrance of the servant with the tea things as a very fortunate interruption. It produced a great and immediate change. The young man's attentions were instantly lost. He took his own cocoa from the tray, which seemed provided with almost as many teapots as there were persons in company – Miss Parker drinking one sort of herb tea, and Miss Diana another – and, turning completely to the fire, sat coddling and cooking it to his own satisfaction and toasting some slices of bread, brought up ready-prepared in the toast rack – and till it was all done she heard nothing of his voice but the murmuring of a few broken sentences of self-approbation and success.

When his toils were over, however, he moved back his chair into as gallant a line as ever, and proved that he had not been working only for himself by his earnest invitation to her to take both cocoa and toast. She was already helped to tea – which surprised him, so totally self-engrossed had he been.

"I thought I should have been in time," said he, "but cocoa takes a great deal of boiling."

"I am much obliged to you," replied Charlotte. "But I *prefer* tea."

"Then I will help myself," said he. "A large dish of rather weak cocoa every evening agrees with me better than anything."

It struck her, however, as he poured out this rather weak cocoa, that it came forth in a very fine, dark-coloured stream; and at the same moment – his sisters both crying out, "Oh, Arthur, you get your cocoa stronger and stronger every evening," with Arthur's somewhat conscious reply of "'*Tis* rather stronger than it should be tonight," – convinced her that Arthur was by no means so fond of being starved as they could desire, or as he felt proper himself. He was certainly very happy to turn the conversation on dry toast and hear no more of his sisters.

"I hope you will eat some of this toast," said he. "I reckon myself a very good toaster. I never burn my toasts; I never put them too near the fire at first; and yet, you see, there is not a corner but what is well browned. I hope you like dry toast."

"With a reasonable quantity of butter spread over it, very much," said Charlotte, "but not otherwise."

"No more do I," said he, exceedingly pleased. "We think quite alike there. So far from dry toast being wholesome, I think it a very bad thing for the stomach. Without a little butter to soften it, it hurts the coats of the stomach. I am sure it does. I will have the pleasure of spreading some for you directly, and afterwards I will spread some for myself. Very bad indeed for the coats of the stomach, but there is no convincing *some* people. It irritates and acts like a nutmeg grater."

He could not get command of the butter, however, without a struggle; his sisters accusing him of eating a great deal too much and declaring he was not to be trusted, and he maintaining that he only ate enough to secure the coats of his stomach – and besides, he only wanted it now for Miss Heywood.

Such a plea must prevail. He got the butter and spread away for her with an accuracy of judgement which at least delighted himself; but when her toast was done and he took his own in hand, Charlotte could hardly contain herself as she saw him watching his sisters, while he scrupulously scraped off almost as much butter as he put on, and then seize an odd moment for adding a great dab just before it went into his mouth. Certainly, Mr Arthur Parker's enjoyments in invalidism were very different from his sisters – by no means so spiritualized. A good deal of earthy dross hung about him. Charlotte could not but suspect him of adopting that line of life principally for the indulgence of an indolent temper, and to be determined on having no disorders but such as called for warm rooms and good nourishment.

In one particular, however, she soon found that he had caught something from *them*. "What!" said he. "Do you venture upon two dishes of strong green tea in one evening? What nerves you must have! How I envy you. Now, if I were to swallow only one such dish, what do you think its effect would be upon me?"

"Keep you awake perhaps all night," replied Charlotte, meaning to overthrow his attempts at surprise by the grandeur of her own conceptions.

"Oh, if that were all!" he exclaimed. "No – it acts on me like poison and would entirely take away the use of my right side before I had swallowed it five minutes. It sounds almost incredible, but it has happened to me so often that I cannot doubt it. The use of my right side is entirely taken away for several hours!"

"It sounds rather odd to be sure," answered Charlotte coolly, "but I dare say it would be proved to be the simplest thing in the world by those who have studied right sides and green tea scientifically and thoroughly understand all the possibilities of their action on each other."

Soon after tea, a letter was brought to Miss Diana Parker from the hotel.

"From Mrs Charles Dupuis," said she, "some private hand."

And, having read a few lines, exclaimed aloud, "Well, this is very extraordinary! Very extraordinary indeed! That both should have the same name. Two Mrs Griffiths! This is a letter of recommendation and introduction to me of the lady from Camberwell – and *her* name happens to be Griffiths too."

A few more lines, however, and the colour rushed into her cheeks and, with much perturbation, she added, "The oddest thing that ever was! A Miss Lambe too! A young West Indian of large fortune. But it *cannot* be the same. Impossible that it should be the same."

She read the letter aloud for comfort. It was merely to introduce the bearer, Mrs Griffiths from Camberwell, and the three young ladies under her care, to Miss Diana Parker's notice. Mrs Griffiths, being a stranger at Sanditon, was anxious for a respectable introduction – and Mrs Charles Dupuis, therefore, at the instance of the intermediate friend, provided her with this letter, knowing that she could not do her dear Diana a greater kindness than by giving her the means of being useful. Mrs Griffiths's chief solicitude would be for the accommodation and comfort of one of the young ladies under her care, a Miss Lambe, a young West Indian of large fortune in delicate health."

"It was very strange! Very remarkable! Very extraordinary!" But they were all agreed in determining it to be *impossible* that there should not be two families; such a totally distinct set of people as were concerned in the reports of each made that matter quite certain. There *must* be two families. "Impossible" and "Impossible" was repeated over and over again with great fervour. An accidental resemblance of names and circumstances, however striking at first, involved nothing really incredible – and so it was settled.

Miss Diana herself derived an immediate advantage to counterbalance her perplexity. She must put her shawl over her shoulders and be running about again. Tired as she was, she must instantly repair to the hotel to investigate the truth and offer her services.

Chapter 11

I T WOULD NOT DO. Not all that the whole Parker race could say among themselves could produce a happier *catastrophée* than that the family from Surrey and the family from Camberwell were one and the same. The rich West Indians and the young ladies' seminary had all entered Sanditon in those two hack chaises. The Mrs Griffiths who, in her friend Mrs Darling's hands, had wavered as to coming and been unequal to the journey was the very same Mrs Griffiths whose plans were at the same period (under another representation) perfectly decided, and who was without fears or difficulties.

All that had the appearance of incongruity in the reports of the two might very fairly be placed to the account of the vanity, the ignorance or the blunders of the many engaged in the cause by the vigilance and caution of Miss Diana Parker. *Her* intimate friends must be officious like herself, and the subject had supplied letters and extracts and messages enough to make everything appear what it was not. Miss Diana probably felt a little awkward on being first obliged to admit her mistake. A long journey from Hampshire taken for nothing, a brother disappointed, an expensive house on her hands for a week must have been some of her immediate reflections – and much worse than all the rest must have been the sensation of being less clear-sighted and infallible than she had believed herself.

No part of it, however, seemed to trouble her for long. There were so many to share in the shame and the blame that probably, when she had divided out their proper portions to Mrs Darling, Miss Capper, Fanny Noyce, Mrs Charles Dupuis and Mrs Charles Dupuis's neighbour, there might be a mere trifle of reproach remaining for herself. At any rate, she was seen all the following morning walking about after lodgings with Mrs Griffiths as alert as ever.

Mrs Griffiths was a very well-behaved, genteel kind of woman, who supported herself by receiving such great girls and young ladies as wanted either masters for finishing their education or a home for beginning their displays. She had several more under her care than the three who were now come to Sanditon, but the others all happened to be absent. Of these three, and indeed of all, Miss Lambe was beyond comparison the most important and precious, as she paid in proportion to her fortune. She was about seventeen, half mulatto, chilly and tender, had a maid of her own, was to have the best room in the lodgings and was always of the first consequence in every plan of Mrs Griffiths.

The other girls, two Miss Beauforts, were just such young ladies as may be met with in at least one family out of three throughout the kingdom. They had tolerable complexions, showy figures, an upright, decided carriage and an assured look; they were very accomplished and very ignorant, their time being divided between such pursuits as might attract admiration and those labours and expedients of dextrous ingenuity by which they could dress in a style much beyond what they *ought* to have afforded; they were some of the first in every change of fashion.

And the object of all was to captivate some man of much better fortune than their own.

Mrs Griffiths had preferred a small, retired place like Sanditon on Miss Lambe's account – and the Miss Beauforts, though naturally preferring anything to smallness and retirement, yet having in the course of the spring been involved in the inevitable expense of six new dresses each for a three days' visit, were constrained to be satisfied with Sanditon also till their circumstances were retrieved. There, with the hire of a harp for one and the purchase of some drawing paper for the other, and all the finery they could already command, they meant to be very economical, very elegant and very secluded; with the hope, on Miss Beaufort's side, of praise and celebrity from all who walked within the sound of her instrument, and, on Miss Letitia's, of curiosity and rapture in all who came near her while she sketched – and to both the consolation of meaning to be the most stylish girls in the place. The particular introduction of Mrs Griffiths to Miss Diana Parker secured them immediately an acquaintance with the Trafalgar House family and with the Denhams – and the Miss Beauforts were soon satisfied with "the circle in which they moved in Sanditon", to use a proper phrase, for everybody must now "move in a circle" – to the prevalence of which rotatory motion is perhaps to be attributed the giddiness and false steps of many.

Lady Denham had other motives for calling on Mrs Griffiths besides attention to the Parkers. In Miss Lambe, here was the very young lady, sickly and rich, whom she had been asking for; and she made the acquaintance for Sir Edward's sake and the sake of her milch asses. How it might answer with regard to the baronet remained to be proved, but as to the animals, she soon found that all her calculations of profit would be vain. Mrs Griffiths would not allow Miss Lambe to have the smallest symptom of a decline or any complaint which asses' milk could possibly relieve. "Miss Lambe was under the constant care of an experienced physician – and his prescriptions must be their rule" – and except in favour of some tonic pills, which a cousin of her own had a property in, Mrs Griffiths never deviated from the strict medicinal page.

The corner house of the Terrace was the one in which Miss Diana Parker had the pleasure of settling her new friends, and considering that it commanded in front the favourite lounge of all the visitors at Sanditon, and on one side whatever might be going on at the hotel, there could not have been a more favourable spot for the seclusion of the Miss Beauforts. And accordingly, long before they had suited themselves with an instrument or with drawing paper, they had – by the frequence of their appearance at the low windows upstairs, in order to close the blinds, or open the blinds, to arrange a flower pot on the balcony, or look at nothing through a telescope – attracted many an eye upwards and made many a gazer gaze again.

A little novelty has a great effect in so small a place; the Miss Beauforts, who would have been nothing at Brighton, could not move here without notice. And even Mr Arthur Parker, though little disposed for supernumerary exertion, always quitted the Terrace in his way to his brother's by this corner house, for the sake of a glimpse of the Miss Beauforts, though it was half a quarter of a mile round about and added two steps to the ascent of the hill.

Chapter 12

CHARLOTTE HAD BEEN TEN DAYS at Sanditon without seeing Sanditon House, every attempt at calling on Lady Denham having been defeated by meeting with her beforehand. But now it was to be more resolutely undertaken, at a more early hour, that nothing might be neglected of attention to Lady Denham or amusement to Charlotte.

"And if you should find a favourable opening, my love," said Mr Parker (who did not mean to go with them), "I think you had better mention the poor Mullins's situation and sound Her Ladyship as to a subscription for them. I am not fond of charitable subscriptions in a place of this kind – it is a sort of tax upon all that come – yet as their distress is very great, and I almost promised the poor woman yesterday to get something done for her, I believe we must set a subscription on foot – and, therefore, the sooner the better – and Lady Denham's name at the head of the list will be a very necessary beginning. You will not dislike speaking to her about it, Mary?"

"I will do whatever you wish me," replied his wife, "but you would do it so much better yourself. I shall not know what to say."

"My dear Mary," he cried, "it is impossible you can be really at a loss. Nothing can be more simple. You have only to state the present afflicted situation of the family, their earnest application to me and my being willing to promote a little subscription for their relief, provided it meet with her approbation."

"The easiest thing in the world," cried Miss Diana Parker, who happened to be calling on them at the moment. "All said and done in less time than you have been talking of it now. And while you are on the subject of subscriptions, Mary, I will thank you to mention a very melancholy case to Lady Denham which has been represented to me in the most affecting terms. There is a poor woman in Worcestershire, whom some friends of mine are exceedingly interested about, and I have undertaken to collect whatever I can for her. If you would mention the circumstance to Lady Denham! Lady Denham *can* give, if she is properly attacked. And I look upon her to be the sort of person who, when once she is prevailed on to undraw her purse, would as readily give ten guineas as five. And therefore, if you find her in a giving mood, you might as well speak in favour of another charity which I and a few more have very much at heart – the establishment of a charitable repository at Burton-on-Trent. And then there is the family of the poor man who was hung last assizes at York, though we really *have* raised the sum we wanted for putting them all out, yet if you *can* get a guinea from her on their behalf, it may as well be done."

"My dear Diana!" exclaimed Mrs Parker, "I could no more mention these things to Lady Denham than I could fly."

"Where's the difficulty? I wish I could go with you myself – but in five minutes I must be at Mrs Griffiths's to encourage Miss Lambe in taking her first dip. She is so frightened, poor thing, that I promised to come and keep up her spirits, and go in the machine with her if she wished it. And as soon as that is over, I must hurry home, for Susan is to have leeches at one o'clock – which will be a three hours' business. Therefore I really have not a moment to spare – besides that (between ourselves), I ought to be in bed myself at this present time, for I am hardly able to stand – and when the leeches have done, I dare say we shall both go to our rooms for the rest of the day."

"I am sorry to hear it, indeed. But if this is the case I hope Arthur will come to us."

"If Arthur takes my advice, he will go to bed too, for if he stays up by himself he will certainly eat and drink more than he ought – but you see, Mary, how impossible it is for me to go with you to Lady Denham's."

"Upon second thoughts, Mary," said her husband, "I will not trouble you to speak about the Mullinses. I will take an opportunity of seeing Lady Denham myself. I know how little it suits you to be pressing matters upon a mind at all unwilling."

His application thus withdrawn, his sister could say no more in support of hers, which was his object, as he felt all their impropriety, and all the certainty of their ill effect upon his own better claim. Mrs Parker was delighted at this release and set off very happy with her friend and her little girl on this walk to Sanditon House.

It was a close, misty morning, and when they reached the brow of the hill they could not for some time make out what sort of carriage it was which they saw coming up. It appeared at different moments to be everything from the gig to the phaeton, from one horse to four; and just as they were concluding in favour of a tandem, little Mary's young eyes distinguished the coachman, and she eagerly called out, "'Tis Uncle Sidney, Mama, it is indeed." And so it proved.

Mr Sidney Parker, driving his servant in a very neat carriage, was soon opposite to them, and they all stopped for a few minutes. The manners of the Parkers were always pleasant among themselves – and it was a very friendly meeting between Sidney and his sister-in-law, who was most kindly taking it for granted that he was on his way to Trafalgar House. This he declined, however. He was "just come from Eastbourne proposing to spend two or three days, as it might happen, at Sanditon, but the hotel must be his quarters – he was expecting to be joined there by a friend or two".

The rest was common enquiries and remarks, with kind notice of little Mary, and a very well-bred bow and proper address to Miss Heywood on her being named to him – and they parted, to meet again within a few hours. Sidney Parker was about seven- or eight-and-twenty, very good-looking, with a decided air of ease and fashion and a lively countenance. This adventure afforded agreeable discussion for some time. Mrs Parker entered into all her husband's joy on the occasion, and exulted in the credit which Sidney's arrival would give to the place.

The road to Sanditon House was a broad, handsome, planted approach between fields, and conducting at the end of a quarter of a mile through second gates into grounds which, though not extensive, had all the beauty and respectability which an abundance of very fine timber could give. These entrance gates were so much in a corner of the grounds or paddock, so near to one of its boundaries, that an outside fence was at first almost pressing on the road – till an angle *here* and a curve *there* threw them to a better distance. The fence was a proper park paling in excellent condition, with clusters of fine elms or rows of old thorns following its line almost everywhere.

Almost must be stipulated, for there were vacant spaces, and through one of these Charlotte, as soon as they entered the enclosure, caught a glimpse over the pales of something white and womanish in the field on the other side. It was something which immediately brought Miss Brereton into her head – and, stepping to the pales, she saw indeed – and very decidedly, in spite of the mist – Miss Brereton seated not far before her at the foot of the bank, which sloped down from the outside of the paling, and which a narrow path seemed to skirt along – Miss Brereton seated, apparently very composedly – and Sir Edward Denham by her side.

They were sitting so near each other and appeared so closely engaged in gentle conversation that Charlotte instantly felt she had nothing to do but to step back again and say not a word. Privacy was certainly their object. It could not but strike her rather unfavourably with regard to Clara; but hers was a situation which must not be judged with severity.

She was glad to perceive that nothing had been discerned by Mrs Parker; if Charlotte had not been considerably the taller of the two, Miss Brereton's white ribbons might not have fallen within the ken of *her* more observant eyes. Among other points of moralizing reflection which the sight of this tête-à-tête produced, Charlotte could not but think of the extreme difficulty which secret lovers must have in finding a proper spot for their stolen interviews. Here perhaps they had thought themselves so perfectly secure from observation; the whole field open before them, a steep bank and pales never crossed by the foot of man at their back, and a great thickness of air in aid! Yet here she had seen them. They were really ill used.

The house was large and handsome; two servants appeared to admit them, and everything had a suitable air of property and order. Lady Denham valued herself upon her liberal establishment and had great enjoyment in the order and importance of her style of living. They were shown into the usual sitting room, well-proportioned and well-furnished, though it was furniture rather originally good and extremely well kept than new or showy. And as Lady Denham was not there, Charlotte had leisure to look about her and to be told by Mrs Parker that the whole-length portrait of a stately gentleman which, placed over the mantelpiece, caught the eye immediately, was the picture of Sir Henry Denham – and that one among many miniatures in another part of the room, little conspicuous, represented Mr Hollis. Poor Mr Hollis! It was impossible not to feel him hardly used: to be obliged to stand back in his own house and see the best place by the fire constantly occupied by Sir Harry Denham.

Note on the Texts

The texts in this edition are based on those published by R.W. Chapman in Volume Six of *The Novels of Austen* (1954). The paragraphing follows the editorial precedent set by Margaret Drabble in the 1974 Penguin Classics edition. The spelling and punctuation have been standardized, modernized and made consistent throughout.

Notes

p. 81, *only a surgeon*: A surgeon was considered a more lowly part of the medical profession until later in the nineteenth century.

p. 89, *empressement*: Eagerness (French).

p. 93, *cassino*: A popular card game at the time.

p. 124, *departed without her*: The fragment ends here. On p. 364 of the second edition of his *A Memoir of Jane Austen* (1871), the author's nephew James Edward Austen-Leigh (1798–1874) provides the following information: "When the author's sister, Cassandra, showed the manuscript of this work to some of her nieces, she also told them something of the intended story; for with this dear sister – though, I believe, with no one else – Jane seems to have talked freely of any work she might have in hand. Mr Watson was soon to die; and Emma to become dependent for a home on her narrow-minded sister-in-law and brother. She was to decline an offer of marriage from Lord Osborne, and much of the interest of the tale was to arise from Lady Osborne's love for Mr Howard, and his counter-affection for Emma, whom he was finally to marry."

p. 133, *the poet Cowper... mile from home*: The quotation is from line 333 of the long poem 'Truth' (1782) by William Cowper (1731–1800), which compares the French Enlightenment writer Voltaire (1694–1778) unfavourably to a simple cottager.

p. 140, *cottage orné*: A picturesque cottage used as a retreat for middle-class families rather than as a home for a labourer.

p. 150, *West Indian*: In this context, "West Indian" refers to an English settler rather than a member of the indigenous population.

p. 153, *Camilla*: A hugely popular 1796 novel by Fanny Burney (1752–1840), named after its main character, who is seventeen during the main action of the story.

p. 160, *Oh! Woman... them than heaven*: Quotations from Canto V of *Marmion* (1808) and Canto II of *The Lady of the Lake* (1810) by Sir Walter Scott (1771–1832).

p. 160, *Burns's lines to his Mary... far between*: The Scottish poet Robert Burns (1759–96) famously wrote poems to Mary Campbell (also known as Highland Mary, 1763–86). The other poets Sir Edward refers to are James Montgomery (1771–1854), William Wordsworth (1770–1850) and Thomas Campbell (1777–1844), whose poem 'The Pleasures of Hope' was first published in 1799.

p. 167, *Richardson's*: A reference to Samuel Richardson (1689–1761), the author famous for his novels *Pamela: Or, Virtue Rewarded* (1740), *Clarissa: Or the History of a Young Lady* (1748) and *The History of Sir Charles Grandison* (1753).

p. 167, *Lovelaces*: A reference to Robert Lovelace, the villain in Richardson's *Clarissa*, who became a byword for a ruthless seducer.

Extra Material

on

Lady Susan,
The Watsons, Sanditon

by Jane Austen

Jane Austen's Life

Jane Austen was born on 16th December 1775 into a clerical family in Steventon, Hampshire. Her father was the rector of the parishes of Steventon and Deane. However, although often living in straitened circumstances, the family were for the time unusually well connected, mainly through Jane's mother, who was distantly related to minor aristocracy and to leading academics at Oxford University. The family also had relatives in India – a fact which later came to play a major role in Austen's life. This circle of acquaintances and connection with the wider world expanded still further as four of Jane's brothers (three older and one younger) progressed upwards in their careers or vocations. Two of them were officers in the navy during the wars against Napoleon, one ultimately rising to the rank of admiral. The other two became clergymen. There was also another brother, born nine years before Jane, who appears to have had some kind of severe handicap; as was common at the time, he was farmed out to distant neighbours, and was never mentioned again by anybody, including Jane in her surviving letters – though she does once talk about knowing manual sign language, indicating that visits may have taken place. Jane also had one older sister, Cassandra, born in 1773, almost three years her senior. She became Jane's inseparable friend and companion. Jane's eldest brother, James, was born ten years before her, in 1765, and had three children – Anna, James Edward and Caroline – all of whom were old enough to remember Jane; James Edward wrote the first substantial memoir of his aunt in 1870, and the other two contributed valuable background information. The second brother, George, about whom nothing is known, presumably never had offspring because of his handicaps. But the third brother, Edward, who fortunately for Jane and Cassandra became a rich landowner, had eleven children, all of whom were born sufficiently before Jane's death to have had at least hazy memories of her. Only the oldest of these, Frances ("Fanny") appears to have written anything for posterity, some fifty years after Jane's death. All of Austen's siblings outlived her; indeed, her brother Francis lived to be ninety-one. Even Jane's hypochondriac mother survived her by ten years, and lived to be eighty-eight. Jane was the only one of the family who died young.

Although Jane's father, the Reverend George, had been a fellow of St John's College Oxford, and membership of the clergy conferred some kind of notional "gentry status", the family was not well off; they had to keep a small farm to help make ends meet, and the house was turned into a kind of "crammer boarding school" for boys. This meant that the two girls were from a very early age surrounded by a house full of boys, and must have been influenced by them; the thought arises that Catherine Morland, the heroine of *Northanger Abbey*, is a reflection of the young Jane, for Catherine too is a clergyman's daughter, and she "is fond of all boy's plays, and greatly preferred cricket... to dolls... she was moreover noisy and wild, hated confinement and cleanliness, and loved nothing so well in the world as rolling down the green slope at the back of the house."

Schooling, Education and Play   Perhaps it was for this reason that their parents banished Cassandra and Jane to a boarding school in Oxford in 1783 which subsequently moved to Southampton, where both Austen girls contracted a fever that was raging in the town; Jane almost died. Following this episode they were brought back home, until they were both sent in 1785 to a boarding school in Reading, which sounds like a cheerfully inefficient institution, and in 1786 both girls came home; any attempt to educate them formally seems to have been given up.

Their older brothers had by this time been admitted to Oxford University, and, during their holidays, put on amateur dramatics in the parsonage barn, sometimes of plays which would be held by the later Evangelical religious movement, and by the Victorian age, to be in rather dubious taste.

Jane's father, the Reverend George Austen, was a priest in the eighteenth-century mould, who enjoyed living, and who had an extensive library, stocked with the latest novels, both comic and otherwise. He would read passages from these to his family after the evening meal, plus extracts from the poetry of Cowper and Crabbe. There is evidence that, from a very early age, Jane was a fluent reader in English, and knew some French and Italian. She obviously was an omnivorous reader, because, from her letters, and from allusions in her novels, we can deduce that not only was she a devotee of the writings of such authors as Shakespeare, Dr Johnson, Fielding and Richardson, but also of so-called "Gothic" novels – the "trash" literature of the time. She was also, throughout her life, a voracious reader of travelogues, including accounts of journeys to Russia and the Far East.

Notable occurrences during this early period were the *Edward and Eliza* adoption of her brother Edward by rich relations – an event subsequently of the most outstanding importance in Jane's life – and her becoming acquainted with her cousin Elizabeth Hancock, later to be known exclusively as Eliza, who had been born in India and was later married to a French count.

Edward first began to spend time with these rich, childless relatives, the Knights, in 1779, when he was twelve and Jane four. He was finally adopted by them in 1783, making him the legal heir to their wealth and large estates. This was, in fact, a more common proceeding then than now; we recall that, in *Mansfield Park*, Fanny Price is adopted by the aristocratic Bertram family.

Elizabeth Hancock was the daughter of Jane's aunt on her father's side, Philadelphia. Philadelphia had married a surgeon in the East India Company, Tysoe Hancock. In Bengal, they became acquainted with Warren Hastings, then already a senior government official, and subsequently to become Governor of India. Elizabeth, their only child, was born in 1761 and was thus fourteen years older than Jane. She married a low-ranking French count, and spent much of her time in France, attending glittering balls and even meeting French royalty. She gave birth to a son who appears to have been physically and mentally handicapped, and did not send him away, but looked after him till he died at the age of fifteen. Her husband, the Comte de Feuillide, was guillotined in the French Revolution, in 1794, and Eliza herself only just managed to escape to England, and started living a luxurious life in an apartment in London, with French servants.

Despite the age difference, she and Jane became firm lifelong friends, and she regularly gave Jane the latest French novels (including possibly the explicit *Les Liaisons dangereuses*). Jane often stayed at her apartment in London, from which she would go to see the latest plays and exhibitions. Later Eliza married Jane's brother Henry, and Jane was present when she died, apparently of breast cancer, in 1813.

Early Writings   The theatricals at Steventon lasted till 1789, when her brother James, who was still at Oxford University, started to produce a magazine called the *Loiterer*, on the model of Dr Johnson's the *Rambler* and the *Idler*. This lasted for fourteen months, and both James and his brother Henry contributed; there have been attempts to prove that an item in it by one "Sophia Sentiment", written in the style of a literary romantic heroine of the period, is by Jane, who at the time would have been thirteen. Whether this is so or not, Jane had, from the age of around eleven, with the encouragement of her father, been writing brash, surreal burlesques and satires of the popular novel of her time, plus highly original and racy knockabout comedy, full of references to sexually unbridled conduct and outrageous behaviour. These juvenile pieces only petered out around 1794, when she began to experiment with novel-writing – although none of her works was to be published till 1811.

There is one short epistolary novel – *Lady Susan* – which could have been written around 1793 or '94, although it has also been dated as late as 1805. If the earlier date is correct, which is most likely, then *Lady Susan* shows Jane beginning to move, at the age of eighteen or nineteen, from adolescent high spirits and farce to the more serious aspects of novel-writing.

Family tradition has it that Jane's first attempt at a novel was *Elinor and Marianne* (subsequently *Sense and Sensibility*), written around 1784 or '85 in the then popular epistolary form, and that she then wrote *First Impressions* (to become *Pride and Prejudice*) in 1796–97, and *Susan* (later *Northanger Abbey*) in 1797–98. These attempts at novel-writing show that, already, between the ages of roughly twenty and twenty-two, she had composed what, substantially rewritten, were ultimately to become three of the greatest novels of the English language.

Real-life Romance   Did Jane Austen have suitors? There is evidence that young men danced with her and presumably flirted with her at balls around Steventon. It should be remembered that Cassandra destroyed a large part of Jane's correspondence, so perhaps there were early letters deemed unsuitable for the world. However, the first surviving letter of her correspondence, written in January 1796, gives an account of what does seem to have been the beginning of a genuine romance with one Tom Lefroy, the outcome of which left her very upset. Tom Lefroy was Irish, and was in England to study in London to be a lawyer. At Christmas, he had come down to visit relations, who were near neighbours of the Austens, and Jane and he were obviously beginning to become close. But it seems Tom had to marry money, and the daughter of a relatively impecunious country parson would not do; his Hampshire relatives never invited Jane and Tom to visit them simultaneously again. Tom resumed his studies, returned to Ireland and ended up, in 1852, becoming Lord Chief Justice of Ireland. Lefroy did comment many years later that he had indeed had a "boyish" love for her. Whatever this means, it seems that Jane for the first time came up against a theme that recurs constantly in her novels – that, in the highly stratified cultural world of her time, love would very often have to give way to money.

In 1797 Cassandra's fiancé Tom Fowle died of fever in the West Indies, where he had sailed in the capacity of temporary naval chaplain. Cassandra seems from then on to have settled into a resigned and disappointed state of spinsterhood; she became the lifelong companion of Jane, who, although having other subsequent romantic encounters, about which little is known, also remained unmarried.

In 1801, just as Jane was beginning to develop as a novelist, *Unhappy Life in Bath* misfortune intervened: her parents unexpectedly announced that her father was going to give up his post as a clergyman – presumably because he was now seventy – and move to lodgings in Bath, taking their two unmarried daughters with them. Jane is supposed by tradition to have fainted when she was told. Preparatory to the move, and to Jane's dismay, her father's library of 500 books and her piano were sold.

Jane apparently wrote nothing for the next nine years (if we accept the earlier date for *Lady Susan*), apart from a short fragment entitled *The Watsons*. A rural existence in a large rectory surrounded by familiar sights and friends and relations who could visit and be visited, with enough space and privacy to allow for her writing, was now replaced by financially constrained exile to a series of small and poky lodgings in a town which was, to Jane, unpleasant. Furthermore, although she went to the occasional ball at the Assembly Rooms, she found town life uncongenial; in one of her first letters on arrival, she describes Bath as being "vapour, shadow, smoke and confusion"; in another letter she talks of "another stupid party last night", and adds, "I cannot anyhow continue to find people agreeable."

No letters exist for the period May 1801 to September 1804, suggesting Cassandra may have destroyed them because they contained anger and bitterness against her parents.

During this fallow period in Jane's life, she and her family used the opportunity to travel widely onwards from Bath to the west of England, and to Wales. Apparently, somewhere in Devon – according to Cassandra many years later – Jane met a man, and they both became very fond of each other; they arranged to meet again the next summer, but the Austens received news that he had died unexpectedly. Nothing more is known of this episode.

Another notable story relating to this period occurred in 1802, when a twenty-one-year-old heir to a large estate, Harris Bigg-Wither (the brother of some of Jane's female friends), proposed to her; she was almost twenty-seven. He was not very bright, had a stammer and could occasionally grow frustrated and belligerent at his inability to communicate. Jane accepted him – but the next morning withdrew the acceptance.

Although she apparently wrote nothing substantial or complete during this period, she revised *Susan* (later *Northanger Abbey*). Her brother Henry, acting as her agent, offered it to the London publisher Crosby, who bought it for £10 and advertised it in the press; however, nothing happened till some thirteen years later, when Jane in desperation bought back the copyright.

In 1805 Jane's father died; in those days the church made no provision for the widows or families of deceased clergymen, and Jane, Cassandra and their mother were in dire financial straits until Jane's older brothers each contributed annual gifts of £50, and in the case of Edward, £100. There would otherwise have been the very real possibility of the two younger women having to sacrifice their independence and work as governesses.

Move to In late 1807 the family moved to Southampton, where Jane
Southampton seems to have been much happier, although still not able to resume creative work.

Finally, in 1809, their rich brother Edward, who had by now *Move to Chawton* inherited the vast wealth and three large estates of his adoptive parents (changing his surname to "Knight" in the process), offered the family the use of a large cottage on one of his estates, at Chawton, in Jane's native Hampshire. This cottage was to be her home until her early death in 1817, and the site of the final extraordinary flowering of her genius.

Jane, Cassandra and their mother moved into the cottage at Chawton in July 1809. It stood at a major crossroads in the village, and coaches would go thundering past day and night, between London and various parts of Hampshire, and as far as Portsmouth, which meant that visiting foreign dignitaries would be transported in state past Jane's window to their official receptions in London. Jane reacquired a piano, and practised for an hour or so in the early morning, then prepared breakfast for her family.

Jane now appears to have regained all her vivacity, and, *Establishment of a* having more space to write, began to revise *Elinor and* *Literary Career* *Marianne*, which was published as *Sense and Sensibility* in 1811; as mentioned above, it had been first drafted, possibly in epistolary form, some sixteen years before. No manuscript survives of any of the drafts, so we can only speculate as to how drastically the story had been revised over such a long period.

Regular contact was re-established with many of their old Hampshire friends, and we gain the impression that Jane was now happy and settled, and profoundly grateful for the miraculous change in her life. Henry had by now married the widowed Eliza de Feuillide, and Jane regularly visited them in London. She was, in addition, kept in touch with events in the wider world by the letters of her sailor brothers.

Although she now launched out on a life of extreme productivity, she still preferred to keep her writings secret from anybody but her family; there is a famous anecdote which claims that there was a creaking door along the corridor from where she wrote, and she insisted that it should be left in this state so that she would know if visitors or servants were approaching; she would then conceal her writing.

Finally, in 1810, Henry offered *Sense and Sensibility* to the London publishers Thomas Egerton – without disclosing the author's name – and it was accepted. However, the arrangement was that the author had to pay the costs of printing. Henry paid these, and acted generally as Jane's agent. After some delay it was published in November 1811, although she declined to have her name on the title page.

Pride and Prejudice and Mansfield Park At the same time she was also very busy revising *First Impressions*, which was finally sold to Egerton as *Pride and Prejudice* in November 1812; as a result of the popularity of *Sense and Sensibility*, the publisher bought the copyright of the novel for £110, which meant that he would print it at his own cost. It was published in January 1813, with "by the author of *Sense and Sensibility*" on the title page; it received excellent reviews – for instance, the playwright Sheridan called it one of the cleverest things he had ever read.

It was possibly by this time that Jane's carefully guarded anonymity began to be breached. While on holiday in Scotland, Henry had heard *Pride and Prejudice* being warmly praised by family friends and their acquaintances, and immediately blurted out that the writer was his sister.

In early 1811 Jane had also begun working on *Mansfield Park* – the first novel that can unequivocally be said to be of her later "Chawton" period, rather than a reworking of an earlier draft. Its material is very different from the rest of the novels, perhaps showing that Jane was beginning to worry about the changing moral climate, and possibly reflecting more the events of the time, rather than those of her adolescence and early adulthood.

About this time too, Jane's beloved cousin, and now sister-in-law, Eliza began to develop signs of failing health. Jane was a frequent visitor to their house in London, and saw her fade away. Eliza finally died in February 1813, with Jane present; she described it a "long and dreadful illness". On Eliza's death, Jane took one of her middle-aged French servants, Madame Périgord, back to Chawton with her for a long, well-earned rest, since she had nursed Eliza devotedly. Jane also left £50 in her will to another of Eliza's servants, Madame Bigeon. Moreover, one of her closest lifelong friends was Anne Sharp, the governess of Edward's children; Jane seems to have been more comfortable with her than with anybody else in the house. This does not sit easily with the popular myth of Jane as a snobbish, remote, strait-laced figure.

Egerton, the London publisher, suspected that *Mansfield Park* would probably not be as popular as the previous two novels, so he once again asked her to print it at her own expense. It was eventually published in May 1814.

By this time word had spread that Jane was an author, and some of Jane's younger relatives – most notably Anna – sent their youthful attempts at story-writing to her, resulting in her famous comments on the most suitable subjects to work on, and her own novels being like "two-inch-wide strips of ivory".

The last one of Jane's novels to be published in her lifetime *Emma* was *Emma*. Jane offered the manuscript to Egerton; however, owing to the comparatively slow sales of *Mansfield Park*, he was reluctant about bringing out a second edition, and procrastinated over accepting *Emma*. Accordingly, in the summer of 1815, Jane and Henry decided to offer both *Mansfield Park* and *Emma* to John Murray, publisher of Walter Scott and reputable learned journals such as the *Quarterly Review*. Jane termed Murray a "rogue", though a civil one; he offered £450 for the copyright of *Emma*, *Mansfield Park* and *Sense and Sensibility*. Henry, as Jane's London intermediary, refused, and once again Jane went for the option of paying for publication, with Murray taking ten per cent of any profits.

Shortly afterwards, Henry became seriously ill, and Jane went to London to nurse him. Then followed one of the most amusing of all the episodes relating to Austen's novels. One of the senior doctors who attended Henry was also a practitioner at the royal court. He became aware, presumably from Henry, that Jane was an author, and the doctor informed Jane that the Prince Regent – whom Jane detested for his extravagant living during a time of war, and for his treatment of his wife, Princess Caroline – was a great fan of her novels, and he, the doctor, would inform the Prince's attendants that Jane was in town. A few days later, the Prince's librarian, the clergyman James Stanier Clarke, called on her and invited her to visit the library at Carlton House. She did so on 13th November, and the clergyman informed her that she was "invited" to dedicate her next novel – *Emma* – to the Prince Regent. Jane's niece Caroline informs us that Jane simply did not want to comply with this, but various friends – and possibly John Murray – informed her that a royal "invitation" was tantamount to a command. Consequently, Jane suggested to Murray that the dedication should be beneath the title, and simply read "Dedicated to HRH The Prince Regent". However, Murray presumably realized that this was not correct etiquette, and besides, a prominent and flattering dedication would attract more readers. Therefore, it might safely be said that the fawning dedication of *Emma* was not Jane's idea, and was regarded by her with some distaste. Jane herself never met the Prince Regent, and although a complimentary copy of the novel was sent to him, there is no evidence that he ever read it.

Murray produced a print run of 2,000, in three volumes, at the price of twenty-one shillings for the set.

Later Years   Shortly before and after the publication of *Emma*, an exchange of letters took place between Jane and Mr Clarke; the self-important Revd Clarke recommended as subjects for Jane's novels, first, the life of a devoted and erudite clergyman, and then he suggested a historical romance about the royal family of Coburg, who were in London at the time. Jane's warm, high-spirited, exasperated replies demonstrate not only her highly developed sense of the ridiculous, but her awareness of her own limitations.

Clarke also offered Jane the use of his pied-à-terre when she was in London, suggesting that the reverend gentleman might have had some designs upon the maiden lady. Jane possibly read Clarke's letters aloud to her family and friends, and they may have added their suggestions to Mr Clarke's farragos, because, a short time later, Jane produced the 'Plan of a Novel, According to Hints from Various Quarters'.

At about this time (March 1816) another dramatic occurrence took place in the Austen family: Henry was senior partner and director of a bank, which now collapsed and was declared insolvent. Although other members of Jane's family – including Edward – incurred significant losses in the crash, Jane lost a mere £13; the profits she had so far made from her novels were all safely invested in government bonds, yielding five-per-cent dividends per annum. Henry, after the failure of his bank, decided to become a clergyman, and was shortly afterwards ordained. He immediately adopted the predominant Evangelical creed and its piety, leading to amused observations from Jane on his sanctimonious sermons.

While in negotiations for the publication of *Emma*, Jane began writing her final completed novel, *The Elliotts* (published as *Persuasion*). In 1816 she also bought back the copyright to *Susan* from the publisher Crosby; it had been purchased by him for the same sum in 1803 and never published; she then revised it in preparation for publication. It was now given the provisional title *Catherine*, and was in the end published posthumously as *Northanger Abbey*. At about this time her health began to fail, and the first symptoms appeared of what modern medical practitioners have speculated was either Addison's disease or a lymphoma.

The last few months of her life were immensely painful *Illness and Death* for her and those around her. Her letters show an admirable courage and gallows humour. At first she tried to pass off her illness as "rheumatism", and that nineteenth-century catch-all, "bile", but she slowly began to accept her situation. In summer 1816 she went to Cheltenham to try the healing powers of the spa waters there, but to no avail.

By early 1817 she was even beginning to find it difficult to walk from one room to another, although in January she managed to commence a novel called *Sanditon*. In March, however, overcome by what she called a "fever and bilious attack" she gave up writing. She was described at the time as being very pale, with a weak voice. From mid-April onwards she spent most of her time in bed, and on 27th April she made her will: the total profits from her novels amounted to eighty-four pounds and thirteen shillings, the equivalent of around £4,000 nowadays. She left everything to Cassandra, apart from £50 for Henry, and £50 for Madame Bigeon, the elderly French servant who had so devotedly nursed Jane's cousin Eliza during her last illness.

She then agreed to be transported to lodgings in College Street, Winchester, to be under the care of the doctors at the local hospital, who had an excellent reputation. Her letters grow warmer, more tender, as she approaches her death, expressing her gratitude to all her family; yet still they maintain a kind of wistful and gentle humour. On 17th July, she spent most of her time asleep, and a sharp decline in her condition was noted that evening; her doctor gave her a painkiller and sedative – maybe opium or laudanum – and Jane died at about four the next morning, still in bed, but with her head on a pillow on Cassandra's knees. She is now buried in Winchester Cathedral. Cassandra later wrote: "She was the sun of my life, the gilder of every pleasure, the soother of every sorrow, I had not a thought concealed from her, and it is as if I had lost a part of myself."

Jane died at the age of forty-one, and her last unfinished fragment of a novel, *Sanditon*, possibly shows a new direction in her work, suggesting that, with a successful publishing career behind her, she was now confident enough and sufficiently in touch with modern trends to begin to branch out into new, more experimental paths.

Posthumous
Publications and
Reputation

Five months after her death, with titles chosen by Cassandra and Henry, *Susan/Catherine* and *The Elliotts* were published together in four volumes as *Northanger Abbey* and *Persuasion* respectively, with a foreword by Henry announcing to the world for the first time Jane's authorship of her previous novels.

There is a slight misapprehension that Jane Austen's novels were remembered only by a discriminating few, until her rediscovery in the 1870s. But already by 1818, just a year after her death, some critical magazines were claiming that she would remain one of the most popular novelists of her time, and the publisher Bentley included all of Austen's works in his "Standard Novels" series of 1833, along with such renowned best-sellers as Mary Shelley's *Frankenstein*. From the 1830s, her novels were being discussed by such novelists as Anthony Trollope and Charlotte Brontë, and her posthumous reputation – and the contradictory views prompted by her books – may be assessed from the amount of reviews and opinions which appeared soon after her death.

Jane Austen's Works

It's often said that the predominant subject of Austen's novels is marriage, and this may have given a slightly distorted and trivialized view of her work, since in her era and social class marriage was a much more ritualized and circumscribed affair than it is now. Members of one of the higher classes could only generally marry within their own class, and among the very highest classes this could even be restricted to a few families, in an attempt to cement dynasties, and unite wealth, land and privilege. Therefore this aspect of her work is not a saccharine romantic affair, but a deeply sociological examination of what made her class tick.

However, another preoccupation of Austen's, deriving from her own situation, was the unfair way the world treated unmarried women, and the dreadful prospect in store for them if they had no private source of income.

As she was a product of the eighteenth century – the era of Gibbon, Hume and Dr Johnson – another predominant theme throughout her novels is the necessity of restraining the excesses of the imagination by means of the reasoning faculty, the education of the overall personality towards this end, and the production of an emotionally and morally balanced person. In this, she could be seen as decidedly anti-Romantic.

The juvenilia date from roughly 1787 to 1793, that is from *Juvenilia* when Jane was eleven to eighteen. They were apparently first written on loose sheets, and then transcribed over a number of years into three large exercise books, titled Volumes I, II and III by Austen herself. The original loose manuscripts no longer exist. The items are all rumbustious, sometimes quite zany and frivolous, and in the main, parodies of the popular novels of the time, with the notable exception of 'The History of England'. However, even these parodies show a development over the years from short, light-hearted, inconsequential scraps to rather longer pieces which, with the eccentricities of plot removed, and the burlesque elements replaced by Austen's mature wit, could conceivably serve as mature short stories or the basis for novels. Some of the contents of Volume II were published in 1922, while the rest of her juvenilia was published between 1933 and 1951. It has been speculated that the family members who recreated her personality from the heights of the late-Victorian era may have been somewhat embarrassed about their aunt's "unrefined" character as revealed in some of these pieces.

Lady Susan, an epistolary novella, was at first dated by *Lady Susan* scholars as having been written about 1805, but current opinion is that it was produced around 1793–94 – in other words, just before the first drafts of Austen's first major novel, *Elinor and Marianne* (subsequently *Sense and Sensibility*). If this earlier dating is correct, *Lady Susan* is Austen's first completed serious work, and it certainly seems to be a transition in style and content between the juvenilia, and the world of the first three novels, which Austen had written by 1798.

Theories have been advanced that Jane's French-speaking cousin Eliza had introduced Austen to Laclos's scandalous novel *Les Liaisons dangereuses*, since, although *Lady Susan* is much shorter, it shows similarities to the French novel in having as a heroine an uninhibited, amoral widow, who is perfectly prepared to commit adultery, destroy relationships and callously ill-treat her sixteen-year old daughter in order to gain wealth and standing in society.

Unpublished in her lifetime, the novella was first printed in the second edition (1871) of J.E. Austen-Leigh's *Memoir* of the life of his aunt.

Sense and Sensibility *Sense and Sensibility* was first drafted around 1796–97, as *Elinor and Marianne*, in epistolary form, along the lines of *Lady Susan*, while the final novel version – published in 1811 as *Sense and Sensibility* – is told in the third person. No manuscripts exist, and it is impossible to know what changes have been made in the story, although the heroines are still called Elinor and Marianne.

The print run was probably around 1,000 copies; it was sold in three volumes at a price of fifteen shillings for all three. It was a great success, and sold steadily, finally selling out in 1813, and netting Jane a profit of £140, enabling her to have a rather less straitened lifestyle. It was published anonymously; apparently Austen did not wish to draw attention to herself and her literary work; her nephew James Edward, in his memoir, tells of the lengths she went to avoid it becoming common knowledge that she was a writer.

The story in outline is that two sisters, Elinor and Marianne (there is a third, the thirteen-year-old Margaret, who plays hardly any part in the story), and their widowed mother, are effectively expelled from their childhood Eden in Sussex by their selfish half-brother and his wife. They are forced to relocate to a cottage near Exeter, and then the husband-hunting begins. Rather schematically, the elder sister, Elinor, is cool and reasoning and displays "Sense", whereas Marianne is the representative of "Sensibility" or the prevailing Romantic spirit of sensitivity to nature, displaying one's emotions, and "wearing one's heart on one's sleeve".

The novel, then, already displays the typical Austen themes of a family of females thrown out of their home, the necessity of hunting for husbands to try to redress the situation, and the equal necessity for curbing the excesses of imagination by reason. After the usual misunderstandings, Marianne's rejection by a heartless young man, and her near-death from fever, the two girls find husbands – Elinor marries a clergyman, and Marianne a retired army colonel, now a minor landowner. The resemblances between this fictional family and the Austen sisters do not need to be pointed out. Possibly because the moral climate had changed somewhat in the years between the first draft and final publication, the broad and explicit humour of the juvenilia and *Lady Susan* has been toned down: the style now is beginning to take the form of epigrammatic wit, rather than broad satire.

The reviews were excellent, and apparently the novel was popular in the highest circles: Princess Charlotte, then sixteen years old, writes of it enthusiastically in a letter, and notes: "Marianne and me [*sic*] are very alike in *disposition*... I must say it interested me much."

Pride and Prejudice was brought out in January 1813. It *Pride and Prejudice* sold out rapidly, and a second edition followed in November of that year.

Reviews were generally excellent, and especially favourable attention was devoted to the figure of Austen's bubbly, witty, vivacious heroine, Lizzy Bennet.

Once again, the customary Austen themes are here in evidence: the pursuit of marriage to avoid poverty, and the necessity of curbing prejudiced imaginings (and possibly in the fifteen-year-old Lydia Bennet's case, animal high spirits and appetites too). The plot centres round the five Bennet sisters, who, if they do not marry money, will be thrown out of their house on their father's death, with ownership of the premises passing to a distant male relative, the unappealing clergyman, Mr Collins. Two wealthy young men, Mr Bingley and Mr Darcy, take up residence for some time in the neighbourhood, and although a connection immediately springs up between the oldest sister Jane and Mr Bingley, the second sister Elizabeth takes a dislike to Mr Darcy for his apparent aloofness and arrogance – a view of him which alters over the novel as she progressively finds out more about him. Mr Darcy is the representative of the "Pride" of the title, while Elizabeth at first is the embodiment of youthful "Prejudice" against him. Of course, finally Jane and Elizabeth both marry the man of their choice, with Elizabeth finishing up with the immensely wealthy landowner Darcy. It should be noted that, as a counterfoil to the main plot, there is a subplot, in which the fifteen-year-old sister Lydia is invited to Brighton, and flirts with many of the army officers garrisoned near the town as a result of the supposed threat of invasion by the French; she finally runs off with the caddish Wickham. What is fascinating is that, although Lydia's elopement is considered a disgrace to the family, it is not the ultimate catastrophe it would be to a Victorian household. Lydia treats the whole thing almost as a joke; Austen tells us she was still "untamed, unabashed, wild, noisy and fearless".

The Watsons   While in Bath, in late 1804, Jane attempted to revive her writing by starting a novel, *The Watsons*, which, however, remains an unpolished fifty-page-long fragment. All the Austen ideas are there, and indeed, it has been called a trial run for *Emma*, although there are still greater similarities with the plot of *Pride and Prejudice*, demonstrating the continuity of the world-view which Austen carried through the fallow years from Steventon to her literary rejuvenation in Chawton. Mr Watson, a widowed hypochondriac – like Mr Woodhouse in *Emma* – has a family of four daughters. However, unlike Emma Woodhouse, the family are all poor, and the sisters are desperately husband-hunting, as – like the Austens' own father – Mr Watson is a clergyman, and on his death the girls will be thrown out of their home. Once again we find the Austen theme of the horror of being left a penurious old maid: the eldest sister Elizabeth comments: "...we must marry; my father cannot provide for us, and it is very bad to grow old and be poor and laughed at." Later she states: "I would rather do anything than be teacher at a school." However, when she had completed the extant fragment, Jane's own father died in January 1805, and perhaps because the subject of a hypochondriac clergyman who might die, leading to his family being thrown out of their home, was a little too near her own family circumstances at the time, Austen abandoned the sketch and apparently never returned to it again.

Mansfield Park   *Mansfield Park* was begun in 1811 and published in 1814, again anonymously. It is possibly the most controversial and, at first reading, the most dense and impenetrable of Austen's novels. Analogous to the situation of Jane's brother Edward, the nine-year-old Fanny Price, a member of a large impoverished family, is adopted by rich relations, Sir Thomas and Lady Bertram. The Bertrams have two sons and two daughters; Lady Bertram is a supine aristocrat who does nothing but lie on the settee all day with her pet dog, while Sir Thomas, although giving his daughters a good factual education, acknowledges near the end of the novel that he has never given them an adequate moral upbringing – one of Austen's principal themes in this work. The only younger people in the house who have any moral discipline are the second son, Edmund, and Fanny, the poor relation. When Sir

Thomas is called away for a long period to the West Indies as a result of trouble on his landholdings there, laxness and indiscipline set in, as Lady Bertram is just not interested in upholding any standards at all. Various unsuitable young men are invited in from the neighbourhood to join in the staging of a morally dubious play in the house (although Austen and her brothers had staged such plays at Steventon with great enjoyment, in *Mansfield Park* these amateur dramatics seem to be an indication of lowered standards of behaviour). The only two who refuse to perform are Edmund and Fanny – though even Edmund is on the verge of acquiescing in playing a minor role. Although Sir Thomas returns unexpectedly early, so that the play is never performed, the rot has set in; the eldest son almost dies through his dissipated lifestyle at university, while the two daughters elope with two of the dubious young men whom they have met during their father's absence. The only two unblemished people are Edmund and Fanny – who of course end up marrying, with Edmund becoming a clergyman. The two characters have been described by some critics as the most boring, irritating, priggish and staid of Austen's heroes and heroines. Fanny herself seems merely a passive observer at times; she has none of the sparkle of Elizabeth Bennet or Emma. Some of the witty but morally lacking young men who are frequenters of the place while Sir Thomas is away may appear far more amusing, entertaining and sympathetic than Edmund and Fanny. Some critics have claimed that Austen was judging the declining state of English social life at the time, including the poor example set by the Prince Regent, whom she detested. Others have suggested that Austen was becoming worried about embarrassing her family, in the rising tide of Anglican Evangelism and social conservatism, by producing any more sparkling and witty productions, such as *Pride and Prejudice*.

However, perhaps because she realized that *Mansfield Park* hadn't been a total success with the public, or because she felt she had betrayed her natural creative instincts, Jane returned to former preoccupations in her next novel *Emma*.

According to Cassandra, Jane Austen began writing *Emma* in January 1814 and completed it in March 1815. It was published in 1816.

The plot revolves around Emma Woodhouse, the twenty-year-old daughter of an elderly, indulgent, hypochondriac widower, who is one of the wealthiest men in the large village of Highbury. A constant visitor to their house – indeed the only visitor who is not elderly – is Mr Knightley, the extremely rich local landowner. Emma, to provide herself with amusement, decides to take upon herself the education and rearing for polite society of an orphan girl, Harriet Smith, who is a boarder at a local, privately run girls' school. Possibly deluded by some of the Romantic novels she has read as a child (compare Catherine in *Northanger Abbey*), Emma assumes Harriet is the illegitimate daughter of a wealthy gentleman, or even a nobleman, and proceeds to separate her from a young farmer who has formed an attachment for her, and to try to pair her off with a series of unlikely and unsuitable men. Finally Harriet, herself misled and encouraged by Emma's false views of her, dares to set her sights on Mr Knightley, and Emma, with a shock that reaches to the depths of her consciousness, realizes that she herself has been subconsciously in love with Mr Knightley for as long as she can remember. The book is further complicated by a series of subplots and a rich array of minor characters including Miss Bates, Frank Churchill and Jane Fairfax. The impression of the dense texture of village life is deepened by the constant mention of characters who never actually appear, such as the Coxes, or Mr Perry, the local apothecary who seems to attend upon everybody in the novel.

Although Austen said that only she would like her heroine, Emma is genuinely kind and solicitous to her dreadful hypochondriac father, even though this is affecting her social life disastrously; in her visits to the poor of the parish, she is described as being "very compassionate", and we are told that "she understood their ways, could allow for their ignorance and temptations... entered into their troubles with ready sympathy, and always gave her assistance with as much intelligence as goodwill". This is in marked contrast to the appalling Lady Catherine de Bourgh of *Pride and Prejudice*, who, regarding the discontented and poor of her estate, would "scold them into harmony and plenty".

The novel sold around 1,300 copies fairly quickly, but then sales declined, and the rest were remaindered in 1821, along with unsold copies of *Mansfield Park*. However, the critical reception at the time was very favourable (including a long, laudatory piece by Sir Walter Scott).

Austen's last two novels were published five months after her *Persuasion*
death. *Persuasion* had been provisionally titled *The Elliotts* by
Jane, and the new title was apparently Henry and Cassandra's
idea – as was *Northanger Abbey*, which had originally been
Susan, then *Catherine*. Although generally recognized as a
masterpiece, there are some passages in *Persuasion* which are
not fully polished, and a few minor plot lines left undeveloped;
this may have been as a result of Jane's encroaching illness,
which sapped her energy.

The heroine of *Persuasion* – whom the Reverend G.D. Boyle,
quoting an acquaintance of Jane's many years later, claims
was Jane herself in some respects – is Anne Elliott, the second
daughter of the coarse and impoverished Baronet Sir Walter
Elliott. Since there is no son, on his death the estate will pass
to a male relative. Some years previously, Anne had been
engaged to a young naval officer, but had been persuaded by a
well-meaning older friend to break off the engagement, since
he had as yet no wealth. Eight years later they meet again
in Bath; he is now extremely rich, through his share in the
"prize" money his ships have accrued – i.e. their percentage
of goods on any foreign vessel captured by them, which
was given to them by the state as a reward, and shared out
among the officers and crew. At first he appears indifferent,
but finally they are reunited and marry. *Persuasion* is the only
Austen novel for which we have any surviving manuscripts,
since a chapter was cancelled, which survives in manuscript
form, and two new chapters added to the published version.

Northanger Abbey was published posthumously together *Northanger Abbey*
with *Persuasion*. It had been written in 1797–98 under the title
Susan, and sold to Crosby Publishers in London in 1803, but
never published. Austen bought back the copyright in 1816,
revised it again slightly, in the process changing the name
of the heroine, and of the novel, to *Catherine*. She added a
foreword apologizing for the fact that many of the references,
particularly to the Gothic novels satirized in the text, were
now some twenty years out of date.

The story is high-spirited and funny, but a common crit-
icism is that it contains two themes that are not well inte-
grated. The heroine, Catherine – once again a clergyman's
daughter – goes off to Bath with friends and, after a
series of misunderstandings, marries a witty and educated
clergyman, Henry Tilney – who is presumably Austen's

idea of what a real clergyman should be, unlike the deeply unpleasant Mr Elton or Mr Collins. However, Catherine is invited to Henry's paternal home, Northanger Abbey, presided over by his father, General Tilney; in this "Abbey", with her imagination misled by the Gothic novels she has been reading, Catherine dreams up secret passages, hidden documents and ghosts, and forms the totally erroneous conjecture that the widowed General murdered his wife. It is part of her growth to maturity, and her acceptance by Henry Tilney, that – another Austen theme – she learns to control her imagination by reason.

The first edition of *Northanger Abbey* was preceded by a short biographical notice from Jane's brother Henry, in which he revealed her identity and gave a brief account of her life. He claimed that she was a profoundly religious woman; however, it should be borne in mind that he himself was by this time an Evangelical clergyman, and so possibly felt constrained to create this gloss on her character – a process to be continued and intensified by her family over the subsequent generation.

Sanditon   Between January and March 1817, just a few months before her death, Austen drafted her last tantalizing fragment, entitled *Sanditon* – tantalizing because it does indicate that, at the age of forty-one, she was beginning to move beyond her traditional themes and territory.

Sanditon is a hamlet by the seaside, which is being rapidly transformed by entrepreneurs into a holiday resort, both for holidaymakers and for hypochondriacs. Stunningly, and with no preparation, comment or surprise on any other character's part, one of the characters who Jane introduces near the end of the piece is described as a "half mulatto" heiress. Although Jane never mentions Afro-Caribbean people in her letters, there were far more in Britain at the time than is commonly realized, mainly serving as domestic servants or cab drivers. Not only London, but such provincial cities as Bath, where Jane had spent several years, had such an ethnic population. Suddenly we are in the world of *Jane Eyre*, or *Vanity Fair*, among characters of a variety of social class and ethnicity.

Select Bibliography

Standard Edition:
The first complete scholarly edition of Austen's complete works, with background material, appendices and notes was produced by R.W. Chapman in six volumes from 1923–54; the third revised edition (Oxford: Oxford University Press, 1988), remains the most authoritative edition.

Biographies:
Austen-Leigh, James Edward, *A Memoir of Jane Austen* (London: Richard Bentley, 1870)

Nokes, David, *Jane Austen: A Life* (Berkeley, CA: University of California Press, 1998)

Shields, Carol, *Jane Austen* (London: Weidenfeld & Nicolson, 2001)

Tomalin, Claire, *Jane Austen: A Life*, 2nd ed. (London: Penguin, 2000)

Tucker, George Holbert, *A Goodly Heritage: A History of Jane Austen's Family*, 2nd ed. (Stroud: Sutton, 1998)

Additional Recommended Background Material:
Austen-Leigh, William and Austen-Leigh, Richard Arthur, *Jane Austen: A Family Record*, rev. Deirdre Le Faye (London: British Library, 1989)

Grey, J. David, ed., *The Jane Austen Handbook* (London: Athlone, 1986)

Lascelles, Mary, *Jane Austen and Her Art* (London: Athlone, 1995)

Le Faye, Deirdre, *A Chronology of Jane Austen and Her Family* (Cambridge: Cambridge University Press, 2006)

Nicholson, Nigel, *The World of Jane Austen* (London: Weidenfeld and Nicolson, 1991)

Olsten, Kirstin, *All Things Austen: An Encyclopedia of Austen's World*, 2 vols. (Westport, CT & London: Greenwood Press, 2005)

On the Web:
www.pemberley.com
www.jane-austens-house-museum.org.uk
www.janeaustensoci.freeuk.com

ALMA CLASSICS

ALMA CLASSICS aims to publish mainstream and lesser-known European classics in an innovative and striking way, while employing the highest editorial and production standards. By way of a unique approach the range offers much more, both visually and textually, than readers have come to expect from contemporary classics publishing.

LATEST TITLES PUBLISHED BY ALMA CLASSICS

www.almaclassics.com